The sign over the building brought Kari up short

Bus Station.

What business would the girl have there? This morning, none of the D'Angelos had mentioned a family member coming or leaving town.

A vague, uneasy feeling stole over Kari. She went through the glass door. The station was a small, functional place, and in no time she saw Tessa standing near the bus bay. With a boy. Luggage around their feet.

They didn't see her approach. Both were absorbed in the contents of the bag Tessa held. They looked like kids exclaiming over Halloween treats. They *were* kids!

"...should be enough snacks to hold us until we get to Albuquerque," Tessa was saying as Kari reached them. "I got those chocolate-covered raisins you like."

"Tessa?"

The blond boy looked up, and Tessa swung around. Her features went dead-white, and her eyes moved like a trapped rabbit's. "Oh, K-Kari," she stammered out. "Oh, hi."

Dear Reader,

A long time ago this born-and-bred Florida girl spent a couple of years living in Colorado. What a shock that was! Snow instead of sand, mountains instead of beaches, and for neighbors, wild animals instead of tourists.

Eventually, circumstances brought me back to my home state, but I've never forgotten Colorado's beauty. So when I started thinking of new places to set my next book, I couldn't help remembering a terrific little family-run resort I'd found on the edge of Rocky Mountain National Park.

The Daughter Dilemma, the first of the HEART OF THE ROCKIES series, is based on those fond memories.

This book introduces you to Nick D'Angelo, the oldest son. Nick has his hands full running Lightning River Lodge, piloting helicopter tours, keeping his teenage daughter out of mischief and fending off his loving family's determined efforts to see him remarried. When Kari Churchill literally drops out of the sky and into his life, he can't wait to see the last of her.

As for Kari, she has her own busy career and her determination to learn more about her late father's final trip into the wilderness. She'd be only too happy to oblige Nick and catch the next plane out of the mountains.

But neither of them stands a chance once the rest of the D'Angelo family decides they're meant for each other.

I hope you enjoy Nick and Kari's journey as much as I've enjoyed writing about them and this fun, energetic family. In books to come, Nick's siblings will find their own Happily Ever After. These strong men and loving women typify the characteristics I so often found in the people who live in those mountains in Colorado—commitment, courage and an endless capacity for love.

Regards,

Ann Evans

The Daughter Dilemma
Ann Evans

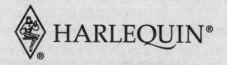

HARLEQUIN®

TORONTO • NEW YORK • LONDON
AMSTERDAM • PARIS • SYDNEY • HAMBURG
STOCKHOLM • ATHENS • TOKYO • MILAN • MADRID
PRAGUE • WARSAW • BUDAPEST • AUCKLAND

ISBN 0-373-71215-4

THE DAUGHTER DILEMMA

It's long past time to say a special thank-you
to fellow Superromance author Kathleen O'Brien.

You convinced me to take the leap off the cliff, and only
your professional insights, unending generosity and dear
friendship keep me from crashing on the rocks below.

Books by Ann Evans

HARLEQUIN SUPERROMANCE

CHAPTER ONE

NICK D'ANGELO was one hour and fifty-seven minutes into Angel Air's deluxe two-hour helicopter tour. One hour and fifty-seven minutes into showing the Pattersons the beauty of Colorado's Front Range the way birds saw it. One hour and fifty-seven minutes into a pounding headache that made him wonder if, at thirty-four, he was getting too old for this job.

Years ago he'd been a chopper pilot in the war, picking scared army grunts off sand dunes no bigger than a pitcher's mound, bullets drilling holes into the side of his Black Hawk. No sweat, that.

But the Pattersons—both the rich, obnoxious father and the spoiled-rotten daughter—were making him crazy.

Dwayne Patterson, seated in the copilot seat of Raven One, was the kind of guy who'd die before he'd admit he was scared to death to fly. Every time Nick put the R-44 into a sharp bank, Patterson's white-knuckled grip dug a deeper furrow into the seat's leather. Nick didn't mind that. Hell, plenty of people got nervous once they climbed into a helicopter. If this guy lost his lunch before the flight was over, Nick would clean it up—then charge him double through the "unforeseen incidence" clause in the release form.

No, the nerves didn't bother him. It was Patterson's constant chatter over the cabin's "hot mike" that drove Nick nuts.

Nick had smiled and nodded in all the right places, glad that his sunglasses hid his boredom. But the guy wouldn't shut up.

As for the man's daughter, Hannah, a more unlikable teenager Nick had yet to meet. Whenever he looked back over his shoulder to see how she was doing, she invariably threw him a pouty, petulant, hurt-baby face. As though the past two hours had somehow been Nick's idea and not Dwayne Patterson's pitiful attempt to bond with his kid.

Hannah Patterson wasn't much older than Nick's daughter, Tessa, but she was miles apart in temperament. Surly. Jaded. Easily bored. In the past couple of weeks Nick had been at odds with Tessa, but nothing in her contrary behavior even came *close* to this girl's attitude.

And he'd been trying so hard to be agreeable to these people, too. He had to. The summer season had been off this year. Too much rain. Too many tourists tightening their belts instead of spending money. But sometimes, Nick thought, you played your best hand and it still wasn't enough to win the pot.

He'd flown these two over some of the prettiest country God had ever created. It was going to be an early autumn—already the aspen were spreading golden blankets across the green velvet slopes. They'd swooped down over abandoned mines and ghost towns. Followed the winding river through the canyons—so close you could make out the bullet-shaped trout in the crystal streams below. Surely that kind of ride beat anything the theme parks were offering.

But neither of the Pattersons seemed the least bit impressed. Hannah just yawned and rolled her eyes occasionally. Daddy should have spent some of his computer software money on charm school.

He felt a fingertip jab hard into his shoulder and turned his head to find Hannah thrusting forward in her seat.

"How much longer?" the girl shouted, though Nick had explained twice that the cabin radio picked up every word and delivered it right into each of their headphones. "I have to pee like a racehorse."

Nice mouth, Nick thought. But Dad Patterson didn't seem to mind.

Instead of answering, Nick pointed out the front right windscreen. Angel Air's heliport was in sight now, the landing pad a stark blue-and-yellow scar against the mountainside. The small office and hangar looked like a Monopoly house, the company's other copter, Raven Two, like a kid's toy.

Somewhere inside the office his sister, Adriana, would be waiting for their return. Probably fuming, if he knew Addy. Which he did.

He pressed the radio switch on the side of the cyclic column that allowed him to talk to the office or any other flight service he might need to raise. "Base, this is Nine-Zero-One-Bravo. Coming in from the west."

"Roger, Nine-Zero-One-Bravo," his sister's voice came through the headphones. "I'll be waiting."

One hour and fifty-nine minutes into the tour now. It would be over soon enough, thank God.

He supposed it wasn't really the Pattersons' fault that he was in such foul humor. It had been a lousy week. Tessa behaving like a royal pain in the butt over some silly dress. Addy pestering him all the time about wanting more flight time now that she had her license.

It didn't help that for the past two days Nick and Tessa had been forced to move into one of the two-bedroom guest suites up at the main lodge. Their own cabin was off-limits right now. Tessa had left the back door open and a skunk had meandered in, then scurried out. But not before getting the hell scared out of it and doing what skunks did best. A good three days, the fumigators had said.

He must be going soft. Over the years he'd slept in barracks cots, hammocks, sleeping bags and once, in a three-foot sand coffin with an Iraqi camel parked on top of him. Now Nick mourned the loss of his own bed. That sag in the middle fit his six-foot, three-inch frame like a suede glove.

Lord, he really *was* getting old.

Rolling his shoulders to work out some of the tension, he thought about how moving back home five years ago had seemed like an answer to a lot of problems. No—in spite of the grim circumstances, it had seemed like *the* answer.

He hadn't expected it to be easy. From the moment he'd returned to Colorado he'd known there would be a heavy load of responsibility. Samuel, his father, had suffered a massive stroke. It had thrown the entire family into a tailspin, forcing Nick to take over running Lightning River Lodge—the family inn and tour company. Everyone had quickly grown to depend on him and eventually they'd weathered that crisis. Most of the time he was confident he could handle anything thrown his way.

Except when he had a week like this one. This week, it seemed as though *ten* of him wouldn't have been enough to go around.

He eased back on the throttle to cut his airspeed for the landing, frowning at the vibration that passed through his fingertips. One of the main rotor blades might be out of trim. Just as well that the Pattersons were the last tour scheduled for the day. Tomorrow he'd take Raven One off-line and check it over.

In deference to Dwayne Patterson's stomach, he set the skids down especially easy on the pad, then cut the rotor. The blades had barely stopped making their whoop-whoop noise before Addy was at the chopper door, helping Hannah Patterson find her feet.

"Well, how was it?" she asked no one in particular. Bright enthusiasm was Addy's idea of good customer service.

Hannah lifted one thin shoulder. "We saw mountains. Big surprise."

The girl pushed past Addy as though she were parting drapes, heading for the office's small bathroom.

Addy smiled at Dwayne Patterson as he stepped out. "What about you? Did you like it? Did Nick point out all the abandoned silver mines? Those are some of my favorites."

"Very nice," the man said absently. He was already consulting his guide book, eager to find the next thrill. "If we take this road, can we get to Estes Park before nightfall?"

While Nick continued to shut down the engine, Addy helped Patterson with his map. She then headed toward the office, presumably to make sure Hannah had managed all right.

Nick came around the front of Raven One. Dwayne Patterson looked slightly uncomfortable, as though he didn't know what to say while they waited for sullen Hannah to emerge.

"Certainly a beautiful day for a flight," Patterson finally said. The clouds bunched along the Front Range were almost purple in the late-afternoon sunlight.

"We'll get a thunderstorm later," Nick said. Addy would lecture him if he didn't make nice with the customers.

"You really think so?" Patterson frowned up at the sky as though he could find an argument for Nick's statement written across the blue canopy. "I hope we can make Estes Park tonight."

Estes Park sat at the east entrance to Rocky Mountain National Park. "You and your daughter plan to blitz the Rocky Mountains in one weekend?" Nick asked.

"Actually, I think Hannah would rather be home with her mother," the man admitted. "Anywhere away from me. I'm recently divorced, and we were supposed to spend the summer together. It didn't happen, and she's still sulking over it." When Nick didn't respond right away, Patterson added quickly, "I needed some time to myself. But I'm making it up to her now. That should count for something, right?"

Personally, Nick didn't think that counted for *anything*. The guy wanted credit for shouldering his responsibility now? After he'd already made it clear to his daughter that she came second in his life? Fortunately he was saved from making any kind of polite answer. Hannah and Addy emerged from the office to rejoin the two men at the helicopter.

The girl headed in the direction of Patterson's rental SUV. When she found the doors locked, she cupped her hands and yelled, "Are we going or not? Come on!"

The car keys quickly appeared in Dwayne's hand. He turned toward Addy and Nick once more, his features sheepish. "Kids," he said, as if that one word explained everything. "You know how they are."

I thought so, Nick wanted to say. *But I guess I'm still learning.* If he'd been really savvy, last night's argument with Tessa might not have happened. "Hard to know what's in their heads," he agreed. "But then, I guess that's the way they intend it."

Patterson nodded, then stuck out his hand to say goodbye.

"Come back again," Addy encouraged. "There's plenty more scenery around here, and next time, see it from the back of one of our horses. Lightning River Lodge has a really fine stable."

The man gave her a noncommittal smile and went off to join his impatient daughter. In another few moments they would be gone, heading back down the winding mountain road and onto the fastest route to Estes Park.

With his arms crossed over his chest, Nick stood beside Addy and watched them go. His sister waved—the quintessential tour guide sending her chicks off to explore new territory.

"Smile," Addy said without glancing his way. "Pretend you're happy."

"I *am* happy," Nick replied. "Happy to see the last of them."

"Well, you didn't have to take them up. I told you I could handle it."

"I wouldn't be so cruel." He turned toward his sister, cocking his head at her speculatively. "The lodge has a really fine stable?"

"I haven't given up on the idea. You and Dad need to hear me out about expanding."

"You want to run the stable or fly?"

"I don't see why I can't do both. Especially since you don't seem willing to let me *do* much flying."

Addy headed toward the office, a trim, dark-haired beauty who had boundless energy and about a million ideas to make the family businesses run better. Some of them were even pretty good.

Nick loved her dearly, but he also knew his younger sister could be foolishly stubborn, shortsighted and impetuous. Only recently had she seemed to settle down, deciding that she wanted a career flying helicopters. Two months ago she'd passed all the tests, accrued enough flight time. But would she stick it out, Nick wondered, when things got boring and a little too routine?

He followed her inside. The office furnishings were pretty sparse—Nick liked things clean and uncluttered. Military style. There was a waist-high counter that created a friendly barrier between staff and customers, a water cooler and a couple of utilitarian chairs. Through the back door lay the hangar area, where both R-44s would be wheeled in tonight before they locked up.

Nick had moved a second desk into the back area for Addy in an effort to show that he took her seriously as a fellow pilot. Not surprisingly, the top of it was nothing but a haphazard pile of clutter.

She plucked a handful of pink slips off a spindle. "As usual, I've been playing secretary." One by one, she handed him the messages. "Leo Waxman says the estimate for rewiring the spa area is ready, and you should be prepared for a shock because it needs major work. Mr. Yokomoto called and wants you to call him back as soon as possible."

She grinned as she handed him the last one. "Aunt Ren said to tell you that there was a wolf wandering near the back door when she took out the trash this afternoon and she's not going back outside until you do something about it."

Aunt Renata and Aunt Sofia, his mother's widowed sisters, had come from Italy to help out after Nick's father had suffered his stroke. Somehow they'd never left. Aunt Sof loved the Lightning River area and considered the breathtaking mountain vistas a little slice of heaven. Aunt Ren, on the other hand, still didn't believe Colorado had ever won statehood. She'd yet to come to grips with the region's abundant wildlife.

"A wolf?" Nick remarked absently as he fingered through the slips. "Probably Leo Waxman's German shepherd. The dog goes everywhere he does."

He frowned at the message from one of their best clients, Kiyoshi Yokomoto from Genichi Tech. Every other week for the past year G Tech had sent a handful of execs to Lightning River for R and R. Part of their stay always included a lengthy helicopter tour. Nick liked them. It was steady, easy money from people who appreciated the beauty of the Rockies.

He settled into his chair, pulled the phone closer and punched in Yokomoto's office number. Kiyoshi seldom called, and Nick felt a nagging sense of doom that sent his headache rippling across his eyelids with renewed force.

"Don't look so worried," Addy said as she plopped into the chair behind her own desk. "He probably just wants to book a couple of extra guests." She went suddenly upright in her chair. "Hey, if that's what it is, we could both take up a Raven. Fly in tandem. That would be fun."

Nick waited for the call to connect. With a scowl, he yanked off his sunglasses and wagged his hand toward the towering pile of paper perched haphazardly on Addy's desk. "Do something with that stuff before it's everywhere."

Addy ignored that advice and reached to pick up the framed picture of her pilot's license that sat proudly on one corner. "You've *got* to let me take up G Tech next weekend, Nick. See this?" she said, pointing to the license. "*This* says I'm perfectly capable of handling it."

A huge, colorfully painted sign hung on the back wall of the office. It depicted a winding river between towering mountain peaks, bisected by a jagged lightning bolt—the family logo. Angel Air, the sign read. And below it: Nick D'Angelo, Owner/Operator.

Nick pointed toward it. "And *that* says I'm still the guy who makes that decision."

His sister sighed in exasperation. Then the call went through and Kiyoshi was on the line. Nick listened to the man's excellent English for a few minutes, made a couple of sympathetic comments, then placed the receiver back in its cradle.

Seeing the look on his face, Addy frowned. "Bad news?"

"Kiyoshi's canceled everything for the next month. The head execs are flying out tomorrow because of some trouble in the Tokyo office."

"Ouch. That's a big one to lose."

"Yeah, that's what I was thinking."

"Well, at least that will give us a little breathing room to concentrate on the Graybeal wedding," Addy said with her usual optimism. "We're going to need all the help we can get to be ready for that one."

Chuck Graybeal, the busiest dentist in three counties and an old family friend, had booked the entire lodge for his daughter's upcoming wedding. The resort had never catered such a large, complex function before, but if everything went as planned, Nick could envision a whole new world of opportunity opening up for the family business. But first, they had to get through this latest hiccup.

He scraped a hand across his jaw, quickly calculating what the lost revenue from G Tech would mean. "The lodge will still be booked pretty solid, but this means Air is going to be hurting for business next weekend."

"We can make it up. Vail's got its big aspen festival coming up. That'll mean lots of tourists checking out the I-70 corridor. Some of them are bound to be looking for a fun way to kill a few hours." Her voice took on more enthusiasm as ideas started to pop. "Maybe we could do a flyer. Blitz the parking lots and shops with a two-for-one deal on an hour flight."

"Pretty short notice."

"You know I'm good at mobilizing, Nick. I can do it."

That was certainly true. When Addy set her mind to something, she was like a laser on a target. "Let's talk about it with the family tonight at dinner."

"Fine," she conceded, but Nick could see the wheels still turning in her head. "Talking about this will be tons better than listening to you and Tessa argue."

"The arguing part's over," Nick said, balling up the messages and lobbing them into the trash can that sat between their desks. "The dress goes back. And you aren't to encourage Tessa to any further rebellion."

Addy shook her head at him. "But—"

He scowled at her and she subsided.

His daughter was fourteen and turning into a lovely young woman that any father would be proud of. But sometimes he wasn't sure he and Tessa were connecting at all. After years of trying so hard, coming so far in their relationship…

"She's growing up, Nick." Addy cut quietly into his thoughts, as though she could read them. Maybe she could. Addy had a way with people.

Nick smiled at her. "I can accept that. But she doesn't need to show everyone just *where* she's growing. That dress was indecent."

"You're such a prude."

"I'm her father. She's too young. You weren't allowed to wear anything that sexy to school dances."

Addy's mouth quirked in derision. "How would you know? You'd already married Denise and left home by the time I was fourteen."

Nick couldn't resist laughing. "Are you kidding? Between your escapades and Matt's overachieving and Rafe getting into trouble all the time, my mailbox was full of letters from Mom and Pop, and I memorized almost every word. The night of your first Sadie Hawkins dance you wore a modest yellow dress with daisies along the neckline."

Addy straightened in surprise. "How do you know that?"

"Because Pop kept asking Mom who Sadie Hawkins was, and she described the dress very vividly to me. Said it looked like melted butter on you."

Addy settled her chin on her hand. "It *was* pretty," she said with a sigh. Then she gave Nick a sly sideways glance. "Too bad I didn't wear it. I switched it for a midnight-blue slip dress with a plunging back. That was the night I let David McKay kiss me for the first time."

Nick thought she looked a little dreamy, maybe even sad, but he gave her a glance that said she was completely hopeless. "No wonder Mom and Pop spent so much time threatening to lock you in your room."

"So is that how you want to handle Tessa? Threaten her with punishment all the time? Make her quake with fear instead of having her respect? Is that the way to raise children?"

"It worked for us."

"Did it?"

He knew what she was getting at. The four D'Angelo offspring—Nicholas, Matt, Rafe and Adriana—had been raised by Samuel and Rose, people with strong values and a belief in exercising firm, loving control over their children. As parents, they had been tough, but devoted. Demanding, but fair.

Nick had always known what was expected from them, where he stood. So had the easygoing Matt, who was now a skilled surgeon living in Chicago. And though she'd been in and out of mischief for most of her growing-up years, Addy had done all right, too.

The real problem had been Rafe. The youngest son had been a black-eyed, black-tempered hell-raiser. As a teenager he'd always been at odds with their father and, after one particularly bitter fight, he'd run away from home.

He hadn't been back since.

"I miss Rafe," Addy said, jogging Nick out of the past.

He made a noncommittal sound in his throat. She and Rafe had been close. He suspected Addy was still in touch—she received mysterious phone calls and the occasional postcard. She'd probably forgive him anything. But he and Rafe had never seen eye-to-eye and he was still resentful that his brother had not returned—even for a visit—during his father's health crisis.

Addy turned to give him a direct look. "Do you think he'll ever come home?"

Personally, Nick didn't think so. His brother seemed content to ricochet around the world without a care for anyone. But he could hear the hope in Addy's voice and a protective instinct rose up in him in spite of his belief that blunt truth always served a person better.

"He'll come home someday," he said. "When he finds the right reason."

That seemed to satisfy her. With a thoughtful nod, she started sifting through the pile of paper on her desk. At least she no longer seemed interested in giving him a hard time about the way he managed Tessa.

He began paging through the log book of upcoming tours. It looked grim. One no-show today. Only three flights scheduled for tomorrow unless someone made a last-minute booking. Enough to give Addy some flight time but not the usual tourist crush that would keep both choppers in the air full-time.

A year ago Nick had added Angel Air to the family business, building the heliport only a mile from the lodge. He'd told himself that it wasn't just that he'd missed flying. Helicopter tours were a natural fit for Lightning River Lodge's well-heeled guests. More and more vacationers wanted to explore the less-familiar wilderness areas that hadn't been over-run by tourists. But so far, this part of the business had yet to turn a real profit.

The phone rang and Addy picked it up. A moment later his sister put the call on hold and motioned toward him.

"It's Mom," she said. "And she sounds out of breath."

What now? Nick thought as he punched the button. Their mother was pretty self-sufficient. After their father's stroke, she'd had to be. With Aunt Sof and Aunt Ren's help, she kept the lodge running in tip-top shape. The front desk, the small restaurant, the fourteen rooms and two suites. If she'd been reduced to calling Nick, God knew what problem she'd run into that she couldn't handle.

Unless it's Pop.

He snatched up the phone. Rapid Italian chattered in his ear. She wasn't speaking to him, but to Aunt Ren in the back-ground. "Mom, what is it?" he cut in. "What's the matter?"

His mother shushed Aunt Ren. There was immediate silence. "Nick, can you come up? I need you. Ah, *Madonn,* I'm surrounded by crazy people here."

"It's not Pop?"

"No, no, no," she reassured him quickly. "Although, if he doesn't stop getting in the way, I may put him *back* in the hospital."

"I'm only trying to help," he heard his father mumble in the distance. Since the stroke, Sam D'Angelo depended on a wheelchair to get around, but after years of therapy, his speech was almost normal again.

"Running over my toe with your chair?" he heard his mother scold. "*That's* your idea of helping?"

"You have big feet," his father replied.

Another string of Italian. No phrase you'd find in a guide

book. Nick pinched the bridge of his nose. Without even looking at Addy, he could tell she was grinning.

"Mom…"

His mother must have realized that Nick's patience today was wearing thin. "The stove. It's broken. How can I cook tonight for our guests?"

That was what this was all about? "So call the repairman."

"You think I don't know to do that? I did call. The stove isn't working because there's a leak. From the bathroom in Number Five."

Nick frowned. That was the guest room directly above the kitchen. Not great to have a leak moving from one floor to the next, but still, the problem was manageable. "Then call the plumber. See if you can get Tom Faraday. He won't charge a fortune for coming up the mountain at night."

"The leak in Number Five is coming from the bathroom in Number Ten. Sofia said she went in there to make up the room and the water was three inches deep. She had to build a dike with every spare blanket we have to keep it from escaping into the bedroom."

Number Ten was above Number Five. If the water leak encompassed all three floors, they were looking at the possibility of serious damage. "Did you turn off the water valve in Number Ten?" Nick asked quickly.

"That's why I'm calling you. We're like weak little birds! Sofia and Tessa went to town to return that dress. Renata and I, we turned the knob a little, but we need a man's strength."

"If you'd just listen to me—" Nick heard his father complain in the background.

"Samuel, I know you can shut it off," his mother said to her husband. "But how am I to get you up there? Carry you piggyback?"

His father's movements were confined to the downstairs part of the lodge now, and most of the time it wasn't a problem. While his parents argued, Nick imagined the entire third floor turning into one big disaster zone.

"What about George?" Nick interrupted, referring to the fellow who acted as both front desk clerk and bellman.

"George left early today. His parents' twenty-fifth anniversary is tonight and he has to pick up decorations. He's such a devoted son…"

"Mom, focus!" Nick said in the sharpest tone he could ever use with his mother. "Who else is around?"

"The Binghams. I think they're in the hot tub. No one else."

"That's perfect. He's probably still in a bathing suit and barefoot. Ask him to go upstairs with you and try turning the valve."

His mother gasped. "I can't do that. They're guests. You don't ask paying guests to do maintenance. What are you thinking, Nicholas?"

"I'm thinking that unless he wants to find his own room flooded, it doesn't hurt to ask. It's turning off one valve, not cleaning up after Mardi Gras. Look desperate. If he balks, tell him we'll comp his room for one night. I'll be up there as soon as I can."

He hung up the phone before his mother could say anything else. Damn, damn, damn, he thought. Can this week possibly get any worse?

Pulling the keys to his Jeep out of his desk's top drawer, he hurriedly explained the problem up at the lodge to Addy. He was just jerking into his worn leather jacket when he noticed a car pull into Angel Air's parking lot.

A young woman got out and hurried toward the office. The afternoon sunlight was still strong enough to reveal that she had a lanky body—lithe and long—with an athletic swing to her walk. She was dressed for hiking, with khakis and boots and a heavy-looking backpack slung over one shoulder. Her blond hair had been stuffed under a baseball cap and spilled out the back in a long, swinging ponytail.

"Who the hell is that?" he wondered out loud.

Addy shrugged. "Could be our ten o'clock that didn't show, I suppose."

"She's too late if that's the case."

The woman reached the office door, stuck her head in first and smiled at both of them. "Hi," she said brightly.

This close Nick could see that she was passably attractive—with a dainty arch to her nose, a charming smile and pretty teeth that indicated somebody had paid a dentist a bucketload of money.

When she looked at him there was a certain sparkle in her green eyes that made his gut take a wild, stray turn. He didn't like the feeling and banished it pretty quickly. After a day like today, he wasn't in the mood for foolishness.

Honey, don't bother, he thought. Whatever you're selling, I'm not buying.

CHAPTER TWO

TWICE SHE HAD ALMOST turned around and headed back to the interstate.

Kari Churchill was a Florida girl, used to the flat, undemanding landscapes of Palm Beach. At home, the closest thing to mountains were the sand dunes she could see from the balcony of her oceanfront condo. But here, all the roads twisted and turned back on themselves, and if you thought you could figure out where you were by watching the sun, you had another think coming. These darned mountains. Beautiful and awe-inspiring, but always in the way.

But she was here now—two years and thousands of miles from the moment she'd made the decision to come. She'd carved out some time at last, though not much of it since her last assignment in Philadelphia had unexpectedly run longer than she'd planned and the next one in New Zealand was right around the corner. Snaking mountain roads, missed highway markers and fluttering nerves were not going to prevent her from keeping the promise she'd made to herself.

No more excuses. No turning back. No matter what.

Right now, however, Kari could see that she might have one last obstacle standing in her way. This man in the Indiana Jones bomber jacket, the strong chin and the tight-lipped smile that practically shouted "Welcome. Now please go away."

From the moment she'd opened the door to Angel Air, she'd sensed a slight tension. The woman, a little younger than the man and a lot more friendly looking, had immediately approached the counter. The man hadn't so much as moved a muscle.

"Can we help you?" the woman asked with a salaried-receptionist smile.

She had the kind of great looks that didn't call for much makeup and a tumble of black hair that sifted prettily across her shoulders every time she turned her head. The name tag over her left pocket read "Adriana."

"I'm Kari Churchill," Kari said, extending her hand. "I was supposed to be here this morning for a flight. I know I'm dreadfully late."

"By seven hours," the man said.

She looked at him more closely as he approached the counter with a slow rippling of muscles. She couldn't help noticing that he was almost offensively healthy looking. As darkly handsome as the woman was beautiful. Kari had a feeling these two were related, but she'd also bet their personalities and management styles were completely different. Adriana looked sympathetic and eager to please, while the hunk here seemed to be silently willing her to vanish.

She stopped focusing on the woman and concentrated on winning over the man. He was obviously the one in charge.

"I know," she said. "And I'm so sorry. First my plane was late, then I got lost. I took my chances that you'd still be open and able to take me to Elk Creek Canyon before nightfall."

"We close at five," he said. Nobody in the room had to look at their watch to know it was nearly that now.

Rule followers! Why did she have to run into one today? Kari suspected flirting would be wasted on him, and she was too tired to try. But it couldn't hurt to be...well, agreeable.

She pulled the ball cap off her head, letting her ponytail swing over her shoulder. She looked up at him and tried to appear both contrite and sweetly feminine. "I know it's getting late. But all the way up the mountain I've been hoping—praying, really—that there would still be time."

"We're not a taxi service, Miss Churchill."

"No, of course not. But—"

"Sorry. Elk Creek Canyon is thirty minutes flying time there and back. Unless it's an emergency, we don't go up after dark."

"This *is* an emergency."

Dark brows lifted as he crossed his arms over his chest. His mouth moved in a fascinating way and she got the feeling she'd amused him. "Ah. What kind of emergency would that be?"

She bit her lip, aware that she'd made a misstep. "Well, maybe not an emergency, really. Not life or death. But it's rather important."

"Then you should have gotten here on time."

It surprised Kari how quickly she could lose ground. What a hard case this guy was! Probably divorced a few times and completely soured on women. She began to feel stubborn.

"You've made your point," she said. "But sunset isn't for—" this time she did look at her watch "—one hour and forty-three minutes. I know because I had to check in with the Park Service on the way up here to let them know where and when I was going into the national forest. If I don't get there before dark, I'll have to re-check-in with them tomorrow. They're very strict about that."

"Yes, I know."

Her cheeks hurt from trying to hold back any outward sign of frustration. "So I'm here now." She pointed out the wide windows. "And I do see a couple of helicopters just sitting out there doing nothing."

"Which is where they'll stay. I'm afraid you'll have to re-schedule. We can probably slot you in tomorrow. Nine o'clock. *Sharp.*"

She didn't want to wait until tomorrow, but she'd never be able to explain to this guy why she wanted to go today. "I can't do tomorrow."

"Then I'm afraid you're out of luck."

"Is there another helicopter tour company in the area?"

"Nope."

"Is there another way to get to Elk Creek Canyon?"

"You could hike in. You'd probably get there by Tuesday. If you didn't get lost."

She frowned at him, refusing to accept that her window of opportunity could be slamming so firmly shut. "Look, can't we be reasonable about this? I've come so far—"

She broke off as he came around the counter and moved toward her. He seemed so full of hard control and dark warning that she wondered if he might be about to physically escort her out of the office. Instead he went past her and flipped the Open sign in the window to the reverse side.

He gave her another tight, meaningless smile. "We're closed."

Kari took a breath and went on recklessly, "I'm prepared to make it worth your time."

Bad idea. Instantly she watched his dark eyes flicker over her—and not in a good way. A cold, jittery, hollow feeling filled her where confidence had once been. Her breath moved inward with slow care. "I mean, I'll gladly *pay* more."

His voice was calmly nonnegotiable. "Sorry. Next time you might want to give yourself more time to get here. Give up those thirty extra minutes of beauty sleep."

Angry and embarrassed, Kari moved toward him. "I didn't

sleep in. I told you, my flight was delayed. And I took a wrong turn—" She broke off, realizing she'd already explained. This guy was just being difficult. She scowled at him, frustrated beyond courtesy. "Just for the record, you have lousy customer service skills."

He tossed a smile toward his office mate, who hadn't said a word in so long that Kari had practically forgotten she was here. "So I've been told. Doesn't change anything. If you still want to go to Elk Creek Canyon, you'll need to come back." He opened the door. "Addy, close up as much as you can, will you? After I get done, I'll come back to help you tie down."

"Nick…" Adriana began.

Kari had come this far—she just couldn't give up now. Refusing to let this stubborn man stand in the way, she caught the edge of the door. He was so close, she noticed that his eyes were the darkest brown she'd ever seen. Nearly black. "I don't want to drive all the way back to Denver."

"Then stay in Broken Yoke."

"That wide spot down by the interstate that seems to be auditioning for ghost town status? You've got to be kidding."

"There are two motels in town. Either one of them would be happy to take your money. Or we can even offer you a room up at the lodge."

"Look, maybe we got off on the wrong foot—"

"I could take her, Nick." The woman he'd called Addy spoke up.

Kari swung around quickly. Ah, bless you, she thought. "You could fly me out there?"

"Yes."

"No," Nick said sharply.

"Why not?" both women said at the same time.

The man ignored his co-worker and continued to address

Kari, his features doing a good impression of a gargoyle. "Addy works for and answers to me. She sure as hell doesn't fly one of my birds unless I tell her she can."

"Hey!" Addy protested, and when Kari looked at her, she could see the woman was now almost as furious as she was. Through the open neckline of her shirt, red splotches marked her skin.

"I have to go. We're closed," Nick said one last time. "Have a nice evening."

Without a look back, he left. There was a long moment of uncomfortable silence as both women watched him disappear. Kari's father had tried to teach her to live by the motto IIPP—Intelligence, Industry, Persistence and Plan. The way to accomplish anything, he'd said. But what should she do when IIPP didn't seem to have any affect on a hardheaded man?

Finally she turned back to Adriana. "What cave did he just finish hibernating in?"

The woman gave her a sheepish look. "He's usually not that bad. I feel I should apologize."

"Are you two related?"

"My older brother, Nick. As you can see, I'm the tolerated baby sister."

"You have my sympathies."

Adriana laughed. "Yeah, sometimes I want to choke him. But you have to take the bad with the good. You know how it is between siblings."

"Can't say that I do," Kari said absently as she glanced around the sparsely furnished office. "I was an only child."

An idea was starting to take shape in her mind. Maybe Kari couldn't win with big brother, but Adriana seemed like a reasonable person. Kari just had to find the right words, the right buttons to push. Her father would have found a way to make this trip happen. So could she.

She moved to the wall where Angel Air's business license was proudly hung. They'd only been in business a little over a year. Nick D'Angelo, Owner.

Ha! Nick D'Angelo, Jerk, was more like it.

She looked back over her shoulder at Adriana. "Does he always order you around like that?"

"When he thinks he can get away with it. He can't help it. Nick's ex-military. And when it concerns his choppers, he's like a hen with baby chicks. I think they're just hunks of metal and Plexiglas. Nick thinks they…breathe."

Kari gave her a commiserating smile. "But you're both licensed pilots, aren't you?"

"Oh, yes."

"Then I don't understand."

"Neither do I. But believe me, I'm going to be addressing this issue with him tonight. No matter what kind of mood he's in."

"Men," Kari complained. "They just won't believe women can do just about everything they can."

"Sometimes better."

They continued to discuss men's shortcomings and what to do about them, laughing over the fact that there seemed to be darned little. Another fifteen minutes went by. Kari discovered that she liked this woman. Adriana D'Angelo was smart, witty and enthusiastic. And, Kari suspected, a bit of a rebel. A trait that might definitely work to Kari's advantage.

"Well," she said at last with a disappointed sigh. "I suppose I'd better head down the mountain before it gets dark."

"Why don't you stay up at our place?" Adriana suggested. "My family owns Lightning River Lodge, just a mile up the mountain road."

"And take the chance of running into your brother? No thanks."

"I'm really sorry you two clashed like that. Reschedule and I promise I'll take you up to Elk Creek Canyon myself."

Kari gave her a doubtful look. "That would be lovely, but do you really think big brother will let you? He doesn't seem to take you very seriously."

That struck a nerve. Adriana colored again. "He will. Please come back."

Kari sent her voice lower, sent her lashes drifting down, too. "I don't know…I had really counted on this…" She let the words float off, hoping that her demeanor spoke volumes.

"I'm sorry. But tomorrow—"

"Will be too late," Kari finished for her. Then she gave the woman a smile filled with friendly regret. "Don't worry about it. It's my fault, really. I should have tried to get on a flight yesterday."

"Is it that crucial to you, getting there today?"

"I'm a freelance journalist and my down time between assignments is pretty small sometimes. But this isn't an assignment. It's personal. Your brother would probably laugh, but this is sort of a pilgrimage I just *have* to make."

"Oh." As Kari had hoped, the woman looked thoughtful, her imagination clearly trying to envision what kind of personal journey this trip could be.

After a suitable silence Kari added, "I don't blame you for being hesitant about flying after dark."

Adriana actually looked distressed now and Kari felt the first stirrings of guilt steal over her. Yes, she wanted to get to Elk Creek today. But was it really fair to trade on this woman's empathetic nature? In spite of her father's best efforts to teach her otherwise, hadn't she always tended to rush into things? For her, hadn't the weakest link in his IIPP motto always been the "plan" part?

"You know what?" Adriana suddenly said in a tone of firm decision. "I think I can get you to Elk Creek Canyon before sunset."

Kari's glance flew upward. "What about your brother?"

"Nick will just have to accept that he can't dictate to me anymore. We're supposed to be in this together. It's time he started treating me like we are."

"He'll be furious."

"Not half as furious as I'll be at myself if I don't stand up to him." She came around the counter, looking so determined that Kari didn't think she could have talked her out of this even if she'd wanted to. "I'll rev up Raven One. You go get your stuff."

TEN MINUTES LATER they were airborne. Stowing her sizable amount of camping gear and her duffel bag in the back, Kari settled into the copilot's seat and slipped on a headset that would allow her to communicate with Adriana through the cabin radio—the "hot mike" as she called it. The tiny Angel Air office dropped quickly out of sight as the helicopter climbed and swung away.

Kari's stomach lurched, but this woman seemed to know what she was doing. Her movements on the controls and rudder pedals were precise, sometimes barely perceptible. She no longer looked like an office receptionist, but a confident, capable pilot.

"I really can't thank you enough, Adriana," Kari said when they'd leveled off.

The woman smiled at her. "If we're going to fly in the face of my brother's wrath together, I think you should call me Addy." She pointed out the front windscreen, where in the distance a rambling three-story building was barely discernable among the tall ponderosa pines. "There's our resort—Lightning River Lodge. My brother's up there right now playing the little Dutch boy with his finger in the dike."

Addy explained about the plumbing problem. "Since our father's stroke, Nick's been the one everyone goes to. And we tend to rely on him for…well, for just about everything."

Guess he's not into delegating, Kari thought. Control freak. Out loud she said, "You know, if he'd just let you take me to begin with, we could have saved some time and hassle. He needs to lighten up."

Addy gave her a look that said that wasn't likely. "He's not usually that cranky, but the week started off badly, and it's been a horrible day. I think you were the last straw. And truthfully, I suspect he just didn't like the idea of me going up after dark."

"Do you like flying?"

"It's great. I'm pretty good, too, but I'll never get better if Nick doesn't stop trying to protect me. Of course, everyone in my family's that way. I'm the youngest." She made an infinitesimal adjustment with the pedals so that the helicopter tilted slightly to the right. "Look there," she said, pointing out the side windscreen. "Elk."

Kari watched a small herd leap away from the noise. "They're beautiful. We don't have much wildlife left back home in Florida."

"This whole area, from Denver to Vail, is some of the prettiest country in Colorado. The area we're flying over right now is the Lightning River Basin." She jerked her chin downward and to the left. "Down there by the river is where my family originally settled when they came here. My grandparents were looking for someplace that would remind them of their home back in the Italian Alps."

"Italian pioneers."

Addy laughed. "That's what my father claims, but I always thought they stopped here because facing the trip over the Rockies looked too intimidating." She tilted her head at Kari. "So what's so special about Elk Creek Canyon?"

"I don't know. I've never been there."

Addy turned her head to see if she'd heard correctly. "What?"

"Are you familiar with Madison Churchill?"

"The writer? Sure. I loved *Strange Disguises*."

"He was my father."

"No kidding," was all Addy said.

The magic of that famous connection received a brief ceremonial silence. Anyone Addy's age probably knew of "Mad" Churchill. He'd been compared to Hemingway, and his books were that rare thing in the publishing world—both popular and well-respected. His stories were vivid, imaginative and bold. All his heroes were the kind of sexy, noble adventurers that men wished in their hearts they could be and women wished they could find and marry.

Well, all but the last one. The hero of *Hours of Ice* hadn't been anyone's idea of a Madison Churchill protagonist.

"Wow," Addy said at last. "All those places he wrote about. You must have had some pretty fantastic vacations, traipsing around the globe."

Kari ducked her head a moment, formulating her response. People often assumed that. You'd think she'd have gotten used to it by now. "Actually, no. My mother hated traveling, so we stayed home most of the time." *Waiting.*

"But I remember reading that he was a stickler for research. That he liked to spend weeks and weeks in the places he wrote about…"

As though realizing that long absences from a husband and father could hardly have meant an idyllic home life for Kari, Addy stopped talking and began fiddling with a couple of the dials and switches on the pilot's console.

"Elk Creek Canyon was the setting for his last book," Kari said, trying to make the woman feel more comfortable.

"Hours of Ice."

"You know it?"

"Of course. I have to admit, though, it wasn't my… It was different than all his others." .

"That's what a lot of people said." And some had said much worse things than that, Kari remembered with a touch of bitterness.

"It sure made news around these parts. Not the book. I mean, what happened. That freak blizzard so early in the season. And then your father, such a famous guy, being lost all those weeks. Finally being rescued. Waiting must have been horrible for you."

"I was out of the country at the time, working on a story. I didn't even know he'd missed the date he was due back. My mother flew out here when the National Park Service called and told her that a full search was on. She had to go through most of it alone."

"Poor woman," Addy said sympathetically. "And then to lose him anyway. I mean, the fact that he…" Her words stumbled as she struggled with a better way to express herself. "It shocked everyone that he…"

"Never regained consciousness," Kari finished for her.

Even in the fading light, Kari could see that Addy regretted bringing up the subject. Her cheeks were like twin beacons.

"I'm sorry," the woman said. "Is it hard for you to talk about?"

Kari shrugged. "Not as much as it used to be. It's been two years since he made the trip."

"So you want to see where he got his inspiration for that book? Minus the blizzard, of course."

"That's one reason. There are others." She grimaced. "I'm sure someone like your brother would find them foolishly sentimental."

"Probably," Addy agreed. "Nick's not much for sentimental stuff."

Kari could well imagine the truth in that statement.

"I've been to Elk Creek Canyon a couple of times," Addy said. "I think you'll be disappointed. It's not very remarkable."

"That doesn't matter to me. I just want to see it. I had planned to have a long conversation with the park office first, get a better feel for my father's itinerary and why he chose that particular place. But my last assignment ran longer than it should have and I had to rely on the newspaper reports I pulled from the Internet to pinpoint just where he camped."

"So you're a journalist?"

Kari nodded. "Magazine articles mostly, so I finally get to travel as much as he did."

"No aspirations to be a novelist, too?"

"Unfortunately, I don't seem to have my father's flair for fiction."

"Tough shoes to fill." Addy smiled at her with kindness. "But maybe someday…right?"

"Maybe," Kari said, wondering if she still believed that. She had a drawer back home full of rejection letters. It had been a long time since she'd tried to write her father's kind of story. Or any fiction, for that matter. In the deepening silence between words, where the truth lived, Kari thought she suddenly knew the answer. *No. I'll never be good enough.*

Dusk was settling, coming fast. Even if the helicopter compass hadn't been positioned almost directly at eye level, Kari would have known they were flying north. The Rockies were a dark, jagged barrier to her left, and behind them the sun had stopped playing hide-and-seek and had disappeared completely.

Addy looked her way again. "So, if you don't mind me asking, why did you wait two years to make this trip?"

A tremor went through Kari as she remembered the two years since her father had died. How unbearable her mother had found the idea of her coming here. There had been so many tears. Countless arguments. And through most of them, Kari suspected that her mother's fears had nothing to do with *her* at all. Forgiveness. Acceptance. Laura Churchill had never been able to find any of that in her heart for the man she'd loved, the man she'd lost long before that final, fatal trip.

Kari cleared her throat. "My mother passed away six months ago. I couldn't have gone before then. She was pretty…frail…after Dad died. It would have upset her too much."

Addy arched an eyebrow her way. "Are you sure you're going to be all right out there? Even without a blizzard, the backcountry's not a place to fool around, and Elk Creek Canyon is pretty remote. I guess you already know that, though, considering what your father went through."

"I'll be fine."

"Still…I don't want to be flying this chopper for search and rescue when *you* fail to check in on your due back date."

"I'll only be out there a couple of days. I have an assignment waiting for me in New Zealand that I can't miss."

"I assume we're the ones picking you up."

Kari nodded. "If your brother has forgiven both of us by then. Tuesday. Nine o'clock. *Sharp*."

They both laughed at her attempt to mimic Nick D'Angelo's inflexible instructions. "Oh, he'll rant and rave for a while," Addy told her. "But he'll come around eventually. He doesn't hold grudges."

"I'll count on you, then," Kari said. She glanced out the left side of the helicopter to see ominous dark clouds rolling over and around the mountain range like boiling ocean waves crashing around a ship.

It occurred to her that she should have checked the weather report for the area. But as usual, she'd been running late. "Should we be concerned about those clouds?"

"There's rain behind them. The weather service didn't indicate the storm was moving so fast."

"Is that a problem?"

"No. But it might make the flight a little bumpy. We can withstand forty knots easily. I should have checked one last time before we left," Addy admitted. "Hold on a minute."

Addy pressed a switch on her cyclic stick, which allowed her to radio the nearest airport. Through her headset Kari could hear the low response between ground control and pilot. The news that a storm was quickly coming over the Front Range gave Kari an unpleasant moment, but Addy didn't seem overly concerned.

In another few minutes rain started to hit the windscreen in a steady pattern, and Kari could feel the wind begin to buffet the aircraft. Addy turned on the overhead cabin light. She made corrections on the controls constantly, seeming to know how to react to the slightest shift in their position. It wasn't until they started to see lightning in the clouds that she looked at all worried.

Kari glanced at the numerous dials spread across the cockpit console, but in spite of all the traveling she did, she didn't know that much about helicopters or how they operated. Nothing looked like a radar screen, or anything that remotely seemed as if it could pinpoint their location.

She gave Addy a hopeful smile. "I suppose you have radar or something to tell you where we are exactly? Just in case."

Addy shook her head. "Sorry. We rely on V.F.R."

"V.F.R.?"

"Visual Flight References." She pointed downward and smiled. "We check out the ground and see what looks familiar." Kari's reaction to that comment made the woman laugh. She added, "Don't worry, we won't get lost. I know every light on the mountain."

But suppose she couldn't see them because of the rain?

"Why don't we head back?" Kari suggested. "If it's raining this hard, I won't be able to set up camp anyway."

"We could set down and try to wait it out."

Just then lightning strobed the sky, flashing eerily into the cabin. When the thunderclap followed it, Addy muttered a curse as Kari clutched the side of her seat. She said nothing, her mouth suddenly too dry to utter words. She should never have pushed for this. Never have taken advantage of this woman.

After a few moments Addy said, "It's probably better if we do turn back. I'm sorry, Kari."

"No, that's fine. I shouldn't have been so insistent."

The woman swung the helicopter in a sharp turn. How dark it was outside, Kari thought. In spite of the landing lights cutting through the night, there seemed to be nothing beyond the front windscreen. Not a flicker of light anywhere.

Except for the lightning that glimmered sullenly within the clouds.

CHAPTER THREE

WITH THE FLICK of a finger on his control box, Sam D'Angelo moved his wheelchair out of his son's way.

They were in one of the lodge's downstairs suites, Nick's and granddaughter Tessa's temporary lodgings until their cabin was habitable again. The plumbing crisis had been dealt with—at least to Nick's satisfaction—but Sam, who had once handled these kinds of little emergencies, couldn't help feeling the need to make sure.

"You turned off *all* the valves in Number Ten?" he asked for the second time. "Just to be safe."

He hated that he couldn't get up the stairs in his own home, his own business. When he'd come back from the hospital, he should have insisted that they put in an elevator. He could have seen the damage upstairs for himself.

Nick was bent over the sink, washing his hands to remove the grease he'd encountered from taking a look at Rosa's stove. "I did, Pop," he said without turning around. "Tom Faraday's on his way. I think a crack in the tank is the culprit, but he'll be able to tell us for sure. Stop worrying."

"You know what water can do to wood when it seeps through tiny crevices?"

Nick straightened, wiping his hands dry. "Gosh, no," he said with a grin. "Not since the last time you put me through Plumbing 101 class."

Sam narrowed his eyes. "Your mother is right. You are becoming a very disrespectful son."

"And you're turning into a bigger worrier than she is."

Sam gave him a severe look.

Nick grabbed the edges of his shirt and pulled it over his head, then slipped on a fresh white T-shirt. From his wheelchair, Sam watched in silent admiration. Nick had inherited Sam's build. His torso was tanned, broad and powerful. A man's chest, the way a man's chest *should* be. The way Sam's had once been years ago.

He couldn't help it, a little twist of envy jolted through him. Bad enough that age took its revenge so soon. That sickness could whittle you down until there was almost nothing left of the person you had been. Sam had cheated death. It had whispered in his ear, but he had refused to listen. He had lived, and for that, he thanked God. But he was only fifty-eight. He missed that lost energy, that effortless strength. He wondered if his son understood how lucky he was to have it.

Nick went to the closet, pulled out his sneakers and sat on the bed. He was halfway through knotting one shoe when the lace popped.

He held the broken piece in front of him, shaking his head. "Perfect," he said. "Just perfect."

Toeing off the sneaker, he kicked them both out of the way and went to the closet to root around for another pair. "I'm telling you," he said as he scooped up his hiking boots. "I don't care if a whole *family* of skunks have taken up residence in the cabin. Tomorrow, Tessa and I are moving back in."

Sam cocked his head. "Why are you in such a black mood?"

"I'm not in a black mood. Brown, maybe. You wouldn't believe—"

He broke off as they both became aware that Tessa stood

in the open doorway. Sam's granddaughter was a beauty even at fourteen. Glossy black hair like Rosa's had been when he'd first met her. And the eyes—like dark fire. Unfortunately the fire lately had all been directed at Nick. Even now, as she addressed her father, her eyes were smoldering.

"Nonna Rosa said to tell you that we're all eating sandwiches tonight 'cause of the stove. Everything else is for guests. She also says the kitchen is closing early and don't either of you touch the zabiglione in the fridge."

"*Donnaccia!* We live under the rule of a petty tyrant," Sam said dramatically, hoping to get a reaction out of the girl. Tessa was his pet, his favorite companion. Surely he could make her smile.

The child had no time for him. Tight lips declared her grievances against her father. She lowered her head, setting her chin. "Can I eat dinner in my room?" she asked Nick.

"I suppose." Nick pulled on one hiking boot. "Still mad about the dress, huh?"

Now his darling grandchild's eyes shot daggers. "I took it back like you told me. That doesn't mean I think it's fair."

"Tessa…"

The girl flung herself away from the door and disappeared.

Nick sighed and looked at his father. "If I'm in a mood, would you really wonder why?"

"She'll get over it. The young suffer a great deal, but their anger dies quickly."

"Addy thinks I'm too hard on her."

It was time, Sam decided, to say a few things that had been on his mind lately. "Sometimes you are. I think you need someone to make what you say to her more pal—" He stopped, trying to envision the right word in his mind. In spite of all the progress he'd made, sometimes the consequences of the stroke still plagued his speech, but Nick knew better than to help him.

The word wouldn't come. After a frustrated moment he said, "To make what you say not such a bitter pill to swallow."

"There are plenty of people around here sugarcoating every word I say to her."

"You need more than that. You need a real mother for the girl. And a wife for yourself, Nick. A helpmate."

There was a swift change in Nick's expression. He stopped tightening the laces on his second boot and looked at his father as though he had suffered another stroke. "*A wife!* That's the *last* thing I need."

"Why? Look at your mother and me. So many happy years. Marriages are made in heaven."

"So are thunder and lightning," Nick said with a bark of laughter. He turned back to his boots, a touch of impatience in the set of his mouth. "I don't think we need to have this discussion. Let's go see if we can talk Mom out of some lasagna."

Sam moved his wheelchair closer. "Don't brush me aside. I'm serious. You think one bad marriage and it's over? Just because you burn your mouth once does not mean you have to blow on your soup forever."

Nick rose, raking a hand through his hair. "I don't know where this is coming from," he muttered. "I haven't been this uncomfortable since our birds and the bees talk."

"Your mother and I—we see you. You take on too much. You share nothing. Not even your thoughts anymore. This mountain is becoming your fortress. I know this is because of me." Sam's right arm was his strongest, and he let his fingers brush against the side of the wheelchair. "Because of this. You think we can't manage without you."

The discussion was sapping his energy. Sam could feel his head drooping a little. In a softer tone he said, "Well, perhaps you are right. Perhaps we can't."

Nick came to the chair and knelt in front of his father. He took his hand in his, massaging the long, bony fingers lightly. "I see improvement in you every day, Pop," he said in a gentle voice. "You keep going, and I'll be out of a job in no time. In the meantime, I enjoy looking after everyone here. I'd be bored without all this insanity."

Sam looked his son in the eyes. "You are a healthy young man. Good Italian stock. You should date."

Nick grinned. "I do. Didn't I take Helen Grabowksi to Broken Yoke's Fourth of July celebration?"

"*Bah!*" Sam said with a grimace. "That woman, she is…she has…" Again he struggled to find the word. When it failed to materialize, he settled on something easier. "Your grandfather would have said she has *la malocchio!*"

Nick's Italian was pretty good, but he'd seldom heard that word. He straightened and placed his hands on his hips. "I don't see how a woman who works at Becky's House of Hair can have the evil eye."

"She giggled all through the national anthem." Sam didn't bother to hide the acid in his tone.

"God help her if it had been the *Italian* national anthem. You'd have had her run out of town on a rail."

"That woman is not your type."

"Type!" Nick exclaimed with more laughter. "I was looking for fun and a little companionship. Not a blood transfusion."

"Nicholas—"

"We can talk about my love life later. Much, much later. I have to get back to the hangar. I'm surprised Addy hasn't called screaming bloody murder because I've been gone so long."

He moved around to the back of Sam's wheelchair, bending forward as he pushed his father out into the hallway. "If you and Mom want to work on finding someone a mate, start with Addy. Get her interested in a man and maybe she'll stop bugging me about more flight time."

ALL THE WAY DOWN the mountain in his Jeep, Nick couldn't stop smiling.

Imagine his father and mother worried about his love life! What was *that* all about? Maybe he hadn't been in the best of moods lately, but how did they figure getting involved with a woman was the answer? If anything, it would just make everything more…complicated.

He should have told his father not to bother. He was no damned good at the husband/wife game. Ask Denise, his ex. She'd have given Pop an earful, although Nick wasn't sure she'd be completely impartial about where the blame lay. Some of the reasons their marriage had failed had been his fault. Okay, a lot of them. It probably didn't matter now which ones. It was enough to say that their quarreling had corroded and eventually killed what they'd once had together.

A new relationship? These days he couldn't find much reason to try. He was too tired. Too set in his ways. Too busy to blow the dust off the old male/female dance steps and find someone new to whirl out onto the floor.

Besides, who in these parts could even inspire him to try?

Pop was right about Helen Grabowski. Way too giddy. Ellie Hancock, the owner of Ellie's Book Nook? Too timid. You had to work hard to get a single word out of her. Paulette Manzoni, the pretty ski instructor he'd met in Vail the last time he was there, had been a possibility. She had a great appreciation for the bed and was Italian, to boot, which would certainly please his parents. Only thing, she collected teddy bears, which was a nice little hobby—until Nick had discovered they took up every square inch of her house.

No. Definitely not.

Broken Yoke, the nearest town, didn't offer much hope. The woman who'd shown up at Angel Air's office today had been right. If something didn't happen soon, the only inhabitants there would be ghosts.

Kari Churchill. Pretty name. Pretty lady, too, although she had one heck of a nerve expecting them to drop everything to fly her out to Elk Creek Canyon. He didn't care for egotists who had so little respect for other people's time. She'd put his back up right from the start with that attitude of hers, and Nick suspected the feeling was mutual.

Too bad, because they could have used the money. But if he was going to be tied up at the lodge, he hadn't wanted Addy taking up that flight. Not in the last hour of good daylight. Not when his sister still didn't know his birds like the back of her hand.

But he couldn't say that in front of her. So he'd probably lost that booking and made an enemy of the Churchill woman for life. Sorry, Pop. Scratch that name off your list of potential mates.

Rain splattered the windshield of the Jeep. In the distance he heard the rumble of thunder. Those clouds he'd seen earlier hadn't lied. He was getting pretty good at predicting storms. Soon he'd be like Great-Uncle Giovanni, forecasting weather with his big toes.

Addy was going to be furious. It took both of them to get the birds into the hangar, him pushing from the tail while she maneuvered the skid dolly. Now they might have to manage it in pouring rain.

He frowned as he pulled into the parking lot. The outside floodlights weren't on and Kari Churchill's vehicle was still sitting there. The lights in the office weren't on, either, but what made Nick's stomach drop right down to his toes was the chopper pad.

Raven One was gone.

Ramming the key into the office lock, he flipped on the lights and strode back to the hangar in less than a dozen steps. It was dark, too. No copter. Nobody in sight.

He ran back into the office. Not possible. Addy wouldn't. She *wouldn't* have taken the copter up with a storm coming in. She knew better.

Didn't she?

His mind stretched back, trying to recall if she'd been standing there when he and Dwayne Patterson had shared that awkward conversation about the weather.

We'll get a thunderstorm later.

You really think so?

Where had Addy been? *On the pad, right?* On the pad right beside him. *No. Not there. Checking on that little witch Hannah Patterson.*

If she *hadn't* known about the coming storm, then she might have gone up. When he'd pulled out of the parking lot, had there been anything but pretty blue sky overhead? He couldn't remember. Would she really have let the Churchill woman talk her into something? *No!* She'd check the weather service. She knows the drill. She knows it…

His legs felt as though they were filled with water as he dropped behind his desk, knocked everything aside and pulled the base radio to his chest. He had to swallow hard.

Focus. Don't lose control.

Oh, damn it, sis! Where are you?

"BASE TO Nine-Zero-One-Bravo. Where the hell are you?"

Ground radio transmissions were normally more difficult for a passenger to hear, nothing more than muffled signals, but Kari didn't miss a word of the angry male communication that practically made her ears ring. And it wasn't difficult to figure out just *who* was trying to reach them.

She and Addy exchanged a look.

Addy pressed the radio switch. "Nine-Zero-One-Bravo to Base. Who wants to know?"

"Damn it, Addy! Where are you?" Nick demanded again. At what had to be the top of his lungs. "I don't think this is funny, Adriana. If you get down here in one piece I'm going to break every bone in your body."

Kari threw Addy a worried glance, but the woman only grinned and gave her a look of mock terror. She pushed the radio button again. "Stop acting like a raving maniac. I'm not hurting your bird. We're flying."

"I don't give a damn about the bird. Are you aware there's a thunderstorm on your tail?" There was a moment of hostile silence. "And who's *we?* It better not be who I think it is."

"She can hear every word, Nick," Addy said patiently. "That's not the way to talk to our paying customers."

"She wasn't supposed to *be* a paying customer. Not today. Get down here."

"Soon, big brother. We've been watching the storm. I think we're outrunning it."

"You think?"

"We're getting a little wind. But stop worrying. We'll be down in about five minutes. I can see the power station lights up on the ridge."

"Okay. Okay," Nick said, sounding a little more calm. "Keep your airspeed up. And don't overdo your cyclic. Pull back too hard and she'll plant your tongue to the roof of your mouth."

"I know that," Addy said in a put-upon voice. "Now leave us alone. You're making me nervous. And you've got to promise to be civil when we get down. No yelling."

"I want you to check in with me every minute until you touch down. Base to Nine-Zero-One-Bravo. Out."

Inside the copter cabin and over the dull whipping of the rotor blades, there was nothing but dead silence for a few moments. Kari's ears were tingling in her headset, but Addy still seemed unfazed. Maybe she was used to going toe-to-toe with her brother. Kari, on the other hand, had a feeling that if she ever *did* get to Elk Creek Canyon, it would be another flight service that would take her there.

Addy sighed. "Nice to know he cares."

"I notice he didn't make any promises about not yelling."

The helicopter started to drift and rock as the weather worsened. It seemed to be at the mercy of a giant's swinging hand, picked up and pushed sideways, then dropped and pulled back in the other direction. Kari began to feel slightly queasy, but Addy seemed determined and calm.

Rain was falling in silver sheets. Kari's eyes were riveted by the sight of it sliding down the windscreen, where it was violently flung away by the wind. They both became silent, tense. Addy was concentrating and Kari was simply too nervous to speak.

In the next moment lightning zigzagged across the front of the helicopter. There was a sizzling crack, so loud and close that Kari couldn't hold back a small yelp of surprise and fear. The aircraft bucked and took such a swooping dive that Kari felt her rear end come up off the seat.

"Son of a—" Addy muttered, both hands moving on the controls to correct their descent. "I think we just took a hit!"

She jerked her chin toward the top of the cabin. Over Kari's head was a small paned opening, like a car sunroof. "Look up there and tell me if you see anything. Sparks. Fire. Anything."

Kari rose as much as her seat belt would allow. At first she saw nothing but darkness. Then a stray flicker of light from one of the exterior lights revealed that the blades were still turning. Surely that was a good sign. "Nothing," she said.

"Something's wrong."

"Are we going to crash?"

"Not if I can help it."

The wind seemed stronger, rising and moaning eerily. Kari watched the sure movements of Addy D'Angelo's pale hands. Up. Down. Back again. Correcting constantly.

A heart-deep fear rose in her. *Please. I don't want to die.*

And then the engine failed.

It lasted only a moment or two. Like a misfire in an automobile. But it was enough to send the helicopter plummeting further still, sinking like a bird dropped out of the sky by a hunter's rifle.

Addy was on the radio instantly, shouting through the headphones. "Base, come in. Springs Flight Service, come in. Mayday! Mayday! Mayday! This is Nine-Zero-One-Bravo. We have engine failure from a lightning strike. Two on board. I think we can make Columbine Meadow. I repeat…"

There was no answer. Was the radio dead?

Kari was numb with fear now. She squeezed her eyes tight for a moment, listening to her own rattled breathing and the woman beside her, who muttered and cursed and talked herself through every movement.

"Autorotate, Addy…. Not enough airspeed and height, but you know how to compensate. Easy. Easy. Nose up. Glide in, glide in. You can do it."

Kari gripped her own hands hard. A flicker of lightning lit up the cabin. In that one brief moment Addy's face looked both beautiful and terrible.

It couldn't end like this. Not like this, Kari thought in anguish. *Father. I'm so sorry. Now I'll never know…*

Addy swung her head to look at her. "Columbine Meadow's less than five miles from Angel Air. We can make it."

The helicopter shook as though it was coming apart. Although she couldn't see anything out the front windscreen, Kari knew the ground was coming up fast in spite of all Addy's best efforts. "Oh, God," she whispered. "Oh, God."

"Hang on," Addy warned her. "Hang on." She had pushed back in her seat, bracing, both hands tight on the controls. "Flatten the glide path, Addy. Raise your collective. Keep your nose up, damn it!"

The earth rushed toward them.

Addy shouted at her through the headset. "If we hit hard enough to split the skids, then our bodies are going to take the force of the impact. Get ready."

The helicopter landed suddenly.

Nothing could have prepared Kari for how crushing it was, how loud, how completely terrifying. Her spine jolted. Her teeth came down hard and cut into her lip, filling her mouth with blood. Something struck her against the right temple. Beside her, Addy D'Angelo gave a short yelp of pain. Above them, the rotor blades still turned, but things banged. Rattled. Screeched in protest.

There was a moment of absolute stunned silence as both

of them realized that they hadn't been instantly killed. That they might even survive this.

Then Addy moaned.

"Addy," Kari said, reaching out to touch the woman's arm. "Are you all right?"

Addy jerked away from that contact with a gasp. "Got to shut down. Get us cooled off." She sounded disoriented and when she reached for the switches, she moaned again. "Oh damn, I think my arm's broken. Maybe both of them."

"Tell me what to do."

"Get out. Leg it out of here."

"No!" Kari told her. *Tell me what to do.*

With her chin, Addy motioned toward the floor on Kari's side. "The fire extinguisher. By your right foot. Do you know how to use one?"

Kari reached for it immediately. It looked no bigger than a bottle of shaving cream. "I'll figure it out."

"I'll shut down what I can up here. Can you move? Get out and go to the back of the fuselage. The engine's below. Don't touch it. Just spray the hell out of it until the canister's empty. Understand?"

Quickly, Kari unfastened her seat belt and slipped the helicopter's door latch. The ground wasn't flat and it took a moment for her to find her feet. The craft sat slightly cock-eyed on a scattered field of rocks, but at least it seemed to be in one piece. From what Kari could see, in spite of what Addy had feared, the landing struts hadn't separated from the fuselage.

It was still raining lightly and Kari shivered with cold. Or maybe it was shock. She realized her hands were shaking, too. So badly she could hardly pull the pin out of the extinguisher. Setting her teeth, she did as Addy had told her. Yellow chemicals sprayed out to cover the engine. When the can finally emptied with a dribbling hiss, she tossed it away. By the time she managed to stumble back inside the cabin, her hands weren't the only part of her that trembled.

She slid into her seat, hearing the quick rise and fall of her own shallow breaths as they competed with the pounding of her heart. "I did it. Now what?" she asked, though she hoped the answer required no more than the strength she possessed right now.

"Good," Addy said. "Just give me a minute."

Kari looked at her companion. She held both her arms against her body like a surgeon who'd just scrubbed for surgery. Her face was pale, but there was no blood anywhere, thank God.

Twisting in her seat, Kari leaned closer. "Let me help you." Addy's left arm looked normal, but there was a good-size knot just past the wrist of her right one. "Do you really think they're broken?" Kari asked with a grimace.

"I don't know." Addy frowned at her. "Your forehead is bleeding."

Gingerly, Kari touched her temple. She could feel a lump forming—it hurt like hell—but when she brought her hand away, there was only a little watery blood on her fingertips.

"I'll survive," she said. "Looks like we both will."

"I can't believe we crashed." Addy's voice sounded sketchy and a little wild. "And that we didn't die. Although we might as well have. Nick's going to kill me."

"After what we just went through, we can deal with him."

Kari leaned across the back of the seat, trying to ignore the throb of pain that suddenly stabbed along her spine. Her camping equipment lay all over the rear seats. She unzipped her pack and dug into the contents, pushing through nylon and tin and packages of freeze-dried food.

"What are you doing?" Addy asked.

When Kari finally found what she wanted, she settled back in her seat. She held up the tent stakes and masking tape she'd rescued from her gear. "I think we should try to splint your arms. Okay?"

Addy gave her a faint smile and nodded.

As gently as she could, Kari placed a tent stake against Addy's right forearm, then wound the tape around it to hold the metal in place. The woman was a trooper. She set her jaw and didn't make a sound except for one hiss of pain that escaped her dry, pale lips.

"So now what do we do?" Kari asked as she worked. "Do you think your brother heard you?"

"Even if he didn't, the airport would have heard the Mayday. Assuming that the radio was still working. It's definitely not now."

"So we'll just sit and wait to be rescued," Kari said, trying for a lighter tone that might keep Addy's mind off the pain in her arms.

The woman closed her eyes and let her head fall back against the seat. She suddenly looked so much younger, smaller. The cabin seemed to swallow her up.

"I'm so sorry, Kari," she said in a thin, quavering voice. "My fault. Not rechecking the weather service was such a stupid mistake. It's basic."

"What are you talking about?" Kari reproached her. "You were magnificent. We'd never have survived this if you hadn't been so calm and in control. Besides, it's really my fault. I'm the one who took advantage of your kindness."

Addy gave her a faint smile. "Don't be so hard on yourself."

"No, I'm to blame here. My father was the most spontaneous man you'd ever want to meet, but even *he* used to complain about how impulsive I am, how disorganized. I could have planned this whole trip so much better. I could have come up here when I had more time to devote to it."

"So why didn't you?"

"Because…" Kari hesitated, then decided to tell the truth. After what she and Addy had just been through, the woman deserved nothing less. "Because today is the two-year anniversary of the day my father hiked into Elk Creek Canyon. I wanted to experience the same set of circumstances he did. Know exactly what he saw. It just seemed important somehow. A way to help me understand…how he could have died there."

"I'm sorry," Addy said again, sounding a little woozy.

"It's all right," Kari reassured her. Lightly she pressed the final piece of tape around her splint. "This is the best I can do under the circumstances. Let's just rest now. There's no point in beating ourselves up for what's already done."

That seemed to help a little. They settled back in their seats. Addy kept her eyes closed. Kari just kept staring out the front of the helicopter. Her temple throbbed. Muscles in her back began to protest. The only sounds were the soft exhalations of their own breaths, calmer now, no longer quick and charged with panic. They were cocooned in a puddle of light inside the aircraft, but outside everything looked as black as a deep well. At least the rain had let up.

Help will be here soon. Just rest. Wait for it.

A few minutes passed. Kari dozed.

The next thing she knew, the helicopter seemed to be shaking again. Her eyes flew open. She felt disoriented. In the darkness beyond the helicopter there seemed to be bright lights everywhere. For a moment she thought the lightning was back. Then she realized that the lights were the twin white beams of car headlights.

Shouts. Movement. *We've been rescued.*

Someone tugged on the door next to Addy. It held stubbornly for a moment, then gave with a squeal of protesting metal. Kari squinted, trying to give features to their rescuer's face, but all she could make out was the silhouette of a man.

Please, please let it be a policeman, she thought. A paramedic. A fireman. *Anyone* but—

"Addy, talk to me!" Nick D'Angelo demanded. His tone was tart, frantic.

No such luck. Big brother Nick had found them.

Kari had a feeling the crash was only the beginning of her problems.

CHAPTER FOUR

"JUST TELL ME you're not mad," Addy pleaded around another sniffling sob.

"I'm not mad," Nick repeated for the third time.

Addy's face crumpled and she bit her lip. "I don't believe you."

Oh, brother. Somebody get me out of here.

Addy looked pale and miserable against the stark white environment of the emergency examining room. Nick hadn't left her side since the ambulance had brought both women into the small hospital. His fear for his sister's injuries had subsided and his heart no longer beat as if he'd been running. But his nerves—his nerves were still jangling.

He almost wished the doctor would order him out of the room and back to the anonymous safety of the waiting area. Not much chance of that. The fresh-faced resident looked pretty meek, no older than Tessa's biology partner in school.

His sister, usually relentlessly upbeat, was an emotional mess. She didn't seem to mind the pain of a broken left arm and a sprained right wrist. She hardly looked at the nurse slipping an Ace bandage over her fingers. But she'd been crying off and on for five minutes—five *long* minutes—and nothing Nick said seemed to help. Frankly, he was running out of reassuring words and sympathetic looks.

This is all that Churchill woman's fault.

The doctor had told him that the woman was going to be fine. Lucky lady, the doc had said. No more than a small bump on the head.

I ought to go down to the end of the hall and throttle the life out of her.

He wouldn't do it, of course. How could he when his own guilt was eating away at him like battery acid? Because when it came right down to it, *he* was the one responsible for this latest disaster.

He should have known his headstrong sister would be looking for any excuse to take up one of the Ravens. All it had taken was a little friendly persuasion from a smoothie like Kari Churchill to push her into defying him.

He should have brought Addy along faster in the business. He should have made her understand that all the "ground school" flying time in the world didn't mean diddily if she couldn't read the sky, didn't know how to smell a stormfront just by sniffing the air. Her instincts needed to be honed until they were razor-sharp.

But he'd been dragging his feet. All the annoying little problems he'd had to deal with lately, plucking at him like greedy children. Zapping his time and energy. It had been easy enough to fall into the comfortable pattern of treating Addy more like a secretary than a fellow pilot. No surprise that she'd gotten tired of waiting and jumped at the first opportunity that presented itself.

With nearly tragic results.

"I know you're mad," Addy croaked. "That's why you look that way."

"What way?"

"Like you've been sucking lemons."

Nick blew air through his cheeks. He rolled his eyes in the doctor's direction, but the man just gave him a sympathetic smile and continued scribbling on Addy's chart.

"All right," Nick said in a firm voice. "I *am* mad. Don't think you're getting away with this stunt. You and I are going to have a long, serious conversation about who's in charge at Angel Air." He softened his words by running the back of a quick, affectionate finger down her flushed cheek. "But not right now. Not until you're healed and feeling yourself again."

Sobering momentarily, Addy nodded. "I understand. I take full responsibility for what happened, Nick."

"Oh, believe me, there's plenty of blame to go around."

"You mean Kari?" his sister protested. "She's not at fault here. It was my idea. After we were up and saw the first signs of rough weather, she even suggested we turn around and come back."

Addy had misunderstood just who he really blamed, but right now, it was easier to find fault with their customer's pushy approach than to admit his own part in tonight's near-catastrophic events. "I'll bet she did."

"I've ruined everything," Addy said, looking very young and vulnerable again. Like a child, she ducked her head to wipe her nose against the shoulder of her hospital gown.

The doctor caught Nick's eye and gave him a reassuring smile. "The meds will kick in soon."

Thank God.

He leaned closer, taking Addy's face in his hands and turning her head to make her meet his eyes. Beneath his hands, her bones felt small and fragile. He realized once again how incredibly lucky they were that she hadn't been seriously hurt. A warm tear slipped beneath his fingers and he wiped it away as gently as he could. "Come on, Addy. Quit crying. You know I can't take weepy women. Everything's going to be all right. Mom and Pop will be here soon."

"I can't seem to help it. You know how your whole life is supposed to flash before your eyes when things like this happen?"

"Yours didn't?"

"It *did*." She grimaced. "And it was so boring, Nick. My life has been one big snooze fest. I've made one bad choice after another. I'm nothing but a small-town girl with small-town ideas, and I'm destined to live and die a small-town life. David was right."

"David who?"

"McKay," Addy said with a put-upon voice. "Who else would I mean?"

"Your old boyfriend from high school?" Nick frowned. God, if she was going to dredge up ancient history from ten years ago, they were going to be here forever. "I thought you hated him."

Addy started to sob again. In an effort to sidetrack her, he touched the edge of her bandaged arm. Her fingers stuck out from the end like undercooked sausages.

"I don't know why you're crying," he said in a lighter voice. "This is going to keep you out of work at the lodge for a few weeks. We'll all be waiting on you hand and foot."

"I must have been bracing too hard for the crash. How bad is the damage to Raven One? Tell me the truth. Did I split the skids?"

"Harry's going to tow it over to the airframe techs tonight. I'll get a better look in the morning."

"What are you going to do about the rest of the week's tours? Me out of commission, and down one chopper?"

"Let's not worry about it right now."

She shook her head. "Why did I think I could actually fly

your birds? Maybe flying isn't my forte. Maybe I don't even *have* a forte."

"Of course you do. If you're going to criticize your ability to fly, then you're criticizing my judgment to take you on as a partner." He reached out to flick a stray tear off the end of her nose, giving her a smile. "And I'm never wrong about things like that, am I?"

"No."

"You'd have been fine if you hadn't taken that lightning strike. I was listening on the radio, remember? You were outrunning it. Doing great."

"I did have everything under control up until then…"

That was more like it. The old Addy was returning. Nick ran a hand over the top of her head. Her hair was a tangled mess. "What you haven't got under control is your ability to keep people from taking advantage of you. I know that sobsister played on your sympathy to get you up there."

Absently his sister shook her head, then sniffled around a yawn. "She didn't. Not really."

They both watched the nurse work on her arm a few minutes. Finally the woman tucked the last bit of bandaging into place. "Did you know Kari is Madison Churchill's daughter?" Addy asked.

"No, and I don't care if she's related to *Winston* Churchill."

"She was awfully calm after we crashed. Didn't panic. She handled the fire extinguisher when I realized I couldn't. She even found a way to splint my arms."

"Which wouldn't have needed splinting if she'd taken no for an answer in the first place."

"You should talk to her."

"Not in the mood I'm in."

"She's just down the hall."

"Good. She should stay there."

She gave him a frowning glance. "You're being completely unreasonable."

Nick didn't need Addy to tell him that. But every time he thought about trying to talk to that woman, he could feel his blood pressure take a leap. He grunted. "I get that way when people put my family in danger."

Addy just looked at him in rueful silence. The nurse's eyes flitted back and forth between them. He could tell that even she thought he was being unreasonable.

He rubbed the back of his neck with one hand. "The FAA reports I'm going to have to fill out, the cost of repairs, the lost revenue… If I don't end up suing her sorry ass for her involvement in this, she should consider herself lucky."

His sister ducked her head and swallowed hard. Then her dark eyes found his once more. "Have you considered the possibility that she could…that she might be the one to—"

"Sue us?" he finished for her.

Hell, somewhere in the back of his mind he hadn't been able to think of much else. For all her youthful inexperience, Addy was an adult. An employee of Angel Air. The company had a responsibility to its passengers to keep them safe.

The Churchill woman could probably make a case if she wanted to—no telling what missteps Addy had already admitted—but he wasn't willing to think about that right now. Addy would open a floodgate of fresh tears if she thought there might be that kind of trouble ahead for the family.

"Adriana!"

"My baby!"

"Adda-girl!"

The family had arrived. He'd hoped he and Addy could get out of here soon, but he should have known better. The D'Angelos—Mom, Pop and both aunts—surged into the room to descend on Addy like a wave. Nick stepped back. Even the nurse stepped back. You didn't stand in the way of a D'Angelo tidal wave.

"I thought we'd never get here," Nick's mother cried. She pressed both her hands to her daughter's face as though feeling for fever. Aunt Renata and Aunt Sofia were like bookends on either side of Addy, full of commiserating sounds at the sight of her bandaged arms.

Unable to get any closer because of the cluster of people and his wheelchair, Nick's father settled for placing his hand along Addy's blanket-covered ankle. "What happened?" Sam demanded. He touched the nurse's arm. "Get the doctor. I want to know about my daughter's condition."

Nick stood back and listened while Addy briefly described the circumstances of the crash. The resident came in and explained about her injuries. The family gasped and made little worried sounds throughout it all, but were finally satisfied to hear that Addy wouldn't even have to spend one night in the hospital. Now that the medication had taken the edge off the pain, she had stopped being so weepy, thank goodness. She would, however, find it difficult to use anything but the tips of her fingers for a few weeks.

"You're sure it's nothing more than that?" Sam asked the doctor, obviously making no effort to hide his frowning assessment of the younger man.

"She'll be back up in the air before the month's out," Nick said for his sister's benefit. Addy gave him a hopeful smile.

"This other woman," his father continued. "She's all right, too?"

It was a surprise to Nick, but evidently no one in the family seemed to find the Churchill woman's part in the accident objectionable. "She's fine," he said in annoyance. "Women like that always land on their feet."

His father's brows shot upward. "That's a pretty strong statement. What's got you so wrought up?"

"None of this would have happened if she hadn't been so pushy." Nick turned his attention back to his sister. He nodded toward her bound forearms. "Looks like those are going to make things awkward for a while."

"Don't you worry," Aunt Renata said to Addy. "We'll feed and dress you, and even bathe you if we need to. Won't we, Sofia?"

"Just like when you were a little baby," Aunt Sofia told her.

At that promise, Addy threw a look of desperation Nick's way. He just grinned and shook his head at her. She deserved it after scaring the hell out of him.

"Who's watching the lodge?" Nick asked. He glanced at his watch. Nearly nine-thirty. The hired help would be long gone by now.

"Tessa's at the front desk," his father replied. "It was quiet when we left. This may be a good time for her to get more involved in the business. Perhaps she can take on some of Adriana's responsibilities. The dining room, laundry…"

Aunt Sofia glanced at Nick. "She could clean late checkouts after school and do turn-down service in the evening."

Nick frowned. "I don't want her doing anything that interferes with homework."

"We'll need some temporary help," his mother said. The consummate field marshal, she was already planning ahead.

"Clay Watts at Eagle's Rest owes me a favor," Nick said. "I'll see if he can send over a couple of housekeepers tomorrow until I arrange something with a temp service."

Nick had started to head out of the room when he nearly

collided with one of the nurses. He thought her name was Sharon—a roommate of one of the nurses he'd dated a few years ago. She'd previously come in to tell them that Kari Churchill was doing just fine down in Exam Room One.

Now she tapped the chart in her hand. "Miss Churchill's going to be discharged in a few minutes. She's asking to see your sister before she goes. Or you."

Nick shook his head. "Tell her that's not necessary."

"Nick!" Addy exclaimed with some of her old spirit. "Don't you dare speak for me."

Nick ignored her. "Tell her if she wants to leave an address, I'll see to it that her stuff on board the chopper gets sent to her."

"After what she's been through, that's no way to treat a customer," his mother scolded.

"And I want to see her," Addy said.

His father looked at him sharply. "You have a responsibility to make sure she's all right, Nick. You know that."

Aware that every eye in the family was on him, Nick lifted his hands in a gesture of surrender. "Fine. I'll check on her before I call Clay."

Dead silence followed. Before anyone could comment, Nick stalked out.

He glanced down the corridor toward Exam Room One. He didn't want to go there. "Play nice with the customers," his sister was fond of saying, but he didn't feel like coming face-to-face again with the woman who had helped bring such trouble to their door.

On the other hand, if he didn't, there could be consequences. The family counted on him to put things right. In all the years the business had been operating, there had never been a single lawsuit brought against the company. His father was especially proud of that fact.

Muttering a curse under his breath, Nick wove down the hall, past harried nurses and around complicated-looking equipment.

Civil, but not subservient. Solicitous, but not admitting to any culpability. He knew how to handle women like Kari Churchill. He scrubbed a hand over his face, annoyed with his own need for an internal pep talk. *Come on. Just get it over with.*

When he walked into the room he didn't see her right away. The doctor was busy giving last-minute instructions. "So don't be surprised if you have an occasional headache over the next few days."

"All things considered, if that's all I have to deal with, I won't complain," Kari replied softly.

Nick moved into her line of sight, positioning himself at the end of the gurney. She turned her head in his direction as the doctor moved away.

He realized suddenly that he hadn't remembered her right. He mentally cataloged her appearance all over again, searching for the hard, tough broad he'd built her up to be in his mind. Right now all he saw was a woman who looked pale and tired and a little shaky. Probably trying not to think too much about what a close brush she'd had with death this night.

She sat up straighter, and he noticed.

Nervous? he wondered. Good. He stopped seeing how sweetly appealing she looked lying there and thought about how pleased she must have been when she knew she'd successfully manipulated Addy.

"Hello," she said, her voice full of wary restraint.

He gave her a short nod of acknowledgment, crossing his arms over his chest. He knew his features were too stern, but his willpower was in full force. "You asked to see one of us?" he stated.

"How's Addy?"

"She's tough. She'll mend."

"Her arms…?"

"The left is broken. The other one's a sprained wrist."

"Oh, thank goodness," she said. "I mean, I hoped it would be nothing more serious than that."

The look of relief in her eyes was touchingly real. He indicated the small bandage covering Kari Churchill's right temple. "I hear you're going to be all right."

She fingered her forehead as if she'd already forgotten the injury. "Yes. It's nothing, really."

"Good."

There was an awkward, tense silence then. He didn't know what she was thinking, but he knew his own thoughts were more charitable than he liked. It had been easier when he'd thought of her purely as Satan's sister.

She licked her lips and offered him a small smile. "We were both very lucky."

"Yep. Definitely a lucky day, I'd say."

As he'd intended, she caught the sarcasm. "Look, I don't want you to think…I realize you didn't want…I guess what I'm trying to say is…I apologize."

He narrowed his eyes and cocked his head at her. "Why would you feel the need to do that, Miss Churchill?"

Her cheeks went a pretty shade of pink under the harsh hospital lighting. "You know perfectly well why," she replied.

"You mean, because you managed to talk my sister into taking you up? Because your determination to get your own way nearly got the both of you killed? Yeah, that might be a reason to apologize."

The pink turned to red, twin flags of annoyance. "Now wait just a minute," she said. "I admit I shouldn't have coerced your sister into taking me. I feel horrible about that. But she's a grown woman. I didn't *trick* her into anything." She chewed her lip a moment, then, as if deciding what she'd been thinking deserved to be said, she gave him a hard, hostile look of her own. "Did it ever occur to you that if you weren't such an overbearing dictator, Addy might not have felt the need to prove herself? She did great up there. Even after the lightning hit us, she was in control. You underestimate your sister, Mr. D'Angelo. If you treated her with a little respect, she might surprise you."

He stared at her, letting the words settle in his gut. It would serve no good purpose to heave into further argument. Truthfully, he couldn't say that he totally disagreed with her. But that didn't mean he had to like it.

Expelling a slow, deliberate breath, he came around the end of the gurney and approached her. She watched him move without flinching, chin tipped up, and if it hadn't been for her white-knuckled grip on the sheet, he'd have bought this defiant, steely charade.

"I'm not here to talk about my relationship with Addy," he said in a quiet, terse voice. "I'm here to make sure you're all right."

"Yes, I can see you're eaten up with anxiety," she snapped.

He counted to ten and tried to wrangle his patience under control. "As the head of Angel Air, I'm naturally interested—"

"Oh, I think I understand what you're *interested* in," she cut in, giving him a narrowed glance. "What you'd really like to know is if I intend to take this little accident any further. Like to court."

"Do you?"

She looked away for a moment. He had to admit, she had a damn fine profile, all haughty elegance and sleek lines.

"I don't think…" She took a deep breath, turning back to look at him with cold disdain. "I like your sister very much. I don't want to hurt her by causing trouble for her family. My injuries are minor, so there's no reason to blow this out of proportion. Accidents happen. Why don't we leave it at that?"

The words were flat, though heat wove through them like a thin ribbon. He stared at her, wondering if he could believe her. No way to tell, really. As sneaky as she'd probably been with Addy, he wasn't sure her signature in blood would suffice.

And then she did a strange thing. She laughed.

Nick frowned at her.

She shook her head. "You know, I don't think I've ever met a man as openly skeptical as you are. If I told you the sky was blue, would you insist on going outside to check?" Without waiting for a response, she waved a slim hand toward the outer corridor. "Find a lawyer out there. As busy as this place is, there's bound to be some ambulance-chaser hanging around who can draw up an affidavit for me to sign." She cocked her head at him. "Just tell me one thing. Are you like this with everyone, or is it just me?"

It was crazy, considering the fact that he was being insulted, that he felt the urge to smile. In spite of the fact that she'd been trouble from the get-go, she had a lively, sharp assertiveness that made him realize that her strong chin and intense gaze weren't to be taken lightly.

Definitely not a desirable response. He searched through the debris of his anger to find a more comfortable reaction. He knew one thing. He wasn't about to discuss his character traits—good, bad or otherwise.

"Let's just agree that this entire experience has been…unpleasant for everyone concerned," he said, trying for a reasonable tone. "But it's over and we can all move on. My company will take care of the hospital bill, of course. If you'll leave word where you'd like your things sent, I'll have them delivered to you first thing in the morning. Will that suffice?"

She looked as if she might object, then took another deep breath. "Fine."

"Good. That should be about it, then."

"Any reason why I can't stop in to see Addy before I leave?"

"I'm sure she'll want to say goodbye. But not too long, if you don't mind. She's very tired."

She frowned, clearly annoyed that he would think her that insensitive. "Of course."

He held out his hand. "I hope the rest of your trip to Colorado is enjoyable, Miss Churchill. Good luck."

She lifted her chin again and took his hand. "Thank you, Mr. D'Angelo," she replied in a tight tone that bore no warmth. Not a flicker. "I'm sure whatever happens during the rest of my stay, it can't possibly compare to what I experienced today."

Nick had a feeling she was referring to more than just the accident, but he wasn't about to comment. He nodded and made his escape.

KARI HAD JUST SLIPPED into her jeans when the nurse came back to the room. Except for a killer headache and some stiff muscles in her back, she felt fine. Maybe a little drained from the ordeal she'd been through, but who wouldn't be? The fact that both she and Addy D'Angelo had managed to come out of the crash in one piece was pretty amazing.

Even more amazing was the fact that she'd kept her conversation with Nick D'Angelo semi-civil. If ever there was a man who could make a woman scream in frustration, he was it.

Of course, she had to concede that he had *some* right to be angry with her. She had taken advantage of Addy, and that knowledge had left her struggling with enough guilt to choke a horse. Her mother had always complained that she was too much like her father. When Madison Churchill set his sights on something, he went barreling in and damned the consequences. Kari had certainly inherited that trait.

The nurse who'd assisted the doctor came into the room. She handed Kari a prescription for a muscle relaxer and a mild pain reliever. "You're all set to go," she said. She handed Kari a third piece of paper. "Nick said to give you this. It's the phone number for a couple of motels down by the interstate."

Kari slipped the prescriptions and the phone numbers into the back pocket of her jeans. She realized suddenly that the nurse, a pretty brunette about her age, had used D'Angelo's first name. "You know Mr. D'Angelo?" she asked.

The woman had already begun to strip the hospital gurney of its sheets. She glanced back over her shoulder. "Everyone around these parts knows Nick. He's been baby-sitting Lightning River Lodge for his family for five years now."

"Has he always been so…"

"Sexy?"

"No!" Kari nearly gasped. That thought hadn't entered her mind. "I was going to say…dictatorial."

The nurse's eyes flickered with honest amusement. "Honey, you'd better have the doc check you over again. Make sure your brain didn't get scrambled. Every woman in the Lightning River area would like to lasso Nick D'Angelo. Myself included." She dumped the soiled sheets into a hamper and smiled at Kari. "I haven't seen him look this grim since his dad had his stroke. You certainly seem to have gotten on his bad side."

"Oh, you mean there's a *good* side?" Kari said. "I sure didn't see it."

"Nick's just protective of his family. He takes his responsibilities very seriously. But he can be a real sweetie."

"I must have missed the sweetness in between all the yelling and threats," Kari said with a laugh. "In fact, are you sure we're talking about the same Nick D'Angelo? The guy I know is the most arrogant, annoying, rock-headed man I've ever met."

"One and the same man, I'm afraid."

That slightly rough-voiced response came from behind Kari, and she started. She turned to find an older man in a wheelchair parked in the doorway. His features were worn and tired-looking, but a spark of vibrant life burned in his dark eyes.

Kari swallowed hard. This had to be one of the D'Angelos. He had the same direct way of looking at a person that Nick had. The same commanding presence in spite of whatever illness had put him in that chair.

But did they share the same temper, too?

The man moved his chair forward, until he sat right in front of her. "I'm Sam D'Angelo," he said in a calm voice. "Nick's and Adriana's father."

She'd been afraid of that.

She wet her lips. "Mr. D'Angelo, you have a perfect right to be upset about what happened. I'd like to explain—"

He held up one hand. "That isn't really necessary. I think I have a clear picture. Adriana shouldn't have taken you up, but she can be very…single-minded and impetuous sometimes." He grinned. "She gets that from her mother's side of the family, I'm afraid."

A little of Kari's anxiety settled. This man wasn't nearly the ill-tempered grouch his son was.

But then he tilted his head at her, as though seeing a very unusual bug for the first time. "Besides, I wanted to meet the woman who has my son in such an uproar. It's been a long time since I've seen him like this."

"Like what? You mean, angry enough to drop me from the nearest cliff?"

"Yes. That's one emotion you seem to have brought out in him. Perhaps there are others."

She frowned, not sure what he meant by that. "I'm dreadfully sorry about all this. I really wish I could turn back the clock twenty-four hours. Addy told me everyone in your family is working double-time in preparation for some wedding your resort is catering. Will you be terribly short-handed without her help?"

"Terribly."

That wasn't the polite answer, certainly not the one she'd hoped for. She flushed, feeling more guilty by the second. "I'm so sorry," she said again. "If there's anything I can do…"

He gave her a sharpened look as the tiniest of smiles twitched against his lips. Kari had the strangest feeling that he'd known she would say just that.

"Perhaps there *is* something…"

CHAPTER FIVE

THE METALLIC RING of his cell phone pulled Nick out of a sound sleep. He fumbled it off the nightstand, resenting the loss of a dream that didn't involve copter crashes and leaky pipes and annoying blondes.

What now? To get temporary help for the lodge, he'd had to track down Clay Wyatt at the nearby Moose Lodge tonight. Then he'd had to make arrangements for Pete Golas, a fellow pilot who owned a flight service in Colorado Springs, to fly his chopper up to help cover the tours they had booked for the next few days. Calling in a favor from Pete might have been overkill, but chopper tours brought in hefty revenue, and he didn't want to lose a single one of them.

When he'd gotten back to the lodge things had seemed fairly calm. As far as he knew, everyone in the family was safe in bed, even Addy. The place had been quiet when he'd finally hit the hay, exhausted. Nobody needed him. For anything.

He'd forgotten about Brandon O'Dell.

"I guess you're in bed," his friend's voice said in his ear. There was no apology in his tone.

"Where else would I be?" Nick mumbled, not bothering to hide his irritation. He squinted through the dark to glance at the bedside clock. "It's almost one o'clock."

"You're turning into an old coot who can't stay up past dark."

"Better than being a jackass."

According to Bran's girlfriend Roxanne, his old army buddy had taken off a few days ago for parts unknown. She'd called Nick yesterday, worried and thoroughly pissed, but he hadn't been able to help her much. He'd promised to call a few places Bran liked to frequent, but with everything that had happened, he'd completely forgotten to do so.

"Roxanne called me," Nick told him around a stifled yawn. "You need to let her know you're all right."

"She's not my wife. I don't owe her anything."

As tired as Nick was, that remark didn't set well. "A jackass *and* a bastard," he said sharply. "You're two for two, man."

Unexpectedly, Bran giggled and Nick knew his friend was drunk.

Bran had never really adjusted to civilian life after discharge from the service. Back when they'd flown Black Hawks in the war, Nick would have trusted him with his life. But too many years of erratic behavior, lost jobs and bouts of excessive drinking had turned the guy into someone Nick didn't know anymore. Tonight he didn't have the patience for him.

Bran's amusement finally wound down. He snorted. "Lighten up on me, you damned spaghetti-bender. I'm half lit, and I don't know what the hell I'm saying anymore."

"Where are you?"

"Fresno, I think. Some hole-in-the-wall hotel."

"You need someone to come and get you?"

"No. I need another drink." The conversation stalled as Nick listened to the clink of glass against glass. If he knew Bran, it would be a bottle of cheap vodka.

"Bran, you've got to get it together," he said in a low, even voice. "You've made too many calls like this."

Nothing but silence after that. Just when Nick wondered

if he'd lost the cell phone signal, Bran said, "I can't seem to do it. Don't want to, anyway." He expelled a long, shaky breath. "You remember how we used to fly our birds down the throats of those sand warriors? They scattered, didn't they? Lord, I never saw men run so fast in such thick dirt. You ever think about those days?"

In the inky darkness, Nick shook his head wearily. They'd had this conversation before, and it never ended well. "Sometimes," he admitted.

"I think about it all the time. Can't seem to stop." Nick heard his friend swallow a gulp of liquor, then gasp as the stuff must have cut a fiery path down his throat. When he could finally speak, he said at last, "When you dream, do you ever see those kids, Nicky?"

Nick's scalp tingled and he flinched. This was territory he definitely didn't want to revisit. "No."

"Liar. I can hear it in your voice."

"Bran, you have to let it go," Nick said quickly, with more sorrow than anger. "There was a war on, and you couldn't tell an enemy sniper from a camel herder. Our guys were scared. But nothing we did, *or didn't do,* would have made any difference that day."

"I tell myself you're right. But that won't make it go away. It won't make *them* go away."

Bran's voice was fierce and broken, and in his own sleep-mussed world, Nick silently cursed his friend for bringing up a past neither of them could do anything about. He didn't need this right now. He didn't want it. He grit his teeth, trying not to feel the memory of those days of the war curl around inside him like a hot, sour wind.

"You need to get help, buddy," Nick said at last. He'd said those words before, but they had never seemed to do any good.

"I want you to come out here. Talk to me. Convince me everything can be all right. Just like old times."

"I can't."

"I quit Pacific Pipe."

Nick rolled to one side. Damn! He'd pulled strings to get Bran that job. Flying repair crews out to remote work sites wasn't exactly glamorous work, but the pay was decent, and it still meant flight time. "Why?" he asked.

"Damn baby-sitting job. No self-respecting pilot would take that kind of work."

Nick bit down on an irritated, impatient retort. His friend was drunk and feeling sorry for himself, and there would be plenty of time to give him hell once he sobered up. "Look, it's late. I'm fresh out of ideas right now. Sleep off the booze. In the morning call Roxanne so she stops worrying. Then call me back if you need to, and we'll work things out. All right?"

"I need to talk to you. In person. You're the only one who ever seems to make sense to me. It's a short flight. Pocket change."

"I can't, Bran. We're short-handed and we have a big wedding booked. Everything's crazy here right now. Maybe in a couple of weeks."

He could tell by the sounds Bran made that he didn't like that idea. But, with so much liquor in him, he couldn't think fast enough to form any real objections.

Sensing victory, Nick said in a stronger voice, "Go to sleep. Things will look better in the morning. You'll see."

Bran started to protest, but Nick cut him off. When his friend was like this, his best approach had always been empathy delivered with a healthy dose of practical planning. He closed the phone and tossed it back on the bedside table. Maybe it was time to arrange professional intervention for Bran's drinking.

Nick ran a hand over his face, knowing he wouldn't be able to get back to sleep for a while. So much for getting a few hours of uninterrupted rest before facing the real world again.

His stomach growled and he realized that he hadn't had anything to eat since yesterday's lunch. He got up, struggling into an old robe. If he'd been in his own cabin, he'd have raided the fridge in nothing more than his boxers, but since he and Tessa were staying in the lodge—their last night, thank God—he didn't want to take the chance of scaring one of the guests.

In the adjoining bedroom Tessa was sound asleep. Nick studied her for a moment, very still, absorbing the sweet innocence of the picture she made there in bed. Just watching her made his chest feel full.

She looked so damned fragile, one hand tucked under her cheek, her lips slightly parted. He slipped a stray dark strand of hair behind her ear. Tomorrow he'd try once more to talk to her about the dress he'd made her return. She was a good kid. Level-headed. She'd understand eventually.

Silently, Nick let himself out of the suite. Lamps burned low along the corridors and on the sofa tables in the lobby. They couldn't afford to have insomniac guests tripping over furniture in the middle of the night. He wove his way across the small dining room and through the double doors that led into the kitchen.

This was his mother's domain, all stainless steel and gleaming copper. Everything in the kitchen was industrial-size, but it still felt warm and friendly. This was where D'Angelo decisions got discussed, argued and laughed over, around the big wooden table that sat in the middle of the room while his mother cooked and his father offered unsolicited advice.

He headed for the refrigerator, then pulled up short as he realized someone had beaten him to the leftovers. Addy was bent over the interior bins.

"What are you doing out of bed?" he asked around a sleepy yawn. "I swear, if you've eaten the last cannoli, I'll break your other arm."

There was a startled sound, then a head popped up over the open refrigerator door. The midnight raider wasn't Addy.

It was Kari Churchill.

A SMALL BUNCH OF GRAPES in one hand, Kari nudged the refrigerator door shut and straightened. There was only dim light in the kitchen, but she couldn't miss the look of shock and disbelief on Nick D'Angelo's face.

In spite of his disheveled hair and bare feet, his commanding presence still managed to unnerve her. She offered him a weak smile.

"You…" he rasped. "What in God's name are you doing here?"

She inhaled a deep, fortifying breath. "I'm sorry. I know it's bad manners, but I'm starving." She held up the grapes. "Your mother offered me something to eat when I first settled in, and I stupidly turned it down. But I got so hungry I woke myself up, so I didn't think anyone would mind if I got a little something on my own."

Nick D'Angelo blinked, then threw one hand up like a policeman halting traffic. "Whoa. What do you mean 'settled in'? Why are you here?"

Kari stared at him like a deer before flight.

Oh, no. Oh, just great. He doesn't know what I'm talking about.

Last night at the hospital Sam D'Angelo had told her he

would talk to his son, but clearly he hadn't. And now, here Nick was, looking angry and confused and dangerous.

He wanted explanations, and Kari wasn't sure she could manage them. A debilitating, crash-induced fatigue had nibbled away the last of her wits.

And worse, how was she to have any credibility at all in her bare feet and a haystack mess of hair and— A sudden thought nearly took her breath away. Addy had loaned her pajamas to sleep in until she could get her own things from the helicopter. The short-shorts and skimpy top were silky and lavender and—Kari glanced down quickly—and *way* too revealing. As surreptitiously as possible, she separated her bunch of grapes into two smaller bunches and held them close to her chest, trying to make it look like a natural maneuver. It didn't. Not a bit.

A soft curse slipped out before she could stop it.

"That about sums up my sentiments, as well," Nick said with a frown. "Care to elaborate on that a little?"

"I'm staying here," Kari said. "Room Eight."

"I left a list of motels for you at the hospital. What was wrong with them?"

"I'm sure they're fine. But…I guess your father didn't tell you."

"Tell me what?"

"I'm not a guest. I'm an employee."

That caught him off guard. He stared at her hard, blinking several times as though clearing his mind. "Like hell you are."

"Your father hired me."

"Well, I'm *un*hiring you," Nick said in a weary tone.

"You can't," Kari protested.

She glanced away, realizing that the conversation had gone downhill faster than a runaway pushcart. She'd always thought she'd inherited her father's gift with words, but around this guy she couldn't seem to string two of them together and make a sentence. It was a new and unsettling feeling.

"Now, look," she said in her most democratic tone. "I know we've both had a tough day, but surely we can discuss this reasonably. Calmly. Without anyone getting nasty…again."

"All right, let's discuss this," he said. After a long moment he said in crisp, succinct syllables, "You are not working here. It is not possible."

She frowned at him, then made the sudden decision to do her best to keep the conversation from turning ugly. Tomorrow, Nick could hash this out with his father. Tonight, she wasn't willing to back down, but neither did she want to argue and end up checking in someplace else in the middle of the night if he decided to toss her out into the street.

"I wish neither one of us had been put in this position," she said. "But I think it certainly *is* possible since your father told me he owns this place. I'm going to be helping out until Addy gets a little more mobile. A week. Less, really. That's all."

"Over my dead body."

"He said you'd say something like that. He's aware that you…that we…didn't exactly hit it off. But he says you're sensible enough to realize that the business needs all the help it can get right now."

"We don't need your kind of help."

"Hey!" She tossed the grapes on the table and crossed her arms over her breasts. "There's no need to be rude. I didn't think it was such a good idea, either, at first. But your father's very persuasive, and it started to make sense."

"Nothing makes sense," Nick muttered, shaking his head again.

"Sure it does. You need another body here while Addy's

out of commission. I hear there's a big wedding coming up that's going to require everyone to do more than their share. And since I feel…somewhat responsible for what happened, helping out would ease my conscience."

"I don't care about easing your conscience. What is it with you? Why won't you just *go away?*"

There was something in his long-suffering and stricken voice that made her want to listen to him, but she'd made the decision to stay, and she wasn't about to let him chase her off. "Your family likes the idea of me standing in for Addy, and what's more, they seem to like *me.*"

She lifted one arm and made a muscle, then smothered another frown. She remembered it as being a lot more impressive. "See this? I got it working out for the Miami Beach Triathlon last spring. I didn't win, but I was second in the swimming leg of the competition. For a little while, anyway."

He was ignoring her, waving away those comments with a flailing hand as though chasing off a pesky mosquito. He shuffled over to a restaurant-size beverage cooler. "We don't need anyone to swim anywhere," he muttered. "In case you haven't noticed, there's no ocean. We're surrounded by mountains."

"My point is," Kari said, coming around the table toward him, "I'm strong. I can do a lot around here. Everyone's on board with it. Even your aunts seemed to like the idea, although they speak with such heavy Italian accents I only understood half of what they said. It's the perfect solution."

Nick stopped in front of the cooler, spread his arms across the front to brace himself, then expelled a huge sigh. The movement caused the belt of his robe to slip its knot. When he turned toward her at last, Kari was treated to a lovely sight—a muscled male chest sprinkled with dark hair. And not a single imperfection that she could see.

Ohhhh….so that's what the nurse meant by sexy. Yes, indeed.

He evidently saw her quick glance. He scowled and tugged his robe back together. He took a couple of steps toward her. She might have found it intimidating if he hadn't been barefoot and his hair hadn't been standing up in all directions like a little boy's.

"It's *not* the perfect solution," he refuted as he jerked a better knot in his belt. "The perfect solution would be for you to go away and leave us alone. We don't need you. I've already made arrangements for temporary help from one of the other resorts."

"Your father says he's going to tell you to cancel that. He thinks if I'm standing in for Addy, that should be enough."

"Addy knows what's required around here. You don't."

"I learn quickly." She tried for a more reasonable tone. "Look, I suspect your father is also trying to make Addy feel less guilty about what happened. She's very upset about not being able to pull her weight. And as I said, working here for a week will help ease my conscience a little, too."

"And as *I* said, I'm not worried about your conscience," he said harshly. "The situation is handled, and I'll make that clear to my father in the morning. After that, you can consider your employment terminated."

In spite of all her best efforts, he was getting to her. She bit her lip, trying to keep anything nasty from coming out of her mouth. "Your father hired me. I think he'll have to be the one to fire me." It was the best she could manage.

"Fine." Nick squeezed his eyes shut for a moment, then raked a distracted hand through his hair. "Fine. I can't deal with any more tonight," he mumbled almost to himself. "Tomorrow, then."

She watched as he slid open the cooler door and pulled out

a beer, mumbling to himself the whole time. The interior light washed his features with an eerie, harsh glow. Without another word to her, he turned to head out of the kitchen, the bottle swaying back and forth between two hooked fingers.

"Good night," she called to his retreating back. "Sweet dreams."

It came as no surprise that the sound of the swinging kitchen door was the only response she got.

HER STOMACH FULL, Kari went back to her room. Damn that Nick D'Angelo! Worry over what would transpire in the morning was sure to keep her sleepless the rest of the night.

Instead she fell asleep almost instantly and didn't rouse again until someone had the gall to knock on her door a short time later.

"Come back later," she croaked, refusing to open her eyes and chase sleep away completely.

"Signorina Churchill," a muffled voice called from the other side of the door. "It's Renata and Sofia. Wake up, please."

Who?

Oh.

Addy had told her last night about her two Italian aunts—the "Zias," she'd called them—widows from Verona or Venice or someplace in Italy that started with a V. The women had come to help Addy's mother a few years ago and never gone back.

Wrapping the blanket around her shoulders, Kari stumbled to the door and opened it a crack. She squinted out into the corridor. Both women smiled at her. Kari tried to sort out in her mind which one was which. Sofia had seemed the shyer of the two, a sweet dumpling of a woman. Renata was thinner, with a long nose and a commanding air about her.

"Can I help you, ladies?" Kari said, yawning.

"Good morning," Aunt Sofia said. "It's time for breakfast."

Kari frowned as she glanced toward the window in her room. There was not one sliver of light anywhere near the curtains. She looked back at the women, who were both fully dressed and seemed ready for anything. Maybe Italians liked to meet the day before it actually *became* a day.

"Very sweet of you," Kari managed to get out. "But I'm really not a morning person. Don't wait breakfast for me. I'll get something later."

The women exchanged a look. Sofia seemed momentarily confused. Renata nudged closer to the door opening. She tucked her chin so she could catch Kari's eye.

"Signorina Churchill," she said in a firm but still friendly voice. "We're not inviting you to breakfast. It's time to *serve* breakfast. To our guests."

"Oh." It was starting to make sense now, but Kari couldn't resist glancing at the glow-in-the-dark alarm clock. No need for that with the aunts around, she supposed. "Who eats breakfast at five o'clock in the morning besides birds and bad women?" she couldn't resist asking.

Renata didn't see any humor in that question. "Our dining room is open to guests from six-thirty until ten. Most of them like to get an early start, so that means we have to get an early start, as well. To—"

"Be ready for them," Kari finished for her, holding up a forestalling hand. "I get it."

"Adriana is a wonderful server," Sofia said with a touch of worry in her voice. "Last night you did say you could take her place."

Kari scraped hair out of her eyes. "No problem. I used to wait tables at a burger barn while I was in college. I can sling hash with the best of them."

"Sling hash?" Sofia asked with a blank look.

"Not fancy enough for Lightning River's menu, huh?"

"We don't have a menu," Renata replied, and Kari thought the woman actually ratcheted up her spine a notch to stand taller. "We offer a few different specialties every day. You'll have to learn how to recite them properly. And to explain what's in them."

Wonderful, Kari thought. Just great. Why hadn't she thought to pack her photographic memory and Italian phrase book when she'd left Florida? "I'm sure I can manage," she said, mainly because Sofia looked really fretful now and Renata had begun to frown.

"Do you know how to do a Windsor napkin fold?" Renata asked, looking very doubtful that the answer would be yes.

"Does it involve more than wrapping a paper towel around a bunch of plastic silverware?"

"Oh, dear," Sofia said.

The two women stood there in confusion for a moment.

Then, as if to defuse any trouble ahead from her sister, Sofia suddenly thrust a couple of hangers in Kari's direction. They held a royal-blue polo shirt with the Lightning River Lodge logo above the pocket and a sharply creased pair of khakis. Kari hooked them with one finger while still managing a death grip on the blanket. "You and Adriana are similar in size. If these fit, I'll see that you get more." She smiled suddenly, her features filled with pride. "Renata's in charge of the dining room, but my specialties are housekeeping and laundry. After breakfast is out of the way, I'll be showing you how to clean rooms."

"Can't wait," Kari said in a weak voice.

"We aren't open for lunch since most of the guests are out during the day," Renata explained. "But you'll have to help out at dinner, of course."

"Of course." Different, fancier napkin folds, Kari bet.

"Can you join us in the kitchen in fifteen minutes?" Renata asked. It wasn't really an invitation.

"I'll make it in ten," Kari replied, determined to fly in the face of every instinct that told her she couldn't possibly.

When the aunts had gone away, she sank down on the bed, then fell against the mattress. The movement brought a twinge of pain to her back, reminding her that the next few days were likely to be difficult.

And for more reasons than her back, it seemed. Memorizing menus. Learning how to do hospital corners on the beds. Scrubbing toilets, no doubt.

Yeah, she should be dead by Monday.

CHAPTER SIX

KARI MADE IT to the kitchen right on time.

Pretty good, considering she'd really only spent about six minutes getting ready. The other four minutes were spent wondering what she had gotten herself into. Was she really going to allow guilt to turn her into a pre-glass-slipper Cinderella?

Uncertainty swamped her until she caught her first sight of Addy. The girl looked even more pale and tired this morning, seated at the big wooden table, her arms angled out in front of her as she slipped slices of apple into her mouth. It was probably the heaviest thing she could hold right now. And yet, in spite of everything, she smiled up at Kari in genuine warmth.

That smile swept away the last of Kari's doubts.

After last night's conversation with Sam D'Angelo, Kari had known she couldn't just walk out of the hospital without a backward glance. She'd once done an article on small business success stories, and she knew that family owned and operated companies like this one usually didn't have a lot of maneuvering room during crunch times. Everyone had to pull their weight. Addy, who was a valuable member of the team according to her father, would be a big loss. Filling in for her seemed the least Kari could do, at least until she had to be on the plane to New Zealand.

Besides, if she was perfectly honest with herself, there were selfish reasons to stay, as well. Free room and board at Lightning River Lodge, with occasional time off, would keep her from dipping into her limited finances while she delved deeper into the circumstances of her father's trip into Elk Creek Canyon. Since she'd missed the opportunity to camp out there on the anniversary date, she could revisit the National Park office and press harder for information about her father's guide.

They certainly hadn't been very helpful the first time, but she'd been in a hurry to make the helicopter flight. Maybe now there would be time to investigate a little more. Find out just why her father had chosen that area, if he had said anything at all that might clear up some of the mystery surrounding his death.

So the next few days would be full and demanding. She couldn't be sure whether Sam D'Angelo had maneuvered her into volunteering or if guilt had just made her jump in with the offer to help out, but it was done now.

The only fly in the ointment was that middle-of-the-night conversation she'd had with the big pooh-bah of this whole operation, Nick D'Angelo. He wouldn't care what everyone else around here thought. He wanted her gone.

She felt the need to mention that to Sam D'Angelo, who also sat in the kitchen, his wheelchair positioned just out of the way of traffic, which consisted of his wife Rose, directing everyone like the leader of a small orchestra, and the hurried movements of Renata and Sofia.

After greeting everyone, Kari found an excuse to speak to Sam D'Angelo in as much privacy as anyone in the family was likely to get—a secluded corner by the vegetable bins.

"Don't worry," the older man said when she finished filling him in. He waved his right hand in the air as though shooing flies, a habit Kari had already noticed in Nick. "I'll handle him."

"He seemed pretty determined not to have me around."

The head of the D'Angelo family winked at her. "There are many roads that lead to Rome."

Kari didn't have a clue what that meant, but she nodded anyway. If the man wanted to champion her cause, she could see no reason to reject the offer. Then there was no more time for speculation because Renata whisked her away to learn the intricacies of the Windsor napkin fold that was used for breakfast.

Things moved more quickly and smoothly than she'd hoped. The D'Angelos and half a dozen employees came and went throughout the early morning, but the handsome, bad-tempered Nick wasn't among them. Kari had finally stopped looking for him every time the double doors on either side of the room swung wide and concentrated on the duties she'd been assigned.

As she had suspected all along, the D'Angelos were a close-knit family who relied heavily on each other. Everyone seemed to have a job to do, including Sam. Rose ruled the kitchen with an iron fist and a twinkle in her eyes. The Zias were like a well-oiled machine, twin dynamos of industry.

They obviously adored Addy, constantly fussing over her and finding ways to make her feel useful. Kari noticed that all the D'Angelos laughed easily, squabbled noisily, and probably would have bludgeoned anyone who dared to upset this balance.

The fact that they welcomed Kari as they would one of their own, both last night and this morning, surprised her a little. Yet it also made her feel warm inside. As an only child, with a father who gallivanted the globe, Kari marveled at this kind of kinship and found herself feeling more than a little envious.

She discovered that the breakfast menu wasn't nearly as

intimidating as she had feared. The fare was mostly American, thank goodness, with only one elaborate frittata thrown in for anyone who opted for a real Italian breakfast.

Thankfully not all of the lodge's sixteen rooms were booked, so the small dining room stayed busy but manageable.

Kari stood straight and recited the menu in precise, clear words, with pauses for effect. It reminded her of her fifth grade spelling bee, which she had aced with the word "cornucopia."

She waited on three middle-aged rock climbers with matching sunburns who didn't seem a bit impressed and ordered juice, coffee and English muffins. To go.

Her second table was more of an annoyance than a challenge. The young couple on their honeymoon had probably only come to the dining room because their bodies had finally insisted on nourishment. Particularly irritating was the attitude of the new wife. She didn't listen to a word, just giggled and snuggled closer to her husband until Kari wanted to tell them both to take it outside.

As Kari stood patiently waiting for their order, the blonde flashed her baby blues at her groom and said in a girlishly high voice, "Oh, I can't decide. You order for me."

For crying out loud, it's only bacon and eggs. Since when did getting married mean you couldn't navigate a simple breakfast without consulting your husband?

Kari was extremely relieved to discover that she *hadn't* actually said those words out loud. The woman only smiled and turned toward her new hubby, waiting. Renata, stationed within earshot, wouldn't have to boil Kari in olive oil after all.

When the husband finished ordering, Kari pushed through the double doors and pulled the pad and pen out of her back pocket. The man had ordered two of almost everything on the menu, and she didn't want to forget any of it.

"*Bene,* Kari," Renata said with a pleased nod. "Very good."

"Thanks," Kari replied, scribbling down the order. She'd bet the new bride wasn't going to be able to eat a tenth of what her husband had requested. Probably hadn't even wanted it. She shook her head. Why hadn't the silly woman just spoken up?

"What's the matter?" Addy asked, catching Kari's grimace.

Knowing Sam had gone to check on the front desk, Kari didn't hesitate to share what she was thinking, having grown quickly comfortable around the women.

"Why does marriage turn women into such idiots?" she complained. "We have newlyweds out there, and the wife wouldn't even order a glass of water without running it by her husband. Once he realized she was going to defer to everything he said, he turned into some sort of knuckle-dragging Neanderthal." Kari puffed out her chest and tucked her chin. In a low voice, hands on hips, she mimicked, "'Is the frittata fried in butter or baked? Wouldn't want my new lady to think it's all right to start packing on the pounds just because she's finally caught me. Ha, ha, ha.'"

She shook her head more vigorously as she handed Rose the newlyweds' breakfast order. "Men can be such jerks. Why do we put up with them?"

The older women smiled, and Sofia even giggled.

Addy cocked her head, an odd grin on her lips. "I don't know why women put up with them," she said. Then she looked just past Kari. "What do you think, Nick?"

Kari whirled, shocked to find that her audience consisted of more than just D'Angelo women. Tucked in one corner of the kitchen was the bread station, and standing in front of the toaster, calmly buttering a slice of toast, stood Nick D'Angelo.

He didn't look as if a smile had ever touched his lips in this lifetime. There wasn't any doubt in her mind that he'd heard every word. Just replaying it in her mind made her nerve ends wince and the pit of her stomach fall away.

He didn't respond immediately. For a long, long moment the only sound in the room was the scrape of his knife against the toasted bread. The tense silence made Kari wish she could grab the knife out of his hand and slit her wrists with it.

At last he said in a voice that was as buttery as his bread, "I think a man would have to be very foolish to stand in a room full of women and try to discuss that issue logically."

"Are you saying you can't have a logical discussion with women?" Kari asked. His tone made her feel stubborn, all of a sudden.

He took a bite out of his toast and chewed so slowly that Kari knew it had to be a deliberate attempt to annoy her. Finally he wiped his mouth with a napkin, brushed bread crumbs from his fingertips and methodically poured himself a cup of coffee from a nearby carafe. Aware of a subtle vibration between the two of them, Kari noticed that the other women were watching him, too. Even his mother, who'd been keeping a keen eye on a rasher of bacon sizzling on the stove.

A ripple went through her poise as he slowly came toward her. "I'm saying that some women tend to personalize every discussion about men," he said quietly, his meaning clear. "They react on an emotional level instead of thinking it through logically."

"Well, I don't think…" Kari scowled. Nick's tone had been easy enough, almost friendly, but suddenly she wished she had never said a word.

"Yes?" he said, tilting his head at her.

"Objectively speaking—" she began, then broke off again because nothing that had been on the tip of her tongue could be considered "objective" at all. Really, it was too much, to be expected to verbally hold your own with a guy who made no bones about how much he disliked you, whose sheer presence could make you feel besieged and cornered.

Evidently he decided to let her off the hook. "Objectively speaking," he repeated, "wouldn't you say that our honeymooners deserve to have a second cup of coffee? That *is* part of the reason you're here, isn't it?"

Her lips compressed, Kari watched him as he went past her, his attention now fixed completely on his sister. "How are you feeling?" he asked, taking a moment to massage Addy's shoulders.

"Sore," she replied. "And tired. I was hoping Mom would serve me breakfast in bed this morning."

"Then you should have slept in the kitchen," her mother said.

That comment brought a laugh from everyone, and some of the tension seemed to dissipate. Kari took a deep breath, snagged a pot of coffee off one of the hot plates and retreated back to the dining room and her newlyweds.

She cursed whatever gods had tossed Nick D'Angelo in her path, then cursed herself for letting him get to her. Whenever she was around him, why did she feel exhilarated and, at the same time, filled with a sharp, nameless anxiety? Kari had known infuriating men before, but Nick D'Angelo was in a league all his own. During her stay here—*however* long it lasted—she'd be well advised to keep her distance.

The newlyweds were still discovering one another and had no interest in more coffee. Since she didn't want to look as though she was avoiding Nick, Kari returned to the kitchen. Sam D'Angelo came through the opposite set of double doors at the same time.

"Where have you been this morning?" Sam greeted his son.

"Checking on the damage to Raven One," Nick replied.

"Talking to the insurance company about what they'll cover."
A slight pause. "And what they won't."

Kari tried to concentrate on the cups of fresh fruit that Renata placed on her serving tray. She didn't let her gaze drift even one degree to her left, but she could feel a flush stealing up her neck. It would probably be a long time before any conversation about helicopters wouldn't make her uncomfortable.

"…should have discussed it with me," she heard Nick say over the noise in the kitchen.

"I'm still the head of this household," Sam said. "I didn't need anyone's permission."

Neither of the men even glanced her way. Kari happened to catch Sofia's eye. The older woman tried to smile at her, but it didn't really work. In front of the stove, Rose seemed suddenly determined to distract her. She pointed to the omelets solidifying in the pan. "These should get your newlyweds' attention," she told Kari. "Even lovers have to eat."

Across the big room Nick and his father were now embroiled in a low, heated discussion. There wasn't a doubt in her mind that it concerned her. She slowed her movements, straining to hear, alternately feeling stung and annoyed.

Renata touched her arm, then slid slices of oranges onto the plates. "You've done very well this morning," she said.

"Thanks. Like riding a bicycle, it all came back to me once I found my rhythm."

"We have check-ins today. Dinner will be busier."

"Oh, boy. I can't wait."

A moment later Rose called across the room, "Nick, stop upsetting your father and come fix this drawer. I'm tired of things falling out every time I open it."

Kari picked up the tray and headed out of the kitchen. She couldn't help smiling a little. She wasn't sure why, but clearly the D'Angelo women were on her side, protective and determined to defuse any unpleasantness. If Nick wanted her gone, he might have to wade through them to make it happen.

As Rose had predicted, the newlyweds discovered their hunger and became demanding enough to keep Kari on her toes. When they finally finished and left the dining room hand-in-hand, she removed the dirty dishes to the kitchen.

The argument between father and son seemed to have been settled or at least deferred. Both men were busy—Nick had gone to get a ladder and Sam was sorting through a small toolbox on his lap, grumbling under his breath in Italian.

Kari joined Renata at the kitchen sink. "Is it safe to be in here?" she asked the older woman in a soft voice.

Renata gave her a sympathetic smile. "Don't let their squabble upset you. Nick and his father often go head-to-head. Usually at the top of their lungs. We're used to it."

"You've all been very kind to me." She grimaced, thinking of Nick. "Well…almost all of you."

"Addy is fond of you," the woman replied, and Kari suspected that was as good a recommendation as anyone was likely to get.

"She's very sweet."

Renata smiled a little, something she didn't seem to do very often. "And we all agree that your presence here may be just the thing our Nicholas needs."

"I beg your pardon?"

"Since you wear no ring, can I assume you're single?"

Kari jerked back a little. Was this woman implying what Kari thought she was implying? "Yes, I'm single," she said. "But wait a minute—"

Renata left her side, heading off for parts unknown. Kari stared after her a moment. Surely the family wouldn't try to play matchmaker for her and Nick. A more futile effort she couldn't think of.

The breakfast rush over, Rose put Kari to work at the electric slicer, cutting meat and cheese. Since she wasn't officially turned over to Sofia until noon, Kari was glad that the wicked-looking apparatus required all her attention. It allowed her to ignore Nick completely.

Well…almost completely. She'd be lying if she said she wasn't aware of him each time he entered the room—coming and going, no longer in conversation with anyone, really, just a solid, silent presence who seemed determined to keep to himself.

She watched him change light bulbs, re-hang Rose's drawer, work on the plumbing under the big double prep sink. And now, his ladder positioned right beside her, he was repairing the refrigeration unit on top of one of the coolers.

Every time Kari slid a glance to her right, she ran into the sight of his firm rear end and long legs covered in comfortable-looking tan slacks on the ladder. Really, it would have taken a much stronger woman than Kari not to notice six-feet-something of incredibly graceful, masculine power.

Her slicing completed, she was seated at the table, wrapping wedges of cantaloupe in delicately thin slices of proscuitto that would then be wrapped with plastic and placed in a cooler. Kari had quickly learned that almost anything edible in the kitchen was up for grabs unless Rose designated it for guests—as long as you asked first.

Just as she heard her stomach growl a second time, Renata motioned toward the bowl. "*Mange!* Eat. You look hungry."

When Kari reached for a spoon from a nearby tray of silverware, Rose was suddenly beside her, offering a small fork with a flourish. "You must always use a fork. The back of the spoon anesthetizes the taste buds."

Kari nodded, then speared several pieces of cantaloupe onto a small plate. In another few minutes, Rose placed an omelet in front of her. Kari had to admit, it was one of the best she'd ever eaten.

"You seem to know a great deal about cooking, Mrs. D'Angelo," she said around a mouthful of cheese-and-mushroom-laced egg.

"I learned from the cradle. It was self-defense. My mother was terrible in the kitchen. She didn't cook, she assassinated food."

"I had my doubts that she was truly Italian," Sam said. "Rosa's mother cooked for me just once, and she told me there were only two things on her menu—Take It or Leave It." When Kari laughed at that, Sam realized he'd found a receptive audience. "The meal was so horrible," he continued, "I thought I would have to have my stomach pumped afterward."

Rose turned, favoring her husband with a mock-threatening look. "I noticed you ate every bite."

Addy grinned at Kari. "That's because he was in love. Weren't you, Pop?"

"I'm not ashamed to admit it," Sam said with a shrug. "I would have eaten the tablecloth to impress your mother."

Sofia, who had been silently polishing the espresso machine, suddenly spoke up. "Tell Kari how you met our sister and convinced her to marry you." She gave Kari a sweet, girlish smile that made her seem years younger. "It's so romantic."

From the top of the ladder, Kari heard a weary sigh. Evidently, Nick didn't find the tale a bit romantic, or he'd heard it too many times to find it interesting anymore. Killjoy, she thought. It wouldn't surprise her to discover that he didn't have a passionate bone in his body.

"It was fate," Sam said, seeming to warm to the subject. "My family owned a few tourist cabins near the Lightning River. It's a very beautiful spot, but also very treacherous. So many storms, and the river used to overrun its banks before the government came in and rerouted it. That's how the river got its name, because it ran so jagged—like a bolt of lightning."

"Skip to the good part," Addy coaxed.

"One day a family checks in for a two-week stay. Tourists from our very own Italy, eager to see the Rocky Mountains with their three beautiful daughters. Rosa was the youngest, so shy and sweet, and I fell in love with her instantly. Unfortunately she didn't return my feelings."

"He was much too bold," Renata said from the sink.

"I was determined," Sam refuted with feeling.

Addy, who had been sorting through bunches of parsley using the tips of her fingers, tapped her father's forearm in gentle reproach. "Just tell Kari what happened to change Mom's mind."

"Patience," Sam said affectionately. "I know how to tell the story." He looked back at Kari. "One day a storm comes up, a very bad one. Everyone stays in their cabins, waiting for it to blow over. I knew it would last a long time and I was in the courtyard, throwing the pool furniture into the pool to keep it from blowing around."

"We do that in Florida before a hurricane," Kari said, which got her a frown from Addy for interrupting. She obviously liked this story as much as Sofia. Atop the ladder, Nick continued to struggle with the cooler motor.

Sam squinted and placed a fingertip to the corner of his eye. "Suddenly I see the car from Cabin Two pull out into the pouring rain. It's Rosa."

Rose had turned from the stove, still whipping eggs into a golden froth. Her dark eyes sparkled as they looked at Kari. "My mother had an upset stomach and I was going into town to get her something for it."

"It was so foolish," Sam said. "I knew the danger. I rushed to my parent's truck to go after her. A few miles down the road I see a tree fall right in front of her car." Sam made a wild pantomime of Rose's driving. "She swerves, and her car goes into the river." He placed one hand against his chest. "My heart nearly stopped right then."

"So did mine," Rose said. "The car began to sink immediately, and I was sure I was going to be swept downriver and drowned. I crawled onto the hood. The next thing I know, I see this maniac inching out onto an overhanging tree limb."

"It's my story," Sam complained. "Let me tell it."

Kari smiled. The head of the D'Angelo family certainly knew how to milk a story for drama. She was enthralled, captured by the images the older man could create with nothing more than his voice and a few hand gestures.

"The wind was whipping water into my eyes so I couldn't see a thing," he said. "The limb was bobbing up and down. It was like riding a tiger, but I couldn't go back." He extended his arm outward. "I stretched out my hand for her to grasp, but she wouldn't take it. She was too afraid that I couldn't hold on to her against the current."

"Anyone would be frightened," Rose interjected.

"Finally I shouted to her, 'Rosa Pascale, take my hand. I am descended from angels who kept dragons from destroying the town of San Marino in the old country. Have faith, my dearest heart. I will not let you go.'"

As if no one knew how the story would end, there was complete silence in the kitchen. Even Nick had stopped tinkering with the motor and was listening, his arms draped over the top of the ladder.

Finally, Addy spoke up. "And you did it, didn't you, Mom? You jumped across the distance and caught Pop's hand."

"It was a leap of faith," Rose said, her eyes fixed lovingly on her husband. She came across the distance that separated them until she stood behind her husband's wheelchair. Then she bent low to capture him in a hug. Softly she said, "Samuel saved my life that day, and he has been my salvation ever since."

Kari had to swallow hard to get past the lump in her throat. The D'Angelos shared such a vivid, open love for one another, and clearly they had no qualms about showing it.

She had never seen that sort of affection between her own parents. Madison Churchill had been gone too often, so that her mother, suffering from the slow starvation of too much time apart, had forgotten how to express emotion freely. She had developed a cast-iron composure that could not be penetrated, not even during the difficult days when her father had been reported missing. Not even when they had brought his body home for burial and Kari had needed her mother's love and understanding the most.

What must it be like to grow up in a family like this? Kari wondered. To know that your parents adored one another? That no sacrifice would have been too much for a husband or wife to make for their spouse? Growing up in a dysfunctional family was certainly not an oddity these days, but Kari couldn't help but think that, in spite of petty quarrels and emotional outbursts that were bound to occur in large families, love ruled the D'Angelos. Their kind of warmth and caring was something special. Something to be treasured. And a dynamic that had never existed in Kari's family.

The silence in the kitchen had suddenly become intimate. Rose whispered something in Sam's ear, and unexpectedly the older man actually seemed to blush as he tilted his head so that his wife's lips connected with his pink cheek.

"And then…?" Kari prompted.

Sam cleared his throat as Rose straightened. "I proposed before I'd even gotten her home to dry off. There were several long discussions into the night between our families, but when her parents and Sofia and Renata returned to Italy, Rosa stayed here. With me."

Kari couldn't help grinning. "That's quite a story."

"And it seems to get…more dramatic with every telling," Nick said from the top of the ladder. To Kari's surprise, he sounded more indulgent than skeptical.

Sam looked suddenly reflective, a little sad. "I remember it as though it happened yesterday."

Kari wondered if he was thinking of his lost youth, how robust he'd once been. Strong enough to pull the woman he loved from a raging river. How it must sting to be confined to that wheelchair.

"What did you mean, your family is descended from angels?" Kari asked.

Everyone laughed, even Nick. Sam shook his head at them ruefully, and Kari suspected this was an old family debate.

"D'Angelo means 'of the angels,'" he explained. "Legend has it that centuries ago members of my family saved their little town from evil, fire-breathing dragons. D'Angelos were the only townspeople brave enough to go out and meet certain death. Somehow they triumphed and that story has been handed down from one D'Angelo generation to the next. I've never had reason to doubt it."

Rose laughed and ran her fingers through her husband's salt-and-pepper hair. "I haven't seen much angelic behavior from him in the past few years."

Kari listened as they tossed comments back and forth a few minutes. None of their words carried heat.

She let her eyes stray upward to Nick. He'd gone back to work on the motor, putting his back into his efforts to loosen some bolt. Through the thin material of his polo shirt, she could see the movement of his muscles sliding back and forth with athletic beauty. His dark, silky hair feathering along the back of his collar was a heart-stirring sight.

For just a moment she could imagine him descended from angels. Heaven had to have a hand in shaping those deliciously handsome features of his. Then she remembered how obnoxious, how arrogant, he could be and her thoughts jerked to a halt.

Nope. No angels in his DNA, she'd bet. More likely there'd been some unfortunate mixup all those centuries ago. *This* D'Angelo was pure dragon.

She forced her attention back to the table. "Did you build this lodge?" she asked.

Sam nodded. "The land was a wedding present from my parents. A few years after we married we sold the cabins that my parents had owned down in Broken Yoke and built the main lodge here. We've made many additions. I always knew I wanted to run my own place." He tossed a knowing grin toward his wife. "And Rosa needed her own kitchen."

Rose was busy inspecting Nick's handiwork on her drawer. She smiled back over her shoulder. "I loved Sam's mother like my own. But every woman wants her own space. Before she died, she gave me her recipes, brought all the way from Italy." Rose indicated a large pot of simmering sauce on the stove's back burner that had begun to fill the kitchen with a intoxicating lemon-garlic scent. "Tonight's specialty is one of hers. Chicken *scarpariello*."

Kari inhaled deeply. "It certainly smells wonderful."

"You like to cook, Kari?" Sam asked. "I'm always telling Nick he needs to find a woman who can cook for him like my Rosa."

Kari's hands stilled on the parmesan cheese she'd begun to grate. It was a simple enough comment, but she wondered if it was as innocent as it sounded. Good grief, was Sam D'Angelo playing matchmaker, too?

Nick evidently suspected the same thing. He stopped fiddling with the motor and glanced down at his father, his eyes slightly narrowed. "Keep to your fairy tales, Pop."

"I don't know what you mean," his father said, the picture of innocence.

In an even voice Nick replied, "I think you do. Hand me a kitchen towel."

Sam rolled backward from the table to snag a towel from the stack that sat on the edge of the vegetable bin. He offered it up to Nick, who took it and immediately went back to work on the motor.

Kari cleared her throat. "Actually, I don't cook that much. When I'm on an assignment, I rely on fast food a lot. And when I'm home, I'm usually on a diet."

Sam looked aghast and thrust his hand out dismissively. "Dieting is like trying to enjoy an opera without the orchestra!"

"You will love my *scarpariello*," Rose said. "I'll save an extra portion for you."

"That's really very kind, but—"

Addy gave her a rueful look. "Might as well give up, Kari. We're Italian. Eating is one of the things we do well."

"You're too thin," Rose said. "We must work on fattening you up."

"I think she looks fine just the way she is," Addy said, throwing Kari a sympathetic smile that said she'd been through this same discussion herself.

Sam gave Kari a sideways glance, as though sizing up a calf at fair time. "Just a little more meat on such pretty bones. A man likes to have something solid to get his hands on." He glanced up at his son. "Don't you agree, Nick?"

Okay. It wasn't her imagination. For some reason these people were trying to plant ideas in Nick's head. Problem was, Kari could have told them that garden didn't have a hope of bearing fruit. The only thing Nick D'Angelo probably wanted to get his hands on was her throat.

She stared down at the crumbling cheese, too embarrassed to look anywhere else. She heard Nick move on the ladder, but she would have burned her eyes out with hot pokers before she'd check the reaction Sam's clumsy efforts had brought to Nick's features.

Awkward seconds ticked by. Kari rose suddenly. Against the cool tile floor, the chair legs made a harsh, awkward sound of protest. "Where do you want this cheese, Mrs. D'Angelo?"

Everyone was silent as Rose indicated she should set the plate on a nearby counter. Kari refused to make eye contact with anyone—especially Nick.

It had been a nice morning, and Kari didn't want to see it spoiled. She took a deep breath and turned toward Sofia. Glancing at her watch, she offered the older woman a bright smile. "Sofia, I think I'm officially farmed out to you now. Shall we go tackle those rooms?"

They went off together, leaving the kitchen to the rest of the family. As the double doors closed behind her, Kari heard

Nick's voice at last. A garbled response she couldn't catch. If he'd bothered to answer his father's question, she'd never know the answer now.

She followed in Sofia's wake, wondering why on earth that should matter to her one way or the other.

SAM HAD ONCE HAD beautiful handwriting. Almost like calligraphy, Rosa had told him. Age and illness had stolen that talent, and last Christmas the family had given him a computer.

He hated it.

It was too complicated. There were too many ways it could fool you. Sam mourned the loss of his overstuffed file cabinet, but would have cut out his tongue before admitting to the family that he was hopelessly illiterate when it came to new technology.

So just before dinner, when Nick came striding into the office they shared, his dark eyes blazing under his brows, Sam wasn't in the mood to placate. He knew what was on his son's mind, and really, it surprised him that Nick had waited this long to finish the argument they'd started in the kitchen this morning. No doubt, only the fact that he'd had a full day of work scheduled had kept him from addressing before now what was really on his mind.

Sam pushed the computer keyboard away and smiled, though he suspected Nick wouldn't acknowledge the friendly greeting.

Sure enough, he didn't. He came right over to the desk, levered one hip against the edge and stared at Sam. "What were you thinking? What's the matter with you?"

Sam didn't pretend to misunderstand. He studied his son sadly. "I could ask you the same question. I have never in my life known you to behave in such a churlish fashion. Tessa has better manners, and she has the excuse of being a teenager."

Nick scowled. "What is it with everyone? Addy's given me grief all day. When I tried to sneak a *tartufo* from Mom, she smacked my hand and said her chocolate was reserved for people with manners. Even the Zias are glaring at me."

"That should tell you something."

"What it tells me is that somehow Kari Churchill has managed to turn my entire family inside out." He ran a hand along his jaw and muttered almost to himself, "Maybe she's a witch and she's replaced all of you with crazy people. No, that's giving her too much credit. She's just a pain in the ass. Like a rash that won't go away."

Sam tilted his head back, letting his lips curve into a wry smile. "She's also performed very admirably today. You saw her in the kitchen. She pulled her weight. Sofia says she wishes all the floor help was as uncomplaining as she is." He tapped the computer keyboard. "She's even volunteered to help me with the D'Angelo family tree. She says she knows a lot about navigating some of the research Web sites. I think all this makes her a valuable asset around here."

"Yeah. In another twenty years she might pay back the money it's going to cost to fix Raven One."

Sam looked at Nick sharply, his features a challenge. "What is your real objection to her?"

Nick gave him a rueful glance, then shook his head. "Nothing. Nothing. She's a candidate for sainthood."

Sam chuckled. "Perhaps not *that* perfect. But she has a charming personality, a delightful sense of humor, and she's very attractive. I'm surprised you don't see that."

"I'll tell you what I see. I see a woman who doesn't think about consequences. She's irresponsible. She put Addy's life in jeopardy yesterday because she's the kind of woman who won't take no for an answer."

"Addy put her own life in jeopardy by behaving foolishly," Sam said, his tone suddenly serious. "We're lucky it didn't come to real grief."

"I realize that," Nick said wearily. He slid off the desk and paced over to the bookcase where framed family photos lined the top shelf. After fingering them a moment, he looked back at Sam. "Forget the fact that you should have discussed it with me. Hiring Kari Churchill—even for a few days—was a mistake."

"Why?"

He was absolutely silent for a moment: unwilling or unable to answer that question. Then he said, "She has the potential to create total chaos. I'm trying to keep things calm around here, and she's too much of a loose cannon."

"Nonsense!" Sam said, shoving his wheelchair away from the desk and angling it toward his son. Now *he* felt angry. "Businesses stagnate in calm. They need crisis in order to grow. Challenges. Injecting new ideas and different situations." He spread his hands out. "It's easy to hold the helm when the sea is quiet. You should welcome this challenge into your life, Nicholas." When his son said nothing to this, he backed off a bit, sending Nick a lighter look. "And haven't you noticed? *This* challenge is wrapped in a very pretty package."

"And that's another thing," Nick complained. "What's with the matchmaking? I'm not interested. I'll *never* be interested."

"Then you are either blind or crazy."

Nick gave him a thunderous look, though the underlying anger seemed to have departed. "Just knock it off. And tell Mom and the Zias to, as well."

"You're just being stubborn."

"And you're just a meddlesome old man who needs to find himself a good hobby." After a moment he sighed heavily and tossed a dismissing hand. "Do what you want with her. Just keep me out of it. The farther we stay away from each other, the better off everyone will be."

"I think you are making a huge mistake."

"I'm not asking what you think. I don't need your advice."

He stalked toward the door, the discussion clearly over.

"That's the thing about advice," Sam called after him. "Those who need it the most generally like it the least."

CHAPTER SEVEN

By THE EVENING of the third day, with a hectic weekend just around the corner, Kari felt pretty proud of herself. She could bounce quarters off the beds she made and had learned to assemble a passable antipasto plate without consulting her cheat sheet. The Pope's Hat napkin fold? No sweat. She'd even managed to recapture Sam D'Angelo's lost computer file of Italian-Americans who had immigrated to the United States the same year as his parents.

She had anticipated being kept busy, but it surprised her just how much time her duties absorbed. While the hired help had regularly scheduled days off, members of the D'Angelo family were expected to forego that luxury during extremely demanding times. And since Kari had taken Addy's place…

The demands of working at the lodge were so great that they kept Kari from her original goal—learning as much as possible about her father's ill-fated trip. Even volunteering to drive Sofia into town one afternoon for an appointment with the doctor had gained her no more than an hour of free time for a quick side trip to the local library archives. She went through a small fortune in quarters copying every newspaper article she could locate about the search-and-rescue efforts for Madison Churchill. But late that night, after soaking in a hot tub to bleed the last of the day's soreness out of her muscles,

Kari had sorted through the information and discovered nothing significant.

She knew it was a foolish dream, but in addition to learning more about his trip, Kari had also hoped to find some mention of her father's journal. The log he traditionally began at the start of every book's creation had not been part of the personal effects given to her mother. That journal—sure to be full of her father's thoughts and observations—had been Kari's last gift to him. That it could simply disappear didn't seem possible, but it was very likely that it had been overlooked during his rescue and now lay disintegrating in some weedy crevice in Elk Creek Canyon.

Her telephone calls to the National Park office turned out to be an exercise in frustration, due to a massive roadblock named Don. The man claimed to know nothing about her father's trip into the canyon and constantly put her on hold as he was sidetracked by tourists who came in for information. A personal visit to that office seemed like the only way to get cooperation, and Kari made a mental note to find some way to squeeze one in at the first available moment.

Of course, even if she'd been able to pinpoint the exact spot her father had camped, she wasn't sure she could arrange transportation out there a second time. At least, not right now. Helicopter charter flights from the Lightning River area seemed to be fully booked by tourists eager to see the golden fall color of aspen-covered slopes.

She couldn't ask Nick to take her, of course. He'd never agree.

No, that wasn't true. He probably *would* fly her out there. He'd just never bring her back.

She knew he still avoided her whenever possible. He and his daughter had moved back to their own cabin, a quick stroll from the main lodge. It might as well have been on the moon. Occasionally Kari saw him from a distance, on his way to make someone else's life miserable. Once, when she'd walked into the kitchen, he and Addy had been in deep discussion about the damaged helicopter. His sister had smiled at her. Nick had not.

It seemed that, for Nick D'Angelo, Kari simply didn't exist. The thought was a relief, but oddly frustrating, too.

His daughter, Tessa, was another matter entirely. After coming home from school and finishing her homework, the girl often came up to the lodge to help out. She and Kari had formed a fast friendship late one afternoon while cleaning a guest room after the last maid went home.

Together they entered Number Fourteen, a bright, airy room on the third floor that overlooked Lightning Lake. Since Kari had delivered room service here just last night, she knew it had been occupied by Mr. and Mrs. Gary Whitaker, the new-lyweds she'd waited on her first morning at the lodge. Evidently, the happy couple hadn't done much sight-seeing. The room was a mess, looking like it had been lived in for forty years instead of just four days. This wasn't going to be a quick turnaround cleaning.

Tessa obviously agreed. She made a loud moaning sound and shook her head. "Oh, great," she said. "There goes any hope I had of going over to my friend's house to watch a movie."

"Our newlyweds," Kari explained as she scooped the wad-ded-up bedspread off the floor. "I guess they were busy dis-covering each other instead of the mountains."

"Gross," Tessa replied as she went into the bathroom. "They used every towel. Aunt Sof hates it when people use our best for floor mats." She came back into the bedroom. "I'll flip you. Loser has to do the bathroom."

Since one of the things Kari had quickly learned about cleaning hotel rooms was just how awful some bathrooms could be, she shook her head and smiled. "Why don't we do it together?"

Tessa agreed and they got started. Once they developed a rhythm, the work went pretty quickly and the time passed around conversations about movies, school, clothes and boys.

The teenager seemed bright and easygoing, and since Kari was privy to many of the family conversations around the kitchen table now, she knew they shared an important common bond—they both had bones to pick with Nick.

Tessa appeared to be in the midst of a rebellion over her father's heavy-handed method of handling problems. "My way or the highway" seemed to be the rule Nick lived by, and as Tessa struggled to find her own identity in a one-parent household, Kari found it easy to sympathize.

She kept most of her opinions to herself, however. The last thing she needed was to do battle with Nick over advice she gave his daughter.

They had just finished making the bed and were dusting down the furniture when Tessa pulled open the drawer of the bedside table and made a little sound of surprise.

"Orphan!" the girl called out.

Kari had learned that items inadvertently left behind by guests—clothing, eyeglasses, paperbacks, anything—were referred to as orphans and were held in a spare closet downstairs until the guest called to reclaim them. The variety of things people could forget had surprised Kari, and she turned toward Tessa, mildly curious to see what the newlyweds had left.

But in the next moment Kari had the quick, unpleasant thought that two people as besotted with one another as the Whitakers might have left behind any number of embarrassing items. Tessa was fourteen, but just how well versed was she in the kinds of things that two lovers might find necessary to bring along on their honeymoon?

She was inordinately relieved when Tessa's hand came out of the drawer holding no more than a simple VHS tape. No sex toys, thank goodness.

Kari went back to her dusting, certain that Tessa would add the item to the housekeeping basket by the door, when she heard the sound of the tape being popped into the VHS player under the television. She turned to discover Tessa just backing off to sit on the bed, remote control in hand.

"What are you doing?" Kari asked.

The girl's eyes gleamed. "Checking it out. It's not marked. Maybe it's porn. Wouldn't that be cool?"

"Tessa—" Kari began, her heart taking a leap. She could be right, and if so, Kari should stop her. The thought flickered through her mind that the last thing she needed was to be caught watching a sex video with Nick's daughter. She made a move toward the machine, looking for the stop button.

But the tape was already rolling. Kari sucked in a sharp breath.

Tessa's mouth dropped open. "Oh, wow…"

The image had come up immediately. It was bright and loud. It started right in the middle of the action. It was a movie, all right.

It was *Bambi*.

Stunned, Kari stopped dead in her tracks and watched as the classic cartoon deer did his best to ice skate on the frozen pond while Thumper the rabbit called encouragement.

Tessa looked momentarily disappointed, while Kari's heart rhythm settled. "Crap," the girl said. "I thought we might get something really wild."

"Bambi *is* wild," Kari said with a relieved laugh, and Tessa joined in.

Her frowning displeasure turned into a smile that dissolved her features into startling sweetness. "This is one of my favorite parts," Tessa said, her gaze on the screen. She looked enchanted, suddenly younger than her fourteen years.

"Mine, too," Kari agreed as she settled beside the teenager on the edge of the bed. Together they watched a few minutes, making comments and sympathetic noises as poor Bambi struggled and slid all over the ice.

Finally, they both agreed that they'd better finish up the room or Sofia would come looking for them. Tessa clicked off the movie. She turned to glance at Kari, a confused look on her face.

"What's the matter?" Kari asked.

"Don't you think it's weird that newlyweds would bring *Bambi* on their honeymoon?"

"I don't know, I think it's sort of sweet. Maybe it's like their *special* movie. The one they were watching on their first date. Or when they fell in love."

Tessa snorted. "I don't think *that* marriage is going to last very long."

How cynical the girl sounded. Kari shrugged. "Who knows? At least they have something in common. It might last forever."

"What marriage lasts forever these days?"

"Look at your grandparents."

"I mean, a modern marriage. Forever is just too long to promise anyone." Tessa rose and popped the video out of the machine. When she turned back, her mouth was tight and sullen. "My dad and mom sure didn't last forever," she said. "And they probably promised each other all kinds of goofy love stuff."

Touched by the sudden, stony grief in the teenager's eyes, Kari came off the bed. "Tessa," she said softly. "I know divorce is hard to accept. But sometimes a clean break is the best solution for everyone. Sometimes it's the only way two people can save themselves. *And* their children."

"Did your parents get a divorce?"

"No. But there were times when I wish they had. When they were together, they were very unhappy, and it made me unhappy, too, to see them that way. I loved them both, and I know that they loved me. Just as both your parents love you."

"I guess they love me," Tessa said a bit hesitantly. "But you know, sometimes I'm not even really sure about that."

Before Kari could make a comment to that dismal statement, the girl had swung away in search of fresh towels.

NICK HAD JUST COME OUT of the Broken Yoke hardware store when he spotted the company van parked across the street in front of the fabric shop. He supposed that his mother had come into town.

She'd mentioned at breakfast that she wanted to dress up the gazebo overlooking the lake. She had it in her head that bare wood didn't make much of a backdrop for a wedding ceremony, and she'd decided to add blue netting and satin bows to the flowers they'd already ordered. Nick had listened with half an ear to her and Addy debating how much and what design might serve best. He knew only one thing—when it came time to hang the stuff, he'd get elected.

He crossed the street, intending to see if she needed any help carting anything to the van, but first he wanted to stop at the National Park office two doors down to check on the brochure rack, to make sure they had enough Lightning River Lodge flyers to get through the fall season. He hit the front door and discovered that the place was unexpectedly empty except for one woman at the information desk grilling Don, the youngest of two park rangers who manned the office. He recognized her right away, and had to resist the temptation to back out of the room unobserved.

Kari Churchill stood in front of the young man, shaking her head at him. "I don't understand how you can *not* have a computer in this day and age," she said, sounding incredulous.

"Ma'am," Don replied patiently, though his frown and crossed arms indicated he was hanging on to that patience by a thread. "I didn't say we didn't have a computer. We just don't use up valuable disk space by keeping old records on file."

"But you have the records from two years ago."

"Yes, ma'am. In log books."

"Then can I see *them?*"

"No, ma'am."

Kari sighed heavily. "Why not?"

"Because even if we had the particular log book you're looking for, anything older than a year gets sent down to Denver for warehousing." Don threw out one arm to encompass the small room with its single counter. "You can see we don't have much space in this office. We're supposed to get a bigger one down by the interstate soon, but—"

Kari held up one hand. "I'm sure it's difficult," she agreed, and Nick remembered that note of weary tolerance in her voice that told him she wished she could stop being pleasant and just make mincemeat out of this guy. She'd used it on Nick that first day in Angel Air's office. "A few days ago I registered for a camping trip into Elk Creek Canyon and spoke to an older man who assured me he knew who was working as a tour guide this time two years ago. I didn't have time to spare right then, but he told me when I came back we could talk."

"That would be Louis, my supervisor."

"Yes, Louis!" Kari said with a new, enthusiastic tone. "He told me he knows a lot of the guides who take hikers into the park, and could probably pinpoint which one took my father."

So that's what this third degree was about, Nick thought. Addy had told him about Kari's determination to find out more about her famous father's last trip.

"Yes, ma'am," Don agreed. "Louis has been working this desk forever."

"Then may I speak to him?"

"No, ma'am."

"Why not?"

"'Cause he's not here."

"When will he be back?"

"Don't know exactly."

Nick barely suppressed a laugh as Kari straightened with a huge sigh and ran her hands through her hair, then clasped them at the back of her neck. She was struggling for composure, but he could have told her she was wasting her time. Don was probably the dimmest bulb the park service had ever given a uniform to.

"How can you not know when your co-worker will be back?" Kari asked, and Nick had to give her credit for perseverance.

When he saw the mulish tilt to Don's chin forming, Nick found himself speaking up. "Because Louis is up in Washington State."

Don looked over Kari's head with a grin that said he was glad to see reinforcements arrive. "Hi, Mr. D'Angelo."

Kari swung a glance over her shoulder, frowning briefly. *She* didn't look happy to see him. As he came up to join her at the counter, she said, "Why is this Louis fellow up in Washington State instead of here?"

"Don't you read the papers?" Nick asked.

"I've been sort of busy lately."

"Big forest fire up in Mt. Rainer National Park. Louis is an containment expert, and any time there's a bad one, they call on him to help out." He smiled at the younger park service agent. "Isn't that right, Don?"

"Yes, sir. How you doing?"

"Just fine. How are you managing all by yourself?"

"Well…" Don flicked a glance toward Kari. "I was doing fine. Until recently."

Kari turned her attention back to Don. "Is there *anyone* else I might speak to?" she asked a little desperately.

Don shook his head. "No one I know. Like I said, I wasn't here two years ago."

Nick touched her lightly on the arm. "Could I speak with you privately a moment?"

She nodded, tight-lipped with frustration. Her eyes blazed with green fire. He had to give her credit, she was one tough lady. He'd read somewhere that Madison Churchill had been an ornery SOB who never let the impossible stand in his way, and he had a feeling his daughter was cut from the same cloth. If her presence at the lodge didn't annoy him so much, Nick might have admired that trait.

He pulled her outside, into the crisp autumn air and onto the sun-drenched sidewalk. She squinted up at him, waiting, one hand shading her eyes.

"Whatever you're trying to accomplish in there," Nick said, "I'd say it's not working."

"I'm not trying to get state secrets. All I want is some idea of who might have taken my father out to Elk Creek. Since it's off the beaten track, he wouldn't have hiked in by himself. But this guy—" She inclined her head toward the open doorway and Don, who had gone back to playing a hand-held video game. "He's as uncooperative as—"

She broke off and actually bit her lip. He had the faint suspicion that she was going to say that Don was as uncooperative as *he* was, but then thought better of it. Maybe he should have been irritated by that, but strangely, he wasn't.

He tilted his head at her. "You know, for a woman who's supposed to make her living getting people to open up and talk, you're surprisingly confrontational."

"I'm not confrontational," she objected. "I'm—" She broke off and folded her arms across her chest, giving him a sour look. "All right. Sometimes I'm confrontational. Is that the point you wanted to make?"

"No. I was going to say that there might be something I can do to help."

She unfolded her arms and looked immediately hopeful. "What?"

"I know a guy in town who runs an independent tour operation, and there's a good chance he'd know who hiked your father into Elk Creek Canyon."

"Will you take me to him?"

"Can't. Walt spends every September with some big-shot who hires him to traipse him through the Rocky Mountain National Park. He probably won't be back until next week."

"I'll be gone by then," Kari said, clearly distressed.

He rubbed his jaw, thinking. "I can get in touch with Walt's wife. Find out when he's coming home and ask him to meet with you if he gets back before you leave. That's the best I can do."

She narrowed her eyes at him. "Why would you do that for me?"

He grinned at her. "Because if you continue to badger Don, he may forget himself and deck you. Technically you're on my payroll, and I don't need any more hospital bills to cover right now."

"You don't have to pay health benefits to part-time employees." She returned his smile. In the bright sunlight, it was something to see, so warm and charming that Nick thought a guy might be willing to do anything for its sake if he wasn't careful. He was fortunate he was so immune to it. "Thank you," she said. "Anything you can do, I'd appreciate. This is very important to me."

"So I gather."

She frowned suddenly and looked at her watch. "I have to go. I told your mother I'd only be a few minutes, and she'll need me. She's buying enough satin ribbon and bolts of blue netting to wrap up the entire lodge."

"Do you need help?"

"I can manage," she said with a shake of her head. "It beats the heck out of making beds and doing dishes."

She moved away, and he watched her go. In another moment or two, she disappeared into the fabric store.

CHAPTER EIGHT

THE NEXT DAY, with the lodge expected to be very full, Sofia asked if Kari would mind moving to a nonpaying room. Kari agreed readily and packed her belongings. After school Tessa came to help her make the switch to a room in the family quarters that lay beyond the kitchen. The girl had volunteered, much to Kari's surprise.

They trudged downstairs, Tessa leading the way while Kari followed with her backpack strapped to her like a pack mule. The girl's dark hair bounced against her back as she made her way down the staircase. Kari watched her duffel bag bang against Tessa's thin leg and was thankful she hadn't packed anything breakable.

Halfway down, Tessa indicated the tote she held and looked back at Kari guiltily. "I hope there's nothing valuable in here."

"Well, if there was, it's trash now."

The girl laughed. "I'm glad you're here."

"You are?"

"Yeah. It means I don't have to pitch in all the time and make like a slave."

"I can certainly tell you're your father's daughter," Kari said. Same delightful way with a compliment.

They'd reached the bottom of the stairs. Tessa paused to

reposition the tote on her shoulder and blew a few strands of silky hair out of her eyes as she gave Kari a sideways glance. "What's with you and Dad?"

"Nothing." Kari said it casually, but she felt such an uncomfortable jolt in her nerve endings that she found herself adding, "Do you mean, why doesn't he seem to like me? I suppose it has something to do with the fact that I'm partially responsible for what happened to his helicopter."

"Yeah, that would freak him out," the girl said. "Dad likes his helicopters almost more than people. They don't talk back or give him grief. Unlike some of us."

Tessa started through the lobby, waving off help from George at the front desk, while Kari stood for a moment to absorb Tessa's observation.

What's that supposed to mean? Was she referring to herself? Or Kari?

She decided to let the comment go. Teenagers enjoyed being mysterious and talking in riddles. And really, in spite of his willingness yesterday to help her find out more about her father's trip, what further confirmation did Kari need that Nick found her presence here objectionable?

They wove past a couple heading out for a hike around the lake, through the kitchen, into the private quarters the family used. Within the larger structure of the lodge, it was like a small house, with a living room, dining room and a long corridor that presumably opened into bedrooms. Tessa led her down the hallway and opened one of the doors, then stepped back so Kari could enter.

Kari almost faltered. This was no unused guest bedroom. This was D'Angelo family territory. *Male* territory.

"Whose room is this?" Kari asked.

"It used to belong to Uncle Matt and Dad when they were

kids. It doesn't get used much anymore, although I hear Uncle Matt's coming home for Christmas and might bring his new girlfriend. I can't wait to see if they'll get to sleep in the same room. But I guess you'll be long gone by then, huh?"

"Yes," Kari remarked absently. "Long gone."

She looked around, noting that the bedroom had been evenly divided for both boys. There were twin beds with matching quilts in bold, woodsy colors, and identical dressers and student desks. Even the bookcases were the same.

One side of the room was devoted to completed science projects, posters of supermodels, comic books and more than an inordinate amount of trophies and plaques, awards for everything from track to cross-country skiing. Clearly, Uncle Matt had been an overachiever.

She wandered over to Nick's side of the room. It was easy to see he'd been enthralled with flying from an early age. The dresser was littered with model airplanes and helicopters. The bookcase held a set of encyclopedias and more books about flying than Kari had ever seen in one place. There were a few trophies, some blue ribbons tacked to the bulletin board, and a boxy stereo that looked like an antique compared to the sleek technology of today's sound systems.

There was also a handful of photographs. Kari picked one up. "Who are these people?"

It was an interesting tableau—a lineup of kids and teenagers in ski wear, obviously standing at the base of a slope. They looked happy and relaxed, smiling for the camera in spite of sunburned noses and the bright bounce of light reflecting off the snow.

Tessa looked over Kari's shoulder, then pointed at the first person on the left. "That's Uncle Matt with one of his girlfriends. Nonna Rosa says he was a big deal with the girls.

That's Aunt Addy. Doesn't her hair look dorky that way? And Uncle Rafe. I've never met him. He ran away from home a long time ago."

That surprised Kari a little. The D'Angelos seemed so close, and in spite of their talkative ways, no mention had been made of a wayward son. "How awful."

"I think it's kinda cool. Scary, but just think, nobody telling you what to do anymore. Aunt Addy hears from him sometimes, so it's not like he's dead or anything."

"Still, it must be very hard on your grandparents."

Tessa shrugged. "They don't talk about Uncle Rafe much. I heard Dad tell Aunt Addy one day that it's just as well. He said Uncle Rafe is a hell-raising, total ass." She looked suddenly cautious. "Don't tell Dad I said that."

"Our little secret," Kari promised with a smile.

Tessa cocked her head, giving Kari a thoughtful look. "I don't know why Dad's so psycho about you. It's not like you killed anyone or anything. I think you're okay."

"Such high praise," Kari said with a rueful laugh.

The girl missed the sarcasm and turned her attention back to the photo, pointing toward a strapping teenager with a broad smile. "That's Dad. A real stud, huh?"

Kari nodded. That was certainly true, but what surprised her more was the delighted look on his face. Who would have guessed that the rude, rough tyrant she'd locked horns with had once been such an easygoing charmer? Maybe it had something to do with the brunette he had his arm around. A girl who managed to look willowy and gorgeous in spite of the bulky ski bib she wore.

"Who's she?" Kari asked.

"My mother. Dad met her in high school. I don't think I look like her, do you?"

"Maybe a resemblance around the eyes." Kari touched Nick's face in the picture. "But you and your father have the same mouth and nose."

Tessa frowned and looked closer at the photograph. "You think so? Dad says I look a lot like my mother. But he doesn't say it like that's a good thing."

"I'm sure that's not true. What father wouldn't want his daughter to take after someone so beautiful?"

"Dad doesn't. He doesn't talk about Mom. And he wants me to stay a kid forever. Do whatever he says, too."

"Sometimes it's hard for fathers to accept that their little girls grow up."

"He'll have to one day," she said, obviously once more enjoying the mysterious teenager role. "And maybe sooner than he thinks." She was silent a moment. When she looked up at Kari again, her forehead was crisscrossed with annoyance. "Dad is so completely unfair sometimes. He was my age when he met Mom and started dating her. But *I* have to wait until I turn fifteen before I can go out alone with boys. It makes me totally uncool with all my friends."

"When do you turn fifteen?"

"Next April. That's…like forever from now."

Kari did her best to hide a smile, remembering how long a few months had seemed when she'd been a teenager. But she knew better than to give Tessa any ammunition to use against her father. She set the photograph back on the bookcase.

She couldn't resist one more question. No one, not even the talkative Addy, had told her much about Nick's ex-wife. "Do you see your mother often?"

Tessa shook her head, and her clean-cut little mouth formed her words with distaste. "She gave Dad full custody five years ago after she ran off with another man. Maybe she just got tired of waiting for me to grow up and stop being such a royal pain in the butt."

Kari looked at Tessa sharply. There had been more bitterness in the girl's tone than she'd intended, Kari was sure. Did Tessa really think that?

The teenager gave Kari a suddenly amused glance. "You know, I heard Aunt Addy telling the Zias yesterday that she thinks Dad needs to get remarried."

"Oh?" Kari replied, keeping her tone carefully neutral though her imagination was speeding like a teenage driver. "Any candidate in particular in mind?"

"I don't know. They clammed up when they saw me. I'm not supposed to know anything that goes on around here."

"Would you hate having a stepmother?"

Tessa laughed. "Are you kidding? I'd love it. If Dad gets remarried someday, he won't have the time or interest in driving me nuts."

Before Kari could pose a follow-up question or two, the teenager moved toward the door. "I have to go," she said. "I have a boatload of homework to do, and Dad will have a hissy fit if I don't make a dent in it before he gets home. Plus I'm making him an early dinner tonight."

In another moment she was gone, and Kari was left to settle in. She unpacked slowly, feeling uncomfortable in a room that so clearly bore the stamp of its previous occupants.

Finally she lay down on the bed, staring up at the ceiling. A model helicopter, a snazzy red one, spun slowly in an invisible air current. She could imagine a younger Nick gazing up at it in the dark, full of enthusiasm and already envisioning a future for himself. Hard to reconcile that image with the stern-faced dictator she knew him to be. Staying in his childhood bedroom, surrounded by the touchstones of his early years, made her feel as though she was trespassing.

Her cell phone rang. Hurriedly she retrieved it from the bottom of her backpack and discovered Eddie Camit on the other end. He was the photographer who planned to link up with her on their New Zealand assignment.

"I hope you haven't packed your snowboots yet," he said.

She and Eddie were supposed to fly up to New Zealand's Mt. Cook, where an anthropological expedition had recently uncovered some bones of early man, the oldest found in that region. "Why? What's wrong?"

"The assignment's off, at least temporarily. The government doesn't like the idea of outsiders getting first crack at the dig. They want local talent."

"But we have a contract."

"Tell that to the government. There's more red tape there than in Washington."

"I was counting on this assignment."

"Patience. I haven't given up yet. I'm pulling all the strings I can."

She glanced around the room, imagining herself staying at Lightning River Lodge beyond the one week she'd planned. Staying in Nick's old bedroom. Sam D'Angelo had already told her she could stay as long as she liked. But with the exception of allowing her more time to research her father's last trip, the idea didn't hold much appeal. "Pull harder," she said.

Apparently sensing some undercurrent, Eddie asked, "Where are you?"

"Colorado."

"Playing Maria Von Trapp?"

"More like Cinderella, before the prince."

"What?"

"You wouldn't believe me if I told you." She sighed heavily. "Isn't there anything else we can do? I'm ready for a new thrill."

"I've put the word out for the both of us. If we really can't talk New Zealand into following through, then there's a possibility I can get us Jamaica."

"Antone Metcalf?"

"Yep. He's about ready to bring up the *Magdalena*. Rumor has it that the ship is loaded with more goodies than they originally thought, and he hasn't given anyone an exclusive yet. How are your sea legs?"

"Say the word, and I'm there."

Eddie laughed. They'd worked on dozens of assignments together now, and they made a good team. She trusted Eddie, felt safe with the guy. He was handsome, energetic and completely in love with a hunky paramedic, Buzz, from his hometown. "I'll be in touch as soon as I find out anything," he promised. "Sit tight and stay safe."

They hung up and, for several long minutes, Kari just stared at that tiny helicopter overhead. As nice as the D'Angelo family had been to her, as much as she knew they found her contribution helpful, she couldn't stay much longer. She was her father's daughter, and traveling was in her blood.

The call to adventure. Discovery of the unknown. The exposure to different cultures. She loved all that. So even if the assignment in New Zealand was on hold, why should she commit to more than the week she'd originally promised Sam D'Angelo?

Of course, there was still *one* good reason to stay. And if Nick came through with this tour operator he knew…

She tugged her backpack onto her lap. Digging deep, she pulled out her worn, dog-eared paperback copy of her father's last book, *Hours of Ice*. The pad of her thumb ruffled the pages lovingly. After so long, she knew it almost by heart now—every page.

She needed to think, but she couldn't do it in this room. This was Colorado, one of the most scenic states in America. It was time to get outside and see more of it. Clear some cobwebs from her brain. Dinner was a few hours away yet, and she was free until then.

Tucking the book under her arm, she headed for the hiking trail Addy had told her wove around Lightning Lake. She waved at George as she passed the front desk. Just as she was about to push through the wide front doors of the lodge, she saw Renata making a beeline toward her.

No, please, she begged silently as she stopped and waited. No dishes to wash or salt shakers that need refilling. I need some private time.

The older woman handed her a sheet of paper. "I've written down tonight's menu for you to memorize. A couple of Rose's specialties might cause you trouble. Do you want to go over it together so you can recite them properly?"

Kari glanced at the page. She wasn't willing to give up the opportunity to escape outdoors. "Let me try them by myself for a while. If I'm completely tongue-tied, I'll come running for a crash course."

Renata gave her a short, pleased nod. "Very well. Good luck."

Kari thanked her, then slipped away. She tucked the menu into the back pocket of her shorts and fled into the sweet, soft afternoon sunlight before the woman could think of anything else that needed doing.

"ROXANNE, I SWEAR TO YOU, he'll be fine. Bran can be a jerk sometimes, but he's not stupid. And he's definitely not suicidal."

Nick sat behind his desk at Angel Air, cradling the receiver against his shoulder and ear as he listened to Brandon O'Dell's long-time girlfriend break into another fit of weeping. He'd made the mistake of calling her to see if Bran had come home or at least been in touch. He hadn't, that bastard, and now Roxanne was sure he was lying dead in some hotel room with slashed wrists. Or that he'd jumped off the top of some building.

Maybe you ought to, buddy, Nick thought. Because when I see you again, you're a dead man.

He realized he was grinding his teeth. He unclenched his jaw and tried to listen for a break in Roxanne's sobbing. He was having trouble focusing. After getting the word from the airframe tech that he couldn't get Raven One back in the air until this weekend was well over, Nick almost felt like weeping himself. But he couldn't desert Roxanne now. The woman sounded nearly hysterical.

She cried and cursed and threatened to pack up her belongings and go home to her parents. Eventually she ran out of air and energy and settled into hiccupping, sniffling misery.

"All right, Rox," Nick said in a dead-calm voice. "You've got that out of your system, and now I want you to listen to me. I'm going to tell you something that Bran isn't ready to admit yet. He may not even recognize the truth himself."

"What truth?"

"That you're the best damned thing that's happened to him in years."

That got her attention. "Did he tell you that?"

"No! We don't have those kinds of talks. But he's come as close to saying it as he ever could, and I know him. There's never been a woman like you for him. Not ever."

"Then why doesn't he come home? I only want to help him."

"Because he's a dope who doesn't deserve you, and *that* he does know. Don't give up on him. I can give you a dozen reasons why he's worth the effort. Just wait him out. He'll come home."

Roxanne's breath caught, and he could hear the pain in her voice. "I love him so much, Nick."

Nick rammed a hand through his hair. How could Bran do this to Roxanne? "I know you do, Rox. And I promise, as soon as I can, I'll come to your place. If he's not home by then—and I really believe he will be—we'll look for him together. And when we find him, we'll help him clean up his act."

"When he comes home, maybe we could do one of those things. You know, where all his friends get together and try to convince him he needs to get help. For his drinking, I mean."

"An intervention? Hell, forget anything that subtle. If you want, I'll hog-tie the SOB, throw him in the back of my Jeep and haul him down to the closest rehab center. It's time he got his head straight before he loses the best thing he's ever had."

That seemed to help a little. Nick kept his promises—he sure as hell didn't let down people he cared about. And Roxanne, aware of so much of the history he and Bran shared, had to know she could count on him to follow through.

She sighed heavily. "He trusts you, Nick. If anyone can make him see reason, you can."

"I know."

They spoke a little more, and after a while Roxanne stopped crying and started talking about a possible future with Bran. It was a good thing, since Nick had just about run through all the sympathetic comments he could come up with. What was wrong with all the females in his life lately? They were either sad, mad or weepy.

When he got off the telephone, he made a few notes of

places he could call to track down Bran. It was time the guy stopped living in the past and started working toward a future. With Roxanne.

He went back to reviewing the repair bill on Raven One. What the insurance wouldn't cover wasn't astronomical, but it wasn't peanuts, either. The worst part, even with the help of his friend's chopper to pick up the slack and take tours, it would be difficult to handle the overflow of tourists who always made the trek to the mountains during fall season change.

He tossed the invoice away from him. Make about a million more beds, Kari Churchill, and you might, just might, cover the cost.

He scowled, telling himself not to think about *her.* It only made the hairs on the back of his neck rise, and he hated that reaction. A man could handle what he could define, and for the life of him, he couldn't get a clear-cut sense of his feelings for her.

He had a sudden, vivid recollection of watching her in the sunlight outside the park office, and then again up at the lodge office last night. She'd been sitting beside his father at the computer. They'd been laughing over the way she mangled Italian words from some genealogy Web site she'd found for him.

Since the stroke, his father had steadily been regaining strength and mobility in his limbs, but with the exception of time spent with Mom, he didn't laugh much anymore. Not like that. Not with the full-throated pleasure that this near stranger seemed to be able to coax out of him. Sam D'Angelo looked charmed, and at first, Nick hadn't liked the idea that this woman might tamper with his father's emotions carelessly. He even had the uncharitable thought that Sam ought to have better sense than to be taken in by her manipulative ways.

But the longer he watched, the more he became aware that there *wasn't* any manipulation going on. Their conversation was relaxed and natural, with nothing remotely false or artificial about it. They were just two people enjoying each other's company, caught up in word games and nonsense and friendship.

For just a moment Nick found himself smiling, too. She had a sweet, generous laugh and a pretty profile, with just a touch of mischief in the dimple that creased her cheek. No wonder his father found her easy to be around.

Something moved inside him, like the first pangs of hunger after a long fast. All right, he'd reasoned, so you're not as indifferent to her as you'd like to be. He had to grudgingly admit that Kari Churchill was doing her best to fit in, to hold up Addy's end of responsibilities at the lodge, and to do it with very little complaining. That had to be the reason why he'd made that offer to talk to Walt, his friend with the tour guide operation. It just seemed fair to give her a helping hand.

Besides, what was wrong with admiring a good-looking woman?

That question came so unexpectedly that he'd stepped away from the office doorway and let his smile fade in an instant. He prided himself on having his life under control, and his reaction to Kari Churchill didn't feel controlled. He'd been almost relieved when Aunt Sof came up to him with a complaint about one of her clothes dryers.

But now he'd reasoned it out. He was just tired. Trying to do too much lately. His fractured thinking had played havoc with the logical, sensible side of his brain that told him his best view of Kari Churchill was yet to come. When she got in her rental car and drove down the mountain for the last time. Now *that* would be something to smile about.

He closed his eyes a moment, concentrating on images of his favorite place in the world, King's Creek Falls. Years ago, when he'd been flying through hot, gritty sandstorms, just the thought of that little patch of heaven had been able to lift his spirits. He was long overdue for a visit. Maybe after the weekend he'd slip away for a couple of hours.

Feeling calmer, Nick lifted his head and immediately saw that someone had pulled into the parking lot. A red, jazzed-up piece of junk that only a teenager could love gleamed in the afternoon sunlight. Nick knew who it belonged to. The local bad boy, Kyle Cambridge.

Moments later he watched the kid make his way up the gravel path. He knew that walk. It reminded him of his brother Rafe's teenage strut. Full of attitude and anger. Cocky and self-confident. Times changed, but surly teenagers stayed pretty much the same.

Kyle opened the office door, nodding curtly toward Nick. The teenager was handsome, too handsome, but Nick couldn't help thinking that he also looked tougher than the last time he'd seen him, too. Guess he spent more time at the gym, now that he'd gotten tossed out of school for drag racing.

Nick had heard all about Kyle's brush with the law from a very biased, unreliable source. Tessa. His daughter was enchanted with this young hoodlum, championing him every time his name came up in conversation. Nick considered that a bad sign. Of all the schoolgirl crushes Tessa could have, she didn't need one on Kyle Cambridge.

The boy was trouble.

And now he was standing right in front of Nick.

Nick tried to keep from frowning, but he couldn't help the prickle that went up the base of his neck. He wished he'd closed up shop early today.

CHAPTER NINE

HALF AN HOUR LATER Nick closed up Angel Air and went home. At the cabin he found Tessa in the most unexpected of all places—the kitchen. Just like her mother, the girl hated to cook and lacked any talent for it. So he was surprised to find her completely surrounded by pots and pans, the counter cluttered with grocery items.

He lifted the lid off a pot simmering on the stove. An undistinguishable brown goo bubbled back at him. "Science project?" he asked.

Tessa made a face. "I'm fixing you dinner."

That was an even bigger surprise. After their recent argument over the dress, there were still so many harsh words never healed between them. Nick arched his brow at her. "You know...the cops will test for poisonous substances."

His daughter's smile ignited. "I'm not going to *poison* you. I *love* you."

Something about looking gift horses in the mouth occurred to Nick, but he couldn't help being skeptical. "Aren't you the same Tessa D'Angelo who swore a few days ago you'd never speak to me again?"

"I'm much too mature to carry a grudge," she said with an indignant sniff. "Besides, I know you only want what's best for me." From the counter she lifted a strawberry, then offered it to him. "Have one."

He popped the fruit into his mouth, trying not to look or sound suspicious. Tessa knew he loved strawberries. Chewing, he asked, "So what's for dinner?"

"Beef stroganoff. Scalloped potatoes. And strawberry trifle for dessert. All your favorites."

Now he was sure something was up. And he had a gut-sinking feeling he knew what all this was about. "Need any help?"

"No. Although dinner will be a little late. My first batch of trifle went all runny and gross on me, so I'm starting over. Is that okay?"

"That's fine. I have a couple of chores I can do—"

"Here," Tessa said, picking up another strawberry and holding it close to his mouth. "Open wide."

Nick caught her hand, withdrew the berry and placed it back on the counter. As much as he loved strawberries, they didn't hold much appeal when they were being used to soften him up. "Easy, Chef," he said. "You're overplaying your hand."

Tessa gave him a disappointed, wide-eyed look. "Huh?"

"All this domesticity when you normally pitch a fit if I ask you to open a can of soup? You want something."

"Can't I just be trying to make you happy? I know I've been a brat lately."

"So all this doesn't have anything to do with a visit I got today?" Nick opened the refrigerator, plucked out a bottle of water, then tossed the screw-top in the nearby garbage pail. He brought his gaze back to Tessa. "From Kyle Cambridge?"

"I don't know what you mean."

Before Tessa looked away for a moment, Nick saw the flash of emotion dance in her dark eyes. Damn! Whether he liked it or not, his daughter cared about that boy. He took a deep breath, knowing that things were going to go downhill fast. "I can't hire him, Tessa."

From under the fall of her loose hair, she gave him a taut, distressed look. "Why not? Because he has a record? Because he got kicked out of school?" Her chin quivered a little, but she stood ramrod-straight.

Nick's gut tightened in the face of her pain, the rigid anger that seemed to be coming off her in waves. It came back in all its force, that fear that no matter what he said now it wouldn't be enough, that no matter how much headway he'd made with Tessa over the years, he still hadn't got the hang of raising a daughter alone.

She continued to stare at him, pale and defiant. He took his time answering her. There were so many word choices he could make, and every one of them might make the situation worse.

"Kyle's recent trouble has nothing to do with why I can't hire him," he said slowly. "We don't need anyone right now at the lodge."

"Aunt Addy can't do much yet. If we have enough help, then why is Kari Churchill still here?"

"That was your grandfather's arrangement, not mine. And we're not paying her." He took a swallow of water.

"You're just making excuses," she said with a vehement shake of her head. "Admit it. You don't like Kyle, and you don't want him hanging around me. How can you be so uptight about him? He's made mistakes, but he's trying to do better. He's looking for work, and I practically promised you'd hire him."

"Then I'm sorry, because now you'll have to tell him you were mistaken." The words came out a shade too gruffly and he tried to soften his tone. "You should have checked with me first."

"Yeah, like I can talk to you about Kyle. Or anything else."

"If he's as terrific as you think he is, he'll forgive you. He didn't seem all that surprised when I told him no."

"That's because he knows how you feel about him." She slapped the dish towel she'd been twisting in her slim fingers down on the counter and gave him a sour, mutinous look. "This is so totally unfair. Didn't you ever make a mistake when you were young? I'll bet *you* weren't any damned saint."

Nick grit his teeth. It didn't make sense that this child could smell like flowers while looking like such a warrior. His gaze locked with hers, though she hung in there, her mouth set.

"Tessa," he said as calmly as he could, "you need to stop now. Before you make this worse."

"*You're* making it worse. How can you be this way? Kyle thinks I'm special. He thinks—"

"What do you mean, Kyle thinks you're special?" Nick asked with a frown.

She looked at him with hard reproach, tears starting to brim. "He likes me. And I like him. It's no big deal. Don't look like that."

But there, damn it, he saw the truth in her eyes again. He stopped being reasonable as he felt the first brush of panic. "You're right," he said at last, looking her straight in the eyes. "I don't want you seeing him."

She reddened and appeared momentarily flustered, swinging away from him to twist the dials on the stove. Evidently fixing dinner had just become her lowest priority.

"I wish Mom was here," she said when she turned back. "She'd understand."

"Well, she's not," he said, inhaling a deep, calming breath. "And I'm afraid you're stuck with me."

Her mouth tightened. A blink. Enough to send a single tear streaking down her cheek. She brushed it away. Then she stalked toward the kitchen door.

He watched her go, feeling hopeless and angry, the blood pounding in his chest.

At the door she turned back to look at him. Her eyes were dark, full of bleak fire. "You won't *always* be able to tell me what to do."

KARI HAD OFTEN THOUGHT nothing could compare to living on the beach in Florida. But after exploring the shady trail that meandered around the lip of Lightning Lake, she could see why Sam D'Angelo had sold his parents' small motel down by the river in Broken Yoke and decided instead to build his lodge on this spot.

As she'd driven up from Denver, the Rockies had seemed unreal, like a backdrop out of some photographer's portrait studio. She'd been impressed by the overwhelming vastness of it all, fold upon fold of jagged mountains that seemed to go on forever. Their raw strength gave no hint of the secrets they had held since the beginning of time. But now, this close and sheltered within the limitless, pristine beauty of the forest that surrounded Lightning River Lodge, Kari found herself enchanted.

The lake sat like a shallow bowl amid the trees, a slight breeze ruffling the surface. The water sparkled under a ceramic-blue sky, so bright, it almost hurt her eyes. Was it a trick of the late-afternoon sun that made the light seem to have substance and texture here? Regardless, the view from the overlooks positioned along the trail nearly took her breath away.

She settled in a sun-flecked canopy of ground-reaching branches. The family had placed a couple of hand-hewn log benches among the ponderosa pines so weary hikers could rest and enjoy their surroundings, but she had them to herself for now. Beyond a low, split-rail fence that warned guests to stay away from the edge of the sloping undergrowth, the lake peeked enticingly through a stand of white-barked aspen, already dressed in gold for the season.

It had been this same time of year when her father had made the hike into Elk Creek Canyon. Had he found this kind of beauty in that place? Before that freak snowstorm had changed everything and eventually taken his life?

Her copy of *Hours of Ice* sat on her lap, and Kari thought again how different it was from her father's usual recipe for a bestseller.

For one thing, it was very short. Almost a novella, really. Unlike his personal journal, the manuscript had been saved from his gear after the rescue. It had been heavily edited by his long-time publishing house and finally rushed to the bookstores after his death. It had been a miserable failure.

But that wasn't the only difference from his other books. Something had happened to her father during those last two weeks of his life. Instead of being packed with all the intrigue and action his books were famous for, the story featured a single character, a man also struggling for survival, a man who seemed to be on a journey of self-exploration and discovery.

Kari felt it was the best thing he had ever written. Powerful. Eloquent. She'd read it a dozen times, and each time the character—a man with a wife and young daughter—seemed to be speaking directly to her. As though her father, facing certain death, had wanted her to know how he felt about them in his heart.

To Kari, that book *was* her father. She couldn't help believing that, somehow, visiting the place he'd spent his final weeks would help her discover some misty, puzzling truth she could sense but never really capture.

After fingering the worn pages a few moments, Kari closed

the book with a snap and set it aside. Whether Nick was able to put her in touch with that tour operator or not, she had to ask Sam D'Angelo for time off after the weekend. If the New Zealand trip really was on hold, there was simply no reason not to make this extra time work for her. She had to get out to Elk Creek Canyon.

But first, she had to get through this evening.

From the back pocket of her shorts, she dug out the menu Renata had handed her. The woman's handwriting was horrible. Squinting and turning the paper this way and that didn't help much.

Most of the selections didn't present a problem, of course. Who couldn't rattle off strip steak and pork chops? It was the Italian dishes that always gave her fits.

Tonight it looked as though there were going to be two. Taking a deep breath, Kari tried out the first one slowly. "'Chicken Napo-le-lana All-a Natalie. Chicken breast topped with poscutto—pro-sciutto—'" she corrected, "—and mozzarella cheese, sautéed in white wine, with a sprinkling of fresh tomato.'"

No good. Too much stumbling. Renata had told her the words should roll off the tongue naturally. Easy for her to say, considering she was a native.

"'Napolean All Natasha,'" she repeated quickly without looking, then frowned. *Definitely not right. Try again.* "Napolinni Alla Natalie."

Worse. Try the other one. Kari looked down at the menu again. Oh, crap.

"'Pag-lia E Fie-no Papa-lina,'" she recited with precise care. "Hay and straw pasta with ham, peas and mushrooms combined with cream and a touch of tomato sauce." She closed her eyes, trying to commit the ingredients to memory.

"Hay and straw pasta with ham, peas and mushrooms combined with cream and a touch of tomato sauce. Pag-li Feno Papa-something."

She checked the menu. *Darn it! Way off this time.*

Frustrated, Kari got up and wandered to the edge of the log railing.

"You can do this, you idiot," she shouted to the open air. "Pagga Feni Papalini. Pagi-something Feni-Papa. Hay and straw with ham— No! Not hay and straw. Why would anyone want hay and straw to eat? Hay and straw *pasta*—"

Completely annoyed with herself, Kari crumpled the menu in her fist and shook it toward the trees. "What's wrong with offering plain old spaghetti and meatballs?" she shouted, the words bouncing back at her even before she'd finished.

"Nothing. That's usually Monday's specialty."

Kari swung around, startled to discover Nick D'Angelo planted in the middle of the hiking trail. He leaned on a short shovel and balanced a fairly large, shapeless bag on one shoulder. She couldn't help it. Her heart gave a few unnecessary beats, he was that darned good-looking.

"I was just practicing tonight's specialties," she explained in a casual tone that surprised the heck out of her.

He shifted the bag for a better grip. "So I heard."

"I thought I was alone out here."

"You probably are now. Every chipmunk and deer within five miles has to be running for cover." He picked up the shovel and started to turn away. "I'll let you get back to your practicing."

With the exception of that brief conversation at the National Park office, this was the most they'd spoken to one another in days. Kari didn't have a clue how to handle an actual conversation with this guy, but she suddenly didn't want to see it end.

"No, wait—" she called out. That tiny, friendly overture couldn't go to waste. Maybe Nick had decided to be nice. Maybe he'd had a change of heart about her. Anything was possible. He turned back and she asked in an agreeable voice, "Did you need something?"

"No. I'll come back later."

"If I'm in your way…"

"You're not."

"I'd be happy to help if I can."

"I don't need any help."

Kari's heart sank. She knew that tone. She recognized that irritable tension on his brow. Something went molten with anger inside her, like lava spilling. Before she could stop herself, she charged up the trail after him. When she swooped around in front of him, he came to a halt. The look on his face was bland and uncompromising.

"You know what I think?" she said, realizing that her tone already sounded as if she'd consigned him to the fires of hell. "I think you may be in charge here, but you're about the surliest innkeeper I've ever met. Norman Bates offered more of a welcome."

"You're not a guest."

He had a point, but in her present mood, she wasn't willing to see it. "Maybe not, but I'm a person, and I think I deserve to be treated like one."

His brow rose. "Miss Churchill, the very fact that you're here, enjoying the hospitality of my family home should be—"

"Hospitality!" she raged at him. "Is that what you call what I've *enjoyed* the past few days? A Victorian sweatshop was probably less demanding than this job. I've been up to my elbows in greasy dishwater, hauled linen up two flights of stairs and cleaned tubs until you could eat off them. You couldn't have a better employee than me, or one who complained less."

She took a step toward him, her hands on her hips. "And that's not all. I've had my cheeks pinched by your aunts until I don't have feeling in them anymore. Your mother keeps trying to sell me on the benefits of calamari, even though I've told her I hate the stuff." She held up one hand. "Do you see these paper cuts? I got them licking stamps and folding letters for your father. He doesn't trust e-mail—even though I've explained it to him a dozen times. We spent two hours last night doing a mass mailing to the members of his old army unit. In case you're wondering, that's four hundred and sixty-eight guys."

"Miss Churchill—"

"Don't take that high-minded tone with me, *Mr.* D'Angelo. Frankly, I'm sick of your attitude. Yes, I made a mistake. Believe me—I still feel guilty every time I look at Addy's arms. But I've tried to make up for what happened, and your family is big enough to forgive me, so why can't you? It's time you took that stick out of your—"

"Miss Churchill—"

"Stop calling me Miss Churchill. You're only doing it to annoy me."

"Kari—"

She stopped for a moment, probably because she was out of breath. Certainly not because she'd run out of complaints against this man. "What?"

He let the bag he'd shouldered slide to the ground, then straightened. His head tilted and he raised one eyebrow. "Working for us is like working in a Victorian sweatshop?"

She ducked her head, suddenly feeling very foolish. What possible good could come of lecturing this man? "I was trying to make a point," she said, unwilling to concede defeat entirely.

"I think you have. I apologize."

"I just—" She lifted her head. "What?"

"I apologize for my rudeness the past few days. It's been a difficult week, but that's no excuse. I know you've been working hard. If I haven't seen you in action myself, I'm certainly hearing about it from everyone else. My family is very fond of you, and I suppose the least I can do is not make you uncomfortable for the remainder of your stay."

She was stunned into momentary silence. Then good manners kicked in. "Thank you," she said in a soft voice.

He shocked her even more by holding out one hand. "Truce?"

She managed a careless shrug as she shook his hand for less than a millisecond, then dropped it. "All right. Sure. Truce."

There was a short, awkward silence while her shock wore off, and Nick seemed to find sudden interest in the nearby pines. She wondered what he was thinking, but before she could even guess, he surprised her by bringing his gaze back to her. His brows were knit like mating caterpillars.

"What's wrong with calamari?" he asked.

She laughed lightly in response. It was so completely *not* what she'd been expecting from him. "It's squid tentacles, for heaven's sake. What's *right* about it?"

He gave her an odd look that made her heart lurch suddenly sideways. Then he bent to pick up his bag and shovel again.

"Can I help you with something?" she asked quickly.

"Know anything about concrete?"

"It makes good shoes for Mafia enemies."

He indicated a section of the split-rail fence along the trail, where one of the supporting posts was sagging outward and looked in danger of toppling. "It also helps keep leaning fence posts from falling down." He gave her a speculative look. "I suppose you could handle holding it upright while I lay some concrete around the base."

"I'm your girl," she said, then immediately wished she hadn't. The words didn't sound quite right. While he settled the bag back on one shoulder, she moved ahead of him, toward the lazy fence post.

He reached her side and she found herself suddenly nervous. "What do you want me to do? Do you need water from the lake? Are we going to mix it up? I've never done that before, but I'm sure I can learn."

He stopped her babbling by holding up one hand. "Relax. We're not laying the foundation for a house." He pointed toward the bag he'd dropped at his feet. "It's premixed. Welcome to the new age of construction."

"Oh."

"Just hold on to the top of the fence post so it doesn't fall over while I dig out around the base. All right?"

"No problem."

Immediately he took the short shovel and began clearing the earth. There were lavender wildflowers clustered around the base of the post. Nick dug them up with ruthless disregard. Kari must have made some small sound of regret, because he stopped and looked up at her.

"What?" he asked.

"Well, they're just so pretty. It seems a shame to destroy them."

He bent to retrieve one of the flowers, then extended it to her. The poor thing already looked wilted. She took it and brought it to her nose. There was no smell.

"It's fleabane," he said. "People used to crush them up and sprinkle them around dog kennels to keep the fleas away. Should I rescue enough to make a bouquet?"

She wrinkled her nose and tossed the wildflower away. "I'll hold out for roses."

He grinned and shook his head at her, then renewed his efforts with the shovel. She noticed how his dark hair gleamed even in this shady clearing. He had nice hands, too. Strong and capable, the kind of hands that saw hard work and yet still managed to look graceful.

"This your first time in Colorado?" Nick asked as he lifted another spadeful of earth.

"Yes."

"Like it?"

"What I've seen of it. This area is very beautiful. The lake. All these massive trees. I saw deer on the trail."

"We'll see more of them as the weather turns colder and they come down the mountain."

"You must love it here."

"I enjoy the peace and quiet, when I can take advantage of it." He lifted his gaze and inclined his head toward her two-handed hold on the post. "Can you tilt it back a little?"

She did as he asked, then watched as he withdrew work gloves from beneath the belt of his jeans and slipped them on. Yes, definitely nice hands. He ripped open the bag of wet cement and poured it into the hole he'd made around the post.

"I imagine running the lodge keeps you very busy," Kari said while he spread the mix around and she made sure the post stayed straight and steady.

"I'm sure you've seen by now that everyone pulls their weight. I try to keep them from running into roadblocks along the way. I guess I'm the facilitator in the family."

"Addy says you're the go-to guy. Your daughter says everyone counts on you to make things right."

He looked up. She sensed surprise, which seemed a strange reaction. "Tessa said that?"

Kari nodded. "Your daughter's very bright and sweet. We make a good team, cleaning rooms for your aunt Sofia."

"You doing all right?" he asked about her hold on the post. When she nodded back, he added with a touch of asperity in his voice, "Tessa's bright—but sweet? I haven't seen that side of her lately. In fact, I came out here to work off my latest frustration with her. She was about ready to burn down the cabin with me in it."

"Nothing serious, I hope."

"Boy trouble. Which she's way too young for."

"Teenage girls can be quite a challenge sometimes."

"So I'm learning." He sat back on his heels, glancing up at her again. "You give your dad much trouble growing up?"

"I didn't see much of my father. He was either off on some adventure or locked in his study, writing." Now seemed as good a time as any to follow up on his promise. "Uh, I was wondering…"

"If Walt's back in town yet? Sorry, no. But his wife swears she'll have him call me the minute she hears from him."

That would have to do, she supposed, but it was still a disappointment. Still holding the post, she looked away. Right now she didn't want to think about her father. She wanted to keep the conversation light and friendly. And it was turning out to be easier than she'd ever thought it could be. A stray thought popped into her head when she turned back to face him. *"Paglia En Ferno Papalini,"* she said, wondering if she'd finally gotten the pronunciation right.

His mouth moved, putting shallow indentions on the sides of his cheeks. "Close. Papa*lina*, not *lini*." He rose, stripping off the gloves. *"Paglia E Fieno Papalina,"* he said slowly.

Then he recited the ingredients with such flawless eloquence that it made Kari's mouth water.

His gaze held hers. Face-to-face with those dark, da Vinci eyes, she found herself nearly speechless. She'd never realized just how black brown could be. She said feebly, "I suppose it's easy if you grow up eating all those things."

His mouth relaxed into a small smile. "It didn't hurt that I was Mom's head waiter when I was in high school. And it's not *inferno,* it's *E Fieno.* Bare your teeth a little when you say it. Like this." His lips twisted. *"E Fieno."*

"E Ferno," she repeated, then shook her head and grimaced. "I can't. The guests will think I've gone rabid if I make a face like that."

"Try again. Not so wide this time." His hand came up unexpectedly, and he placed thumb and forefinger against either side of her mouth, pushing back slightly against her jaw. His fingers were still warm from the glove. Or was she just imagining that? "Let your lips spread more," he instructed. *"E Fie…no."*

There was nothing in his face to make her think he found anything strange about this small intimacy. Just a little language lesson, she told herself. Nothing provocative. But she felt the shock of his touch all the way down to the soles of her feet.

She didn't want to like it. But she did.

And then, for just a flicker of a second, she sensed he felt it, too. He went very still, searching her eyes for more clues to just what was going on here. She couldn't help him much. She was suddenly having thoughts about Nick D'Angelo that threatened to imperil her immortal soul.

"E Fieno," she said at last, her voice a little hoarse. She cleared her throat. *"Paglia E Fieno Papalina."*

He dropped his hand, nodding approval. "By George, I think she's got it."

In spite of those playful words, he seemed more than ready to put that odd moment behind them. His mouth had tightened. Once more he looked like a man who'd been born without smile muscles.

"Just about finished?" She glanced toward the pool of cement. If he'd decided to ignore those few moments of nonsense, she could, too.

"Yes."

"That wasn't too difficult."

"No. That should do it."

Those crushing monosyllables. Were they deliberate? She couldn't tell.

She glanced at her wristwatch, though she barely registered the time. "I suppose I should get back. You know those Victorian sweatshops. They whip you if you're late."

He placed his hands around the post about the same time she lifted hers. In another few minutes it would probably set well enough to stand alone. Nick didn't look up at her, as though the fence post had become the most important thing in his universe. "You go on. I'll finish up here. And thanks for the help."

She backed away to scoop her book off the bench. "Thanks for *your* help."

"You'll do fine tonight."

There wasn't anything left to be said. Back to business, it seemed. Maybe he wasn't interested in seeing her staked out naked on an anthill anymore, but he didn't seem interested in seeing her at all, evidently.

She'd just started to make her way back up the trail when Nick's voice stopped her.

"Kari, hold up."

She turned, waiting.

"How would you like a different assignment tomorrow?"

"Such as?"

"Vail's Aspenfest starts this weekend. The whole valley will be swarming with tourists. Addy has this crazy idea that we can drum up a little business for Angel Air if we blitz the town with flyers for helicopter tours. Aunt Sof was going to help us, but she doesn't like to leave the cleaning crew on their own. Feel like tagging along?"

"I thought the, uh, accident left you short one helicopter?" She didn't like reminding him of that disaster, but she couldn't help wondering.

"There aren't too many tours scheduled at the moment. A friend of mine brought his chopper up to help out, and Pete says he'd rather be kept busy than sit around with nothing to do. Besides, I covered for his vacation last summer, so he owes me. And I don't want to disappoint Addy's efforts to make the company money. She feels bad enough as it is."

"Oh. Won't the lodge be too busy to spare me?"

"I have some pull with the boss," he said. Then he shrugged. "I just thought you might like to have a little more time outdoors."

The offer seemed friendly enough, though his tone was all business. A warning danced at the edge of her consciousness, almost out of reach. *Don't read too much into this, Kari. Don't.*

She shook her head. "I'm not sure…"

"That's fine," he said with a shrug, as if her decision didn't really matter to him one way or the other. "If you change your mind, we're going to meet in the lobby first thing in the morning."

CHAPTER TEN

WHAT REMAINED OF THE DAY went quickly after that. Kari was so busy helping out in the dining room that she had little time to think about the interlude with Nick on the trail. By the end of the evening she had offered *Chicken Napolelana Alla Natalie* and *Paglia E Fieno Papalina* more than a dozen times, and not once had she stumbled over the words.

Addy spent some time pestering Kari to change her mind about joining them on the trip into Vail the next day. In spite of her bandaged arms, she'd managed to create and copy hundreds of flyers that could be distributed to every shop, restaurant and hotel. She was like a general marshaling troops.

But extended time spent in Nick's company seemed like a poor idea to Kari. One small argument could destroy a peace as fragile as the one they shared. No matter how much longer she stayed at Lightning River, she didn't want to go back to those brittle looks, that insufferable attitude of superiority, those embarrassing, awkward moments when she wished she could be any place else but in his presence.

As for that indefinable *something* that had seemed to flash between them out in that shady oasis—forget it. It hadn't happened. Too much imagination and too little stimulation in her life lately probably accounted for that fantasy.

After the last of her duties, Kari made a quick escape to

her bedroom. She pulled out the Arapahoe National Forest maps she'd picked up at the ranger station and spent an hour studying them. Just when she was about to turn off the light and call it a night, there was a knock on the door.

As soon as she opened it, Rose D'Angelo pulled her into a smothering hug, then held Kari away at arm's length.

"You poor dear," she exclaimed. "Why didn't you tell me?"

Kari struggled not to look thoroughly confused, but it was useless. "Tell you what?"

"That you can't eat calamari."

That's not quite what I said, Kari wanted to say, but she was busy trying to absorb the fact that Nick had ratted her out to his mother. Did Rose think she'd been complaining? Was she upset? Strangely, it didn't seem that way.

"I didn't want to offend you," Kari hedged.

"Oh no, dear, no. Not at all. I shouldn't have pushed. Nick told me you mustn't eat it."

She couldn't imagine what tale Nick had spun for his mother, but if it kept Kari from coming face-to-face with that disgusting stuff again, she was perfectly willing to play along.

She patted the older woman's arm. The kind concern darkening her eyes was really very sweet. "It's all right, Mrs. D'Angelo. I just have to…watch what I eat."

Rose seemed satisfied. "*Bene.* In the future, you must say something. I have such an urge to fatten you up. But Nick says to leave you alone, that you're fine just the way you are."

Nick D'Angelo said that? Wow. She must have done a better job holding that fence post than she'd thought.

When Rose finally turned loose of her and padded down the hall, Kari remained in the open doorway, still contemplating the conversation.

Nick had actually stepped in to help her with his mother,

and *without* making her look like the bad guy. And that remark about her figure—that was probably as close to a compliment as the man ever came. Nick D'Angelo was one surprise after another.

Before she could give it too much thought, Kari went down the hallway and knocked on Addy's bedroom door. She opened it with a sleepy yawn. "What's up?"

"I've changed my mind. What time do we meet in the lobby tomorrow?"

THE NEXT MORNING, Kari helped Rose stack stationary boxes filled with bright yellow flyers into the back of the resort van. Addy, still restricted because of her injuries, held the door open with one hip, already issuing instructions on the best way to blanket the festival. When the last box had been loaded, the three women stood under the portico and waited for the rest of the volunteers on this mission.

Kari had been surprised to discover that Rose intended to join them, since she seemed so firmly entrenched in the demands of the kitchen. "Who's doing the cooking this morning?" she asked Nick's mother.

"Renata. She likes to take charge once in a while, and I need a day out in the fresh air."

Kari inhaled deeply, letting the autumn scents—leaves and wood smoke and crisp air—sift into her system. "It should be beautiful today. I haven't been outdoors much lately."

Rose looked at her with one brow raised in an arch of concern. "Kari, if you want time off, or feel we have been too demanding, please, you must say so. Sometimes we forget just how time-consuming it can be to run this place."

"I hope I didn't sound like I was complaining," Kari said. "Your family's been very kind to me. I'm certainly not overworked, and even if I were…" She hesitated, not wishing to bring up memories of the helicopter accident.

Rose was evidently too sharp to miss Kari's quick glance at Addy's sling-covered arm. "You are doing us a favor," she said firmly. "Not doing penance."

Kari nodded, amazed again at how practical this woman could be. And how forgiving. Remembering her own mother's intolerant stance on so many things, Kari thought Nick and Addy had been extremely lucky to grow up in the D'Angelo household.

A long minute passed. No sign of Nick, who Kari assumed would be driving them to Vail. When she saw Addy glance impatiently at her watch, Kari couldn't resist satisfying her curiosity.

"Who are we waiting for?" she asked.

"Nick and Tessa," Rose responded.

"The day's getting away from us," Addy said, clearly eager to get started.

"They'll be here soon," Rose said. Kari had learned long ago that Rose D'Angelo was one of the most patient people on the planet.

Addy, however, was not. She made an annoyed sound through her nose. "If Nick can convince Tessa to come out of her room."

"What's wrong with Tessa?" Kari asked in surprise.

"Nothing," Addy said as she slammed the rear door of the van closed with one thrust of her hip. "At least, nothing that having a different mother wouldn't take care of."

"Addy…" Rose said, a warning in her tone.

"Well, it's true, Mom," Addy complained. "Pulling this latest stunt is really too much, even for Denise. She has to know how much she's hurt Tessa." Aware that Kari couldn't possibly know what she referred to, Addy threw a chagrined glance her way.

"Tessa has a long weekend free from school coming up, and she's been counting on spending that time in Boston with her mother. It was all arranged. But Nick told us this morning that Denise called last night and canceled. Tessa can't come because Denise and her husband are going to Vermont. How's that for motherly love?"

Rose fixed a harsh stare on her daughter. "Denise has tried to be a good mother since the divorce."

"When it suits her," Addy said. "Mostly she's just been selfish and thoughtless, and if you ask me, she doesn't deserve to have a daughter if she—"

"Adriana!" Rose said more sharply. "Denise is Tessa's mother, and you should remember that."

"Well, it makes me mad. The woman needs to get her priorities straight."

Rose had been using a whisk broom to sweep stray crumbs from one of the front seat cushions. Finishing the job, she stowed the broom under the seat and turned back to her daughter. "Our job is to remain supportive, but impartial," she told Addy. "It serves no purpose to poison Tessa's mind against her mother."

Addy looked sullen. "I never say anything to Tessa. And it seems to me that Denise is doing a perfectly good job of poisoning Tessa's mind without any help from us."

"Enough!" Rose said in the strongest tone Kari had ever heard the woman use. "I'm going to check on them. Practice being silent."

She headed in the direction of Nick's cabin. They watched her go, and the moment Rose had trudged out of sight, Addy grinned at Kari. "Mom tends to insist on finding the good in people. Even when there isn't any."

"Was Nick very angry with his ex-wife?" Kari couldn't resist asking. Having fallen victim to Nick's wrath herself, she could imagine the explosive reaction that change in plans would have brought. Especially coming on the heels of his own difficulties with his daughter yesterday.

Addy's response surprised her, however. "Nick never lets Denise get him worked up anymore. But he was worried about Tessa. Said she was so crushed by the news that she locked herself in her room and refused to come out." Addy leaned against the side of the van. Shaking her head, she said, "Nick's certainly had his hands full lately."

"Tessa seems very troubled sometimes, and your brother doesn't seem like the kind of man to…" She trailed off, not wanting to voice a complaint against someone so clearly beloved by Addy.

"Put up with a lot of foolishness?" Addy finished for her. She smiled, indicating that she understood completely and even agreed. "He isn't. I've lectured him until I'm blue in the face, but he'll do it his own way." She shrugged. "And truthfully, Nick does try. He really does. And I've never heard him say one bad thing to Tessa about her mother." Addy laughed. "It's probably hardest for me and Pop to hold our tongues. We both knew that marriage was doomed for failure, but Nick wouldn't listen."

Kari brushed a speck of dirt from her jeans, wishing she didn't feel compelled to ask. Finally she accepted it. She wanted to know. "What drew the two of them together?"

"You mean, besides hormones?" Addy asked with another knowing smile. "Denise was a beauty even in high school. Destined for a career in modeling, or so everyone thought. She never wanted kids, never wanted to settle down, but she did want Nick the moment she saw him. They dated for years, and when he joined the service, I think she saw that as her ticket out of the mountains. Only problem, the life of a military wife isn't exactly glamorous. Eventually she found someone who could give her what she wanted." Addy made a face. "I suppose that's not completely fair. Nick says Denise did try to make a go of the marriage. He was gone a lot, and she was stuck being both mother and father to Tessa."

Given the dynamic of her own parents' marriage, Kari could certainly understand the frustration Nick's ex must have felt, the burden it must have placed on her.

With a glance down the empty path that led to Nick's cabin, Addy gave Kari a confiding look. "Nick once admitted to me over a bottle of Chianti that he regrets the way he handled things with Denise. He was never completely open with her. After what he'd been through in the Gulf War and Bosnia, he put even more emotional distance between himself and Denise. He says they should have ended it sooner, instead of pretending things could get better."

"Nick doesn't strike me as the kind of guy to give up easily."

"He isn't," Addy agreed. "He doesn't take commitment lightly either, and once he's made one, he'll move heaven and earth to honor it."

"I suppose there are worse traits he could have." When Addy gave her a sudden, sharp look, Kari added quickly, "I mean, he seems completely committed to making the lodge profitable. And making sure your family is well taken care of."

"I think he has control issues. Pop says it's just the D'Angelo stubborn streak in him." She straightened. "Whatever it is, looks like he was able to talk Tessa into coming."

She inclined her head toward the path that led to Nick's cabin. Kari turned and watched Nick, his mother and Tessa make their way to join them on the front drive. Nick's and

Rose's features were blank, but from the look of Tessa's red-rimmed eyes, it was clear the girl was miserable. The tight slash of her mouth indicated that coming on this trip was the last thing she had in mind.

No one said a word, and to keep from becoming part of these awkward family moments, Kari quickly jumped into the van and maneuvered into the third seat.

Nick drove, and Addy, apparently excited to be doing something constructive and determined to keep the mood upbeat, chattered all the way down the mountain. Everyone listened politely to her instructions and nodded their heads in unison like dashboard puppies.

They drove through the tiny town of Broken Yoke, then swung onto the interstate and eventually into Vail Valley. Nick's attitude was a disappointment. He remained quiet and preoccupied. However cordial he'd been to her yesterday afternoon, he seemed to have fallen back into ignoring her most of the time. The hope that they were beyond petty grievances withered and went to dust, though she supposed that his thoughts were preoccupied with Tessa's attitude.

She sat up front beside her father, but her attention seemed riveted out the side window. She made no effort to contribute to the conversation. Father and daughter spoke, but their exchanges were brief and painfully polite.

They passed East Vail and traffic picked up considerably. The true heart of the town, Vail Village, didn't allow anything but foot traffic, so Nick parked on the nearest side street. They all piled out, and almost before everyone had stretched out kinks and adjusted clothing, Addy was awkwardly passing around large handfuls of the flyers.

It was early yet, but plenty of people were already on the streets. Somewhere up ahead in the village, a polka band was tuning up. Although there was no snow on Vail Mountain, the chairlifts were running. With its heavy influence of Bavarian-style architecture, the town was a little too cute, a little too *planned* for Kari's tastes, but the crisp snap of fall air and clear blue sky overhead made her glad she'd come.

Addy was still the majordomo. "Mom, why don't we work that parking lot?" she suggested, motioning toward a lot filled with an ocean of cars. She glanced at Kari and Tessa in turn, then inclined her head toward the cluster of shops, restaurants and hotels within the village. "Why don't you two hit all the stores on the pedestrian mall? See if they'll let you put flyers by the registers. Pass out as many to the tourists as you can, too. And don't forget—charters aren't cheap, so pick out people who look like they can afford us."

Nick had a huge stack of the flyers under one arm. "I'm going to the Visitor's Center. See if I can make a deal for some free advertising."

Addy looked pleased. "Let's all meet back here in an hour to see how we've done. Stop frowning, Nick. I know this will work."

He shook his head and gave her a rueful smile. It was the first one Kari had seen this morning. "Only for you, Addy. No one else could get me out here shucking our wares like someone in a Turkish bazaar."

Addy laughed, balancing a stack of flyers on her extended arms. "If this gets us more business, next time I'm going to try a contest or something. Maybe the winner could get a half hour flight up the Front Range."

"You should make the prize at least an hour's flight," Kari suggested as she withdrew more flyers from the stack. "It needs to have a perceived value. I once did an article on market research companies, and they have a slogan in the business—Peanut Prizes, Monkey Customers."

"See, Nick?" Addy said with a grin. "There may be all kinds of things we can do if you'll just let me."

"Let's just get through this first," he said, and the look on his face made Kari wonder if she should have remained silent.

"Stubborn as always," Addy said, heading off with her mother by her side. "Good luck, everyone! One hour."

Kari and Tessa trooped up the sidewalk obediently. The street was lined with small businesses, the practical everyday kind found in most towns. Nothing as tony or tourist-oriented as they were sure to find in the heart of Vail Village.

The first place they came to was an optometrist, not a likely candidate for flyers.

Tessa looked peevish about going in, but Kari was determined. "Let's see what kind of reception we get and work on our pitch while we're at it."

Sure enough, the office manager said no to the flyers, and they were back on the street in no time. If Tessa had been unenthusiastic before, she was ready to mutiny now.

"This is stupid," she said. "We sound like total losers."

"We'll get better," Kari replied in a firm voice. "We just need to practice a little."

She headed off again, and Tessa fell reluctantly into step beside her. It was going to be a miserable morning if the girl didn't snap out of it, Kari thought. She tried to come up with a topic they could discuss, but she hadn't been a teenager in a long time and she was awfully rusty when it came to small talk.

Finally she took in a deep lungful of air. "The mountains almost take your breath away, don't they?"

"Uh-huh."

Kari pointed toward a huge mountain face off to the right,

completely covered in yellow aspen and dark evergreens like a patchwork quilt. "Have you ever seen anything so beautiful?"

"Only every year around this time."

Oh, yeah, she was her father's daughter. They had non-communication down to an art form.

A couple of teenage girls outfitted in dirndl dresses and holding tap shoes passed them, evidently headed for some dance group.

"I wonder if one of them is Heidi," Kari remarked when they were out of earshot.

"Heidi who?" Tessa said in obvious irritation.

"Heidi. You know, from the children's book?"

"No."

Guess kids don't grow up reading about Heidi and her adventures in the mountains anymore, Kari thought. Probably too tame for this generation. She decided to take a chance. "Tessa, do you want to talk about what's bothering you?"

"No."

She stopped and turned toward the girl. "I'd like to point out that I'm not your father *or* your mother. As far as I know, I haven't done anything wrong lately, so a little friendly conversation wouldn't go amiss. It might make this job go a little faster. And it will definitely take your mind off other problems."

Tessa gave her a wide-eyed, horrified look. "Did my dad tell *everyone* about Mom's phone call?"

"He didn't tell me anything. I overheard your grandmother and Addy talking about it."

The girl seemed immediately contrite. "Sorry."

"Are you sure you don't want to talk about it?"

"No," Tessa said, but in the next moment, she shook her head wildly. "I hate my parents. Mom is totally selfish. She makes promises all the time and never follows through. And Dad…Dad is so mean and bossy and…and he's worse than she is!"

Oh, boy. Kari was almost sorry she'd said anything. "Any particular reason why?"

"He knows I don't want to be here today. But he made me come."

"He probably thought it would be better for you to be out with us than sitting at home by yourself."

Tessa expelled a tragic sigh. "I wasn't going to be by myself for long. A bunch of us were supposed to go kayaking today on Lake Dillon. But Dad said I couldn't go. He *says* it's because he wanted me here with him, but I know that's not it."

"Then what do you think the reason is?"

"It's because there were going to be boys there and no adults to supervise us." Her mouth pinched. "I guess he thinks that somehow I'm gonna have sex in a kayak."

Kari didn't know what to say. She didn't have parenting instincts to guide her, and taking the girl's side in this could be dangerous. "Tessa…" she began, despising herself for sounding so tentative.

"Oh, I don't want to talk about it," the teenager said, and threw up her hands in disgust. Her voice shook as if she were trying to bring it under control. "Mom might not want me around, but Dad treats me like a baby, and he'll never be any different. Let's just do this and get it over with."

Kari groaned inwardly as she watched the girl take off down the street. She was no good at this sort of thing, no good at all.

She caught up with Tessa and, without any further conversation between them, they placed flyers in three shops. They skipped a hardware store, a bar and a small café that weren't open yet. By the time half an hour had passed, they'd barely made it into Vail Village.

"We should split up," Tessa suggested. "We'll never get everywhere if we don't." She pointed to the opposite side of the street. "I'll take that side, you take this one. We'll meet in half an hour…" she glanced back, pointing toward the first place they'd gone into, the optometrist, "—back where we started. Okay?"

Kari hesitated. She couldn't argue with that logic, but she wasn't sure they should separate. The crowd had grown in the time they'd been at this, and it would be easy to get lost. On the other hand, Tessa wasn't a child, and the street was narrow enough that they could keep each other in sight.

She nodded and gave Tessa half the stack of flyers. "Just don't go any farther than the covered bridge," she said.

Tessa rolled her eyes. "God, you sound like Dad."

"A half hour," Kari stressed.

The girl nodded and jogged across the cobblestone street, dark hair bouncing on her shoulders. Kari watched as she disappeared inside a skiwear shop.

It wasn't a bad plan. Without Tessa's surly presence by her side, Kari was able to make real headway. She placed flyers in every single shop on her side of the street and began to think she'd missed her calling in sales. Tessa seemed to be having similar luck. Every so often Kari caught sight of her across the crowded throng of festival-goers, and she occasionally smiled and lifted her hand to give Kari a thumbs-up signal.

In the last shop she went into the woman behind the counter was especially enthusiastic. She'd always wanted to take a helicopter ride over the mountains. Kari gave her the speech Addy had prepped them with, then improvised a little when the woman seemed ready to take off right there and then. When Kari emerged on the street again to meet up with Tessa, she'd left the last of her flyers propped by the register.

The atmosphere was infectiously playful on the pedestrian mall. There were street performers and craft booths and so much music that Kari found herself humming a dozen different tunes while she waited for Tessa. The smell of corn dogs and popcorn made her stomach growl. She was thirsty and beginning to think about lunch.

Five minutes passed. No Tessa.

Deciding not to wait any longer, Kari crossed the street and went into the last shop on Tessa's side of the block. The bright yellow flyers sat at the cashier counter, so Tessa had to have been there. Kari went back outside to scan the street.

They'd agreed to meet at the optometrist's, and Tessa had probably decided not to wait for her. Glancing at her watch, Kari saw that the half hour was well up. In fact, in another ten minutes, they were all supposed to meet back at the van. She wove quickly through the crowd, back the way she'd come.

By the time she backtracked all the way to the optometrist's office, Kari was starting to worry. Now that she'd left the main street of Vail Village, the crowd had thinned a little. In the distance up ahead Kari could make out the lodge van and two figures standing beside it. Addy and Rose.

No Tessa in sight.

Her heart had begun to beat with a hard, steady rhythm now. There had to be someplace else the teenager had decided to place flyers. She and Tessa were only temporarily separated, that's all. She just needed to look a little harder.

She certainly wasn't willing to go back to the van alone to tell Nick she'd misplaced his daughter.

DARN IT, TESSA. Where are you?

Another ten minutes had passed. The first stirring of panic shivered up Kari's spine. She heard a noise behind her and turned to see that the café they'd previously bypassed had opened now. In agonizing slow motion, a lanky teenage boy was flipping chairs upright around umbrella tables.

Kari walked over to him. "Have you seen a girl come by here recently?" she asked. "Shoulder-length dark hair, wearing a red T-shirt. Maybe carrying a handful of yellow flyers. Kind of cute."

"Yeah, I saw her," he said. "She wanted to buy a soda, but I told her the manager's not here yet with the key to the beverage cooler." The boy's face screwed up. There was nothing but smothered anger in the set of his mouth. "The old fart thinks I'll drink up all his beer if he doesn't lock it up like Fort Knox."

Lord, save me from sullen teenagers, Kari thought. Trying to hang on to her patience, she offered him a sympathetic smile. "Did you happen to notice which way she went?"

"Sure." The kid rubbed the side of his nose with one finger, flicked away some foreign object, then used that same finger to point in the direction of Vail Village. "I sent her up there."

"Up to the village?" Kari asked.

"Nah, not that far." He pointed again. "She can get something there."

Kari lifted her hand to shade her eyes. The Black Diamond, a hole-in-the-wall local bar they'd decided to bypass earlier, now looked open for business. Kari swung back to the boy. "You sent her to a *bar?* She's only fourteen!"

The kid blinked stupidly. "Well, she sure didn't look it."

You idiot, Kari wanted to shout at him, but there was no

point wasting time. She took off up the sidewalk, pushing past tourists and anyone else who stood in her way.

Don't panic, she told herself. Don't panic. There was no reason to think anything would be wrong. So how come her breath felt as though it had been squeezed into one small box in her chest?

She hit the front door of the Black Diamond hard, almost knocking down a couple of men heading out. Then she had to stop to let her eyes adjust to the low lighting.

The place lacked the monied ambience of some of the bars they'd passed in Vail Village. This was a local watering hole, closed up against the sun and smelling faintly of beer and body odor. It was too early for there to be much of a crowd, but a couple of die-hard drinkers looked up as she came in.

Then she saw Tessa, talking to the bartender.

Not wanting to look as uneasy as she felt, Kari walked slowly up behind the girl. Tessa didn't notice her. She was too busy being angry at the bartender. "Why not?" Kari heard her ask the man.

"Because you shouldn't be in here," the bartender said, calmly wiping out a beer stein with a hand towel. He'd probably been face-to-face with underage drinkers a million times. "Now skedaddle, before you get me in trouble."

Kari moved into the girl's line of sight and touched her arm. "Tessa, let's go."

Tessa looked momentarily contrite. "I just wanted a soda."

On the other side of the girl, a beefy guy in cowboy denim suddenly came off his bar stool and leaned close. Even in the dim lighting, his bloodshot eyes made it clear he'd had more than one beer already today.

"Aw, give her a soda, Hank," he told the bartender. Then he winked at Tessa. "Hell, give her a beer on me, if she wants one."

He patted Tessa's arm, then let his stubby fingers stay there. She went taut, glaring at the man. "Hey!" she said. "Don't do that."

Kari moved to slowly brush the man's hand away. The guy was drunk, not very coordinated, so he didn't look as though he was going to be much of a problem. "Thanks anyway," she said to him. "But we really have to go."

She nudged Tessa in the direction of the door.

The drunk looked offended. "I'm only being nice," he complained.

"Leave her alone, Bobby," the bartender told him. "The kid's jailbait, you idiot."

Bobby grinned at Kari. "Yeah, but *she* isn't," he said, and suddenly his fingers latched on to Kari's arm.

"Tessa, go outside," Kari ordered in the calmest tone she could manage. "Now."

"But—"

"Go outside. I'll be right out."

Tessa hurried out the door. Kari turned to face the drunk, giving him a small smile. "Okay, big guy. You can let go of me now."

"I don't see why I should," Bobby said, looking as disappointed as a kid who'd had his toy taken away from him. "You're a lot prettier than that little squirt, and I'll bet you know more, too. Like what to do with that pretty little mouth of yours."

With Tessa safely out of harm's way, Kari was starting to feel cranky. She'd fended off enough unwanted advances from men in her time, and they always left her feeling slightly soiled. "I do know more than she does," Kari agreed. "I know what will happen if I start screaming bloody murder and the barkeep has to call the cops. He doesn't want trouble, and neither do you. Right?"

"Let her go, Bobby," the bartender spoke up, clearly on her side now.

"Let me buy you a beer."

The guy's fingers tightened on Kari's forearm. Tomorrow she'd have a bruise from his careless, beefy grip, and she didn't like that.

"Let…go," she said firmly, tired of being nice.

"I just want someone to listen to me for a while. Someone who doesn't make judgments."

"Then get a dog."

She pulled her arm out of his grasp. He started to make another grab for her. She turned toward him, brought up both hands and shoved hard against his chest. Off-balanced, Bobby lost hold of his beer, stumbled and went down. He landed on his back. His beer splashed across his denim jacket and the glass rolled against the foot rail of the bar.

Several things happened at once. Kari made a move for the door, only to find her ankle suddenly snagged in the drunk's hand. He roared his anger, trying to rise. The bartender was cursing now, and Kari struggled to hang on to her balance while twisting out of Bobby's grip. Something moved in the corner of Kari's vision, but her hair had fallen into her eyes during the scuffle, so she couldn't see much.

Then suddenly, Nick was there.

He brought one booted foot to the drunk's chest, then planted it across his neck. The look in his eyes was full of non negotiable intent, as though he'd found a particularly obnoxious bug he'd enjoy swatting. He looked so annoyed, Kari was warmly reminded of the first day she'd met him.

"If you're smart, you'll stay down," Nick told Bobby grimly. "And let the lady go."

Bobby might have just been looking for a sympathetic ear

but he clearly knew he hadn't found one in Nick. He released his hold on Kari immediately and settled back on the floor like a whipped dog offering submission to the leader of the pack.

Then Nick had hold of her and was dragging her out of the bar. Kari was getting tired of being latched on to, but she could tell by the tight line of Nick's compressed lips that he wouldn't be willing to hear any complaints. They burst out into the bright sunlight as though they'd just traversed the darkest tunnel.

"Where's Tessa?" Kari asked.

"With Addy and Mom."

"I can explain—"

"Be quiet."

He yanked her along the sidewalk, then down the side of the building, where a small alley made a quiet, private alcove. He pressed her against the brick wall, then held her there by placing a hand on the wall on either side of her. His face was so close that her vision blurred, but she could tell he was annoyed. No, make that furious.

Slightly out of breath, Kari tilted her chin up. "This was not my fault—"

"Do you know what I want to do to you right now?"

"Something horrible?"

"Yes."

So she was going to get the blame for this little fiasco. He probably thought she'd *taken* Tessa into the bar. "Look, if you're going to chew me out, don't both—"

She gave a tiny, startled gasp as Nick's lips connected with hers.

His mouth moved over hers with hot, hard intent, but surprisingly little of the anger she expected. He tugged at her lips, opening them with his tongue, only enough to provoke her.

She moaned against that delicious assault, and to say she was shocked would have put too mild a spin on it. If Nick hadn't pressed her against the wall, she would probably have slid down it in a mindless heap.

Lost in pleasure, Kari could barely think. She supposed she should have stopped him. Maybe even her hand came up to push against his chest. Then the fight drained out of her. She couldn't have walked away from him if the alley had been on fire.

Just when she started to return his kiss, he dragged his mouth from hers. He stepped back so abruptly that she nearly lost her footing. She stared up at him, but could see no apology in his eyes. She wasn't sure she wanted any.

"Well…" She cleared her throat, nervous as a racehorse at the starting gate. Just where did they go from here? "I, uh, I was expecting a lecture, but if that's your idea of a tongue-lashing…"

Without a word, he swung away from her abruptly and headed back down the alley.

"Nick, wait—"

By the time she reached the sidewalk, Nick had blended into the crowd and was heading toward the van.

CHAPTER ELEVEN

AT FIVE O'CLOCK they headed home, glad to see the end of a long, tiring day that felt as though it had lasted a decade. The drive back to the lodge would pass quickly, but not fast enough to suit Nick.

Addy occupied the passenger seat up front, and kept turning around to carry on a conversation with Rose in the back seat. They sounded as excited as school children and considered the day a success. Thankfully, they didn't seem to need him to hold up his side of the conversation, so he could pretend to be absorbed in maneuvering the heavy traffic along Interstate 70.

He stole a glance in the rearview mirror to the third seat. Tessa had fallen asleep almost immediately, and her head now lay on Kari Churchill's shoulder. After that scare in the bar, she'd stayed glued to Kari like a puppy for the rest of the day. Right now she looked so sweet and trusting in the innocence of dreams that Nick could almost forget he was still mad as hell at her.

As for Kari—all quiet in that corner of the van. He didn't dare find her eyes in the mirror. He didn't want to face what he suspected he'd find in her features. The questions. The confusion. Maybe even a little hope.

Women were like that. They couldn't just live in the moment. Show them a little attention and they inevitably had to pull out the label-maker and start classifying things, sorting them into tidy little piles. She'd want answers. And he didn't have them.

He took a deep, troubled breath, then exhaled. How could he explain that kiss, when he couldn't begin to understand it himself?

You blew it, D'Angelo. What in hell were you thinking?

Maybe that was the problem. He hadn't been *thinking* at all. He'd just been reacting. All those years of practicing iron control. A lifetime of calm, rational behavior. Gone. Out the window.

It hadn't started out that way. He'd been heading up the street to find Tessa and Kari when his daughter had run up to him, white-faced and breathless, jabbering something about Kari having saved her from being attacked and now needing help herself.

He hadn't known what to expect when he'd hit the front door of the bar, squinting through the dark, the fine edge of fear and rage flooding his veins. He just knew that years of pure, protective male instinct kicked in about the time he saw Kari give the drunken cowboy a shove. Then he'd stalked across the bar to finish the job.

It had been appallingly easy. The guy had been all bluster and show, but not completely stupid. He knew enough to stay put on the floor. The moment it was over Nick's blood should have settled, his vision should have cleared, but it hadn't. He'd just grabbed Kari's wrist and pulled her outside, feeling her pulse thrumming under the pad of his thumb in perfect rhythm with his own.

That kiss sure hadn't been planned, either. Heat lay against her cheeks. Her hair, free from the punishing ponytail she usually wore, was a silky, disheveled cascade around her shoulders. She'd looked annoyed and beautiful, the temptress from last night's dreams who just wouldn't disappear, damn it.

It had been so long, *so long* since he'd wanted to kiss a woman as badly as he'd wanted to kiss Kari Churchill. So it had just…happened.

Yesterday by the lake he'd accepted that he was attracted to her and that maybe she'd been on that same path of discovery, too. He'd had a feeling all along that things were going to explode in some unpredictable way between the two of them, and today he'd wanted her hot, erotic taste in his mouth. He relished the near pain of sudden and very real desire, and when she'd started to respond, he'd been delighted.

Wanting, needing—those were the kinds of things that could cause a man to make mistakes. Big ones. He still wasn't sure where he had found the strength to pull back, because that kiss had threatened to get away from him in the end. But he'd come to his senses, thank God.

After they'd rejoined the others at the van, Kari hadn't said two words to him. By unspoken agreement, for everyone's sake, they passed off the incident in the bar as a harmless annoyance. They ate lunch at one of the outdoor cafés in Vail Village—Addy already plotting her next mission—and in very little time the episode seemed forgotten.

But he knew Kari hadn't forgotten a thing.

Under the guise of checking traffic, Nick glanced in the rearview mirror. She didn't meet his eyes, but the pensive line between her brows and the fierce tightening of her mouth left him certain she was replaying that kiss in her mind.

His grip tightened on the steering wheel. He'd have to think of some excuse. Something besides the truth—that every time he looked at her lately he found himself feeling hot, aroused and confused. That he hadn't been able to resist kissing her any more than he could stop breathing.

Luckily she'd be gone soon enough. Looking for the next great adventure, if what Addy said about her work was true.

Good. That was fine with him. He didn't want her at the lodge. Or on their mountain. Or even in Colorado.

And especially not in his thoughts.

"WHEN I GET MARRIED, I'm going to elope," Addy said. "No way am I going to go through all this expense and work."

It was Sunday morning in the lodge's kitchen. The breakfast crowd had left, and now most of the family, with the exception of Nick and Tessa, were seated around the center table, creating small candy baskets for the big Graybeal wedding next week. Even Sam was there, scooping half a dozen sugar-coated almonds into the baskets while Addy struggled to hold the netting together with her fingertips as Kari tied them up with tiny satin bows.

"You will not elope," Sam decreed. "You will be marched down the aisle like a proper bride with your mother and me on either side. You are our only daughter, and we won't be denied that pleasure, will we, Rosa?"

Rose's expertly fashioned bows made Kari's look like the work of a deranged seamstress. Without even glancing her daughter's way she said, "Stop tormenting your father, Adriana. You know you'll have the biggest wedding this area has ever seen." Then she looked up and frowned at her husband. "Samuel, I told you to stop eating those almonds. They're for the wedding guests."

"I was only checking to be sure they are good quality," Sam complained.

Renata, seated at one end of the table cutting lengths of satiny ribbon, gave an unladylike snort. "A liar should have a good memory. A moment ago you said you were counting them."

Sam gave his sister-in-law a mock-evil look and everyone laughed. Nick came into the kitchen about that time, heading right for the coffeepot. Kari noticed he had on his bomber jacket, the one he usually wore if he was going to work at Angel Air. She hadn't spoken to him since they'd returned from Vail. Just as well. What could she have said, anyway?

Uh, you want to explain that kiss, buddy? 'Cause darned if I have a clue.

Maybe some things were better left unexplored.

He stood watching all the activity for a moment, sipping his coffee slowly. Wordlessly his mother scooped up a Danish from a nearby plate of pastries and handed it to him. From the corner of her eye, Kari watched him eat it slowly. He didn't say anything to anyone, least of all, her.

"How's Tessa this morning?" his mother asked him at last.

"Quiet. I let her sleep in late. I'm going to call Denise tonight to see if we can't arrange a visit for the Christmas holidays."

"That should give her something to look forward to," Addy remarked. Taking note of his appearance, she added, "Are you going down to the hangar this morning?"

"Uh-huh. Seems like one of your flyers did the trick. There was a message on the recorder this morning. Honeymooners staying in Vail are coming up to take an all-day tour, and since Pete is already scheduled to handle the two or three we have booked today, it looks like I'm going to be playing tour guide, too."

Addy's excitement was impossible to stem. "I knew it! I just knew it! You see? If you'd just listen, I've got a million great ideas for business."

Nick came up behind her, grabbed her neck in a loose vise,

and planted a kiss on the top of her head. "Yeah, and occa-sionally one of them makes it all the way through that thick stubborn skull of yours and actually comes out making sense."

The teasing was part of the sibling camaraderie they shared, and Addy obviously took no offense. For just a mo-ment Kari wondered what her own childhood might have been like if she'd had a devilish older brother to share it with. Someone to deflect some of her mother's bitterness over their father's neglect. Someone to share dreams with. But most of all, someone who might make you feel less alone. Addy was really very lucky.

Nick frowned at the center of the table, where a small mountain of pale blue-netted clusters lay stacked. "Making confetti baskets, huh?"

Like the rest of his family, he was evidently no stranger to the Italian custom of giving candy to each guest as a token from the bride and groom. Rose had told her that they were supposed to represent a mix of the bitter and sweet things in life, but Kari would have bet money Nick didn't buy such sen-timental nonsense.

"Six hundred of them," Addy complained. "Thank goodness Kari's here to help out." She lifted one of her bandaged arms. "With this boat anchor, I'm hopeless at making little bows."

Nick didn't say anything. Kari felt sure he was resisting the temptation to state the obvious—that Addy would have man-aged the bows just fine if Kari *hadn't* come into their lives in the first place.

No one in the family seemed to hold grudges, but Kari was reminded of the consequences of the accident often. Every time she helped Addy button her blouse, unscrew a bottle cap, or complete one of Renata's more intricate napkin folds, Kari felt the guilt over Addy's injuries strike her anew.

Nick reached down to run a hand through the blue netting. He shook his head. "Eloping would be a lot cheaper."

"That's what I think!" Addy said, clearly glad to have found an ally.

Sam made a displeased sound and settled back in his chair. "What is wrong with my children? Next to the birth of your child, the marriage ceremony is the happiest moment of your life. It's meant to be savored. There should be tears and joy and wine and…and good food. You don't treat it like you are going to get a fishing license."

Both Renata and Sophia nodded in agreement. Kari kept her head down, focusing on knotting a particularly stubborn ribbon around a tiny basket.

"Easy, Pop," Nick said with a light laugh. "I don't know about Addy, but for me, getting married again is the furthest thing from my mind. In fact, I think it might be off my radar screen completely."

There was a small sound of annoyance and Kari was aware that Rose had turned toward her son. "What?" she asked him in surprise. "What does that mean? You don't intend to remarry?"

"Probably not," Nick said. "Sorry."

"And why not?" His father jumped in, obvious irritation making the older man's voice sound slightly hoarse.

"Tread lightly, Nick," Addy advised, clearly aware that their parents were likely to object to his answer.

Nick took his time responding. He sipped more coffee, finished the final bite of his Danish and wiped his hands on a napkin.

Kari felt a tightening in her stomach. What did she care if Nick had decided to choose the single life forever? She reached for more ribbons.

"I guess…" Nick said slowly, as though still thinking it

over. "I guess I just haven't found the right person. Maybe she's not even out there."

There was a long moment of silence. Then Sam snorted. "Ridiculous! Marriage is not about finding the right person. It's about *being* the right person. If you—"

"Whoa," Nick said, holding up his hands. "You asked, I answered. End of discussion." He placed one hand on his sister's shoulder. "Pick on Addy. She's the one still carrying the torch for some guy from high school."

"I am not!" Addy protested, but the sudden color that bloomed in her cheeks told a different story. She gave her brother a hot, angry look. "At least I'm not so emotionally scarred by my first marriage that I won't even consider the possibility of a second."

"Nothing wrong with being cautious," Nick said, and this time his tone was low and serious.

"'*Chi non fa, non falla,*'" Rose quoted solemnly. Then for Kari's benefit, she translated, "'Those who do nothing make no mistakes.'"

Nick placed his coffee cup in the big sink, then turned back to everyone. "Gotta run," he said. "Don't count on me for lunch. It'll be dark by the time I finish up."

There were several good-natured sounds of disappointment from the D'Angelo clan. Kari had learned that there was nothing they liked better than to debate and hypothesize and generally put each other's lives under the microscope. Nick wouldn't give them any further openings. With a friendly wave, he disappeared out the double doors.

Kari sat there, staring at the candy basket in front of her. Ever since Nick had kissed her, her thoughts had been in chaos. She'd spent a sleepless night trying to figure it all out, what to do, if anything. Nothing on Nick's face this morning had given her the slightest clue. In fact, had he avoided looking at her entirely?

She felt suddenly annoyed and frustrated. Were those comments he'd made about never finding the right woman meant for her benefit? Did he think she needed to be warned off, in case she was the type of woman to get…ideas? The man was impossible! What right did he have to be kissing her, anyway?

It wasn't as though she'd *enjoyed* it. Well, all right, that wasn't true. But it wasn't as though she'd *asked* for it.

So why *had* he kissed her?

Making the sudden decision to find out, Kari slid her chair back. Several pairs of dark D'Angelo eyes turned her way. She made a lame excuse about needing to make a phone call and disappeared out the same double doors Nick had exited.

She hurried past the lobby and down the front flagstone steps. Nick was heading in the direction of his Jeep. When Kari called his name, he swung around. The tiniest of frowns crossed his brow, then vanished as if on command.

"Could I speak to you a moment?" she asked as she reached his side.

"I need to get down to the hangar."

"This won't take long. Now that she was face-to-face, she suddenly felt hesitant and wondered how to begin. "I, uh, I wanted to talk to you about what happened in that bar?"

He straightened imperceptively. "What about it?"

Ease into this slowly, Kari. Don't get him riled right off the bat.

"Well…first, I wanted to say thank you for helping out with that guy."

"No problem," he said with a shrug. "You had a handle on it. I just made sure he understood the wisdom of leaving well enough alone."

"It really was quite ridiculous. Everything got out of control so quickly. Is Tessa all right?"

"She's fine. Trying to pretend it didn't happen. She knows she shouldn't have gone into that bar. She's lucky I'm in a forgiving mood."

"If it makes any difference to you, I don't think she went in there with mischief in mind. She wanted a soda, and she just wasn't thinking."

He gave her a small smile. "Thanks for saying that."

She cleared her throat, forcing herself to look him directly in the eyes. "I, uh, I also wanted to talk to you about that…the fact that you kissed me."

He went very still for a moment, gave her a hard look, then scowled. "Yeah, I kissed you," he said in a casual, noncommittal tone. "It happened. There's no reason to blow it out of proportion."

"I don't think it's blowing it out of proportion to ask why you did it."

He made a small movement—impatience, annoyance?—and looked away. Then his gaze swung back, locking with hers. "Who knows? The adrenaline was flowing. I wanted to thank you for helping Tessa out of what could have been a bad situation. Let's not overthink this."

"I've been given thank-you kisses a few times in my life. That sure wasn't one."

A shuttered look came over his face. "Well, when you figure out what it was, Doctor Freud, let me know. In the meantime, I have work to do."

He turned to head toward his Jeep. Kari latched on to his arm. "Nick—"

He turned back to her. "Look—" he said, clearly out of patience. His gaze dropped to her hand. The sleeve of her blouse had inched up her arm, revealing the bruise she'd gotten yesterday, now turned several shades of purple. He frowned down at it, muttering a curse. "Did I do that?"

"No. It's a souvenir from our drunken friend Bobby."

He shook his head. "I should have pulverized the guy. Drunk or not."

"Nick—"

A couple of guests came laughing down the front steps, backpacks and guidebooks in hand. Both Nick and Kari smiled as they passed by.

As soon as they'd disappeared around the corner, Nick twisted a little so that once more they faced one another. "All right, you want to know why I kissed you?" he asked, seeming to have come to some decision to stop playing games. "Because I wanted to. Plain and simple. I'm a man, you're an attractive woman. It's not any more complicated than that." He raised an eyebrow and added calmly, "Unless you want to pretend that you hated it."

"No, I didn't hate it. Just the opposite, in fact. But I think we should talk about it."

"Well, I don't," he retorted.

"I don't want to go back to fighting with you, avoiding you. Can't we be adult about this?"

He put his hand through his hair in a loose, fretful way that told her he wasn't finding this conversation at all to his liking. But they'd gone this far, it seemed silly to go back now, to pretend as if nothing had ever been said.

She took a deep breath. Might as well go for broke. "I'll go out on a limb here and admit that I'm sexually attracted to you," she said, trying to keep her eyes level with his. "I think you feel the same way. But I'll be leaving soon—my next assignment is coming up—so there's really no point in exploring a relationship."

"No point at all," he growled.

"And if what you said in the kitchen is true, you aren't interested in getting involved with someone, either."

"True," he agreed suddenly. "I have my hands full running this place. I don't need a relationship right now."

"So neither one of us is going to…I mean, whatever we feel…there's no reason to act on it…to take any of this any further… Right?"

"None that I can think of."

"Good. And we can still be friends."

"Yes. Unless you try to dissect this any more. God, I feel like I'm on *Oprah*."

Had they crossed some bridge of understanding? Then why didn't it feel better than this? she wondered. "I just want to be sure we're clear."

She watched Nick's jaw tighten. "We're clear as glass. Friends. No touching. No kissing. No *relationship*. Just friends. Anything else?"

"Well, there is one thing. I need a favor."

"You want a signature in blood?"

"Nothing that dramatic. I'd like you to fly me out to Elk Creek Canyon."

A silence fell between them as his gaze roamed her face. It wasn't awkward, but Kari found herself holding her breath all the same. "All right," he said at last. "When?"

"Tomorrow morning. Your father has given me an entire day off."

He nodded shortly. "Meet me in the lobby at eight. Try not to be late this time."

THE SOUND OF SOFT, girlish laughter woke him.

At first Sam thought it was Rosa. But when he opened his

eyes, he discovered he was still in the lodge library and had evidently fallen asleep in his wheelchair. Dreaming again. Lately it seemed as if dreams were all he'd been left with.

He hated that the stroke had taken his health and destroyed his belief in his own invulnerability. The weakness in his left hand and leg. The inability to wrap his mind around certain words. But most of all, the lack of a sex life.

He and Rosa had always enjoyed active, healthy sex in spite of bad backs and extra pounds and workdays that had left them both reeling with exhaustion. He had always been a man who knew how to please a woman in bed. He had made Rosa gasp in excitement and blush like a Key West sunrise. When they had sex, it was thrilling and considerate, wild and loving.

But since the stroke, there had been none of that. Rosa had replaced their soft, inviting double bed with two singles that were as cozy as side-by-side cemetery plots. After a chaste good-night peck on the cheek, Rosa retreated to her bed while he remained trapped in his. For his sake, she'd said, but it didn't feel that way. He missed the familiar contours of her body pressed against him, still warm from the heat of the day. He missed the tickle of her dark hair along his cheek and her intoxicating scent that seemed to pour straight into his veins. He missed *her.*

He was only fifty-eight, still a young man! But in this household he was treated like an aged family dog—loved and petted and gently cared for so that no harm was done—and he was sick of it. Sick of it.

He heard that light laugh again, and knew he was not dreaming this time. The library was tucked out of the way, a quiet, sheltered time-waster of a room, its many well-stocked shelves bewitching guests into daydreams and loitering.

Countless games of chess and backgammon had been played here over the years on the leather-and-mahogany board his grandfather had brought all the way from Italy. On the cold days of winter, a fire always burned in the hearth.

Through the gloom of soft afternoon light, Sam saw two figures huddled side-by-side on a love seat against the far wall. Tessa and some boy. He watched them silently for long moments, then felt his blood heat as the boy reached out a finger to touch Tessa's lips. Presumptuous brat! How dared he assume such familiarity?

But Tessa didn't object. She merely blushed and ducked her head. When she lifted her face again, the boy tipped closer and put his mouth against hers. Sam, who believed in love and all the trappings, nevertheless found his heart hammering in his chest now. The pup had gall! Tessa was little more than a child.

He cleared his throat loudly. As expected, the teenagers jumped and looked around guiltily. As soon as they spied him, they popped to their feet like matching jack-in-the-boxes.

"Nonno Sam!" Tessa exclaimed in a high, excited voice. "Kyle and I were just—we were just studying." To lend credibility to that claim, she lifted a schoolbook off her lap and waggled it in his direction.

"Biology, no doubt," Sam said, making no pretense that he was fully aware of what they'd been up to. He scowled at the blond boy, giving him a look that had once been able to set his own sons to quivering, though it seemed to have little effect on this youngster.

Tessa, on the other hand, had the good sense to look unnerved. She hurried across the room.

"We didn't see you there," she said. "You scared us." She was not a good enough actress to pull off the silly laugh that accompanied that explanation.

"Catch you later, Tessa," the boy said, quick to seize his chance to escape.

"Okay, later," his granddaughter echoed back faintly, and Sam wondered if she was already missing his support.

She moved to the chair beside him, folding herself into it like the teenager she was, all elbows and knobby knees and attitude. She didn't look at him, and when she settled finally, her chin rested on both her balled fists.

He said nothing.

"Well," she said at last. "Let's hear it. Although I think lecturing is really Dad's department."

Sam's eyes rested on her profile with an intimacy like a caressing hand. She was trying so hard to erect a barrier of studied indifference between herself and the world. But when had he, her favorite member of the family, become the enemy?

"I don't lecture," he said. "I…advise."

She cut a quick glance his way and he saw a flash of amusement cross her features, a glimpse of the old Tessa. It disappeared quickly. Her mouth found its favorite shape again, the corners turned down in exasperation and displeasure. He knew she'd been bitterly disappointed to have her visit with her mother canceled, but he wasn't sure he could speak to her about that issue.

"We weren't doing anything wrong," she said suddenly.

He pasted on a confident smile, though Tessa still refused to look at him. "Good to hear," he said. "I would not expect any granddaughter of mine to behave foolishly."

She snorted delicately. "Then you have more faith in me than Dad."

"Your father only wants to protect you."

Her head swung around. There was such vulnerability in her open features. "From what? Kyle's just a boy, not a monster."

"*Mia bella,* it's not Kyle that worries your father," Sam said. "It's you."

"I don't get it."

Of course she didn't. Not now. Not yet. "You care about this boy. Perhaps you dream it can be something more one day. But you're rushing into something beyond your understanding. You don't know how powerful these feelings can be. In a couple of years, you'll be better equipped to handle someone like Kyle, but not yet. You are too young."

She got up fast, facing him with a look so full of misery that it shocked him a little.

Oh, damn.

"Tessa—"

"I thought you'd be the one to understand," she said. There was a tremor in her voice that could easily become tears. "But you don't. No one does."

She ran out of the room, leaving him to stare after her.

Sam started to follow, then let his hand drop from the control switch of his chair. No point. Tessa was as swift as a startled gazelle and there were so many places he could not follow now.

He tried to summon the energy to think, but his brain felt suddenly thick and unbearably slow to form anything substantive. An enormous sense of defeat overtook him. He had always shared a special bond with his granddaughter, but Tessa would not come to him again. Not about this.

Finally he did nothing but sit in his chair and watch the fading sunlight slide down the bookshelves on the opposite wall. In this house he served no purpose. He could not run his business or please his wife or comfort his granddaughter.

He really was useless after all, it seemed.

CHAPTER TWELVE

"There it is," Nick said. "Elk Creek Canyon."

Kari looked out to the left of the helicopter's Plexiglas windscreen, barely suppressing a little sound of surprise. The canyon wasn't what she'd expected.

A broad, open bowl of land tucked between modest, nondescript mountain peaks, Elk Creek was unimpressive. Its slopes offered abundant shelter in scattered stands of evergreens and spruce, but there were few aspen, and most of the ground cover lacked the showy colors of autumn. A creek wove through the canyon like a tiny etched line of silver, its only point of geographical interest.

Though vast and as rugged-looking as the rest of the national forest, Elk Creek Canyon seemed relatively tame. It certainly didn't look as though it would present much of a challenge for an outdoorsmen like her father. What could have drawn him here? And more importantly, how, in spite of sudden blizzard conditions and a broken leg, could Madison Churchill have lost his fight for survival here?

She looked over at Nick. "It's not the way I imagined it," she told him. "I thought it would be much more…imposing. Maybe just a steep ravine with sheer rock walls and no conceivable way out."

"It will look very different in another month or so. At this elevation, and the way the canyon's situated, it can get a hundred and fifty inches of snow before May." He made adjustments to bring Raven Two into a sharp, banking turn. "Where do you want to set down?"

She didn't know what to tell him. The canyon was larger than she'd expected. None of the reports and newspaper articles she'd read had ever mentioned where exactly the search-and-rescue team had finally located her father. "Do you have any idea where they found him?"

He shook his head. "Sorry, I'm no help to you there. Pop suffered a second stroke the week before your father turned up missing, and the whole family was down in Denver at the hospital. We weren't keeping track of the news. It wasn't until we got home that we heard about Madison Churchill having to be air-lifted out."

Momentarily she felt bleak and unsettled. Had she overestimated her ability to carry out this chosen course? "Then I suppose anywhere will be fine," she said, trying not to sound dispirited. "I thought I might hike a few of the trails. Just get to know the area better."

She watched the ground come up as he set the helicopter down gently near the creek on a flat, granite boulder as broad as a billboard.

Meeting him at the hangar this morning, Kari had wondered if Nick would have any difficulty keeping to the agreement they'd made. Friends, and nothing more. She even suspected that he might try to fob her off on Pete, the helicopter pilot who'd been helping him out.

But if Nick had any trouble, it didn't show. He'd been polite, asking a few questions about their destination and her father, pointing out sights along the way.

She wondered why her own heart wouldn't stop beating so

fast. It was more than coming to this canyon at last. Sitting next to him in the tiny cockpit of Raven Two had been maddening this past hour—a constant test of her self-control. The powerful awareness of his physical presence. The way the morning sunlight caught and emphasized the masculine stubble along his cheek. His every movement on the controls deft and sure, all that promise of easy grace fulfilled in every muscle.

Nick cut the engine. She twisted in her seat to grab her backpack from the rear of the craft, almost relieved to make her escape. She settled back when he touched her arm and spoke to her through the hot-mike headset she still wore.

"Mind if I ask what you're trying to accomplish by coming out here?"

His expression said he honestly couldn't fathom the answer. Kari wasn't sure she knew how to respond. What would a practical, logical man like Nick D'Angelo make of the idea that some journeys just needed to be taken?

"I'm not even sure, myself," she admitted. "I just know I had to see this place. I always thought of my father as such a strong person, almost indestructible, really. Since his death, I've tried to imagine how it could have all gone so wrong. I had hoped that coming here would give me some answers."

She stared out the front windscreen, trying to picture the ground covered with dangerous mounds of snow and ice, offering no protection and only a cold, lonely death. On such a beautiful fall day, with a cobalt-blue sky overhead, such harsh consequences didn't seem possible.

"You sure you want me to leave you here?" Nick asked.

"I've got everything I need," she said, tapping her backpack. "And it's only for a few hours."

"I don't like it," Nick said, shaking his head slowly. "I've flown plenty of hikers into the backcountry so they could explore remote trails, but I've never brought anyone in this deep before. Certainly not alone."

"I'll be fine."

Before he could say anything else, she slipped off her headset, unlatched the door and jumped to the ground. Nick leaned across the seat and said something to her, but without the hot mike and with the whoop-whoop noise of the rotor blades as they cycled down, she couldn't make out his words.

"What?" She had to raise her voice to be heard.

"I said, I could stay if you need me to."

The offer took her by surprise and made her feel strangely fragile. She saw concern in his eyes and was touched by it. "Thanks," she said, "but truthfully, I'd rather do this alone."

He nodded shortly—all business again—and pushed back in his seat. His hand flipped switches on the instrument panel and the rotor blades increased their speed once more, making conversation almost impossible.

"Stay on the trails and take it slow," Nick yelled at her. "Remember you're up ten thousand feet and the altitude can get to you. So can the sun, so use your sunscreen. I'll be back at four o'clock." He turned to look at her. "You'd better be here."

She smiled and nodded, holding her hair out of her eyes as the rotor blades whipped the air furiously. "Gee, you sound like you're actually worried about me," she shouted.

"Bad for business if I lose a customer," he yelled back.

The moment she closed the passenger door, he lifted off.

Squinting against the sun, she watched until he was no more than a black speck against that perfect, cloudless sky. And then…nothing.

It surprised her, just how alone she felt in that moment.

Nick didn't know why he should be concerned about her.

Kari Churchill was a grown woman, a woman whose career took her to some pretty out-of-the-way places. So a beautiful, clear day spent alone in the wild backcountry of the national forest ought to be a cinch for someone like her.

That seemed like a sensible argument, but he worried all the same. He did a hundred small chores around Angel Air. There was plenty enough that needed doing, and with Pete's help he made quite a dent in some of them. But invariably he found himself checking his watch, wondering why the time hadn't passed more quickly. When three o'clock came, he was inordinately pleased that he could legitimately rev up Raven Two again.

He made the canyon in record time, setting down on the same smooth, flat rock he'd used before. Kari was nowhere in sight and his heart gave a curious little bump.

If she had run into a bear, or lost her footing along one of the trails and tumbled down a ridge…

He told himself to relax a little, go easy. The canyon was big, and he was early. Still, the blades hadn't completely stopped turning before he jumped down from the cockpit.

Shading his eyes against the strong afternoon sun, he scanned the area. He saw her then, making her way around an outcropping of rocks that formed a natural semicircle near a small pool at the river's edge. He walked across the dry boulder field to join her.

"Hi," she said as he approached. "I'm not late. You're early."

She'd set her hair free. The play of light made it look as though liquid gold spilled across her shoulders. Her face, unadorned by makeup and tinted pink from the sun, gave her the wholesome girl-next-door look that any photographer in his right mind would love. She wasn't cover-girl beautiful, but damned close. Some wayward emotion he couldn't name lifted his senses like a tide.

But as he moved near, he realized something was wrong. Sometime during the hours she'd been out here she'd lost that eager, nervous anticipation. It was more than just the weariness he'd expect from a day spent hiking the canyon. She seemed tense, a little vulnerable. In her eyes he caught a glimpse of something profoundly desolate.

"Did you find what you were looking for?" he asked.

She shook her head. "No. If anything, I've got more questions than ever."

"Want to talk about it?"

"I'm not sure I'd know how to express it."

"Start with something simple."

To encourage her, he lowered himself to a nearby ledge. The granite felt warm from the afternoon sun. The light was a sulky amber color, making the marsh grasses along the creek's edge seem dull and lifeless.

She sat on one of the boulders on the other side of the pool. Lowering her hand, she let her fingertips trail in the water. Her skin was so translucent he could see the veins on the back of her hand like an etching.

"What do you see?" she asked him, glancing down.

He tilted slightly to take a closer look. The water was crystal-clear, only a few feet deep. He wasn't surprised to spot one or two speckled fish swimming lazily in the current. "Trout," he said. "Heaven on a dinner plate."

"Do you think you could catch one?"

"Not without a rod."

"My father could have," Kari said, lifting her head. He must have looked skeptical, because she added more firmly, "I'm serious. Did you ever read *Mixed Signals*? It was one of his earlier books."

"No."

She didn't look offended by that admission. Instead she said, "The main character is an Amazon river guide. In one chapter he catches fish with a piece of string and a bent safety pin. He even seasons it with river algae. Dad was a stickler for research. He told me it was the best fish he'd ever eaten." As though impatient, she shook the water from her hand. "He would have known how to survive in this place, Nick."

He inhaled a deep breath and forced himself not to sound too pessimistic. "It's different in the winter, Kari. And he was injured."

Straightening, she shook her head. "He'd have managed. The creek runs too fast to freeze over, so there would have been water and the possibility of food. He knew how to build a shelter. I'm not saying he wouldn't have suffered, but…it shouldn't have killed him."

"You may have seen your father as invincible, but he wasn't. Even the most skilled outdoorsman can get in over his head out here."

"I know you're right. I guess that's not really what's bothering me. I'm just trying to—"

She stood suddenly, brushing at her jeans with an irritated slapping motion. He heard her sharply indrawn breath against the hush of fading sunlight.

"Kari?"

"I shouldn't keep you. We should go. It's getting late."

The words were crisp, determined. He didn't try to stop her when she hopped down from the rock, slipped her backpack over one shoulder and began to pick her way across the boulder field back to Raven Two. The conversation had started to make him feel distinctly unsettled. The quickening of his pulse every time he looked at her hadn't helped, either.

He was glad to leave this place behind, and he could tell that she was, too. They lifted off. After fifteen minutes of awkward small talk, he turned to look at her. Her jaw was clenched so tightly, he could see the muscle jumping over and over again.

"You all right?" he asked.

A hesitation. Then, "I know this is probably asking a lot, but… Is there any way we could *not* go back to the lodge right now? I don't feel ready to face anyone. Not just yet." She added a weak smile. "Does that make sense?"

He realized that he wanted to say no. He didn't want to spend any more time with Kari. He wanted to be away from her. Away from the unwanted temptation she presented. His heart could do with a little hardening, he realized. But against all will and common sense, he heard himself say, "I know just the place."

HE TOOK HER to King's Creek Falls.

Wedged into a little valley between two saw-toothed peaks, the falls weren't immediately visible when he set Raven Two down in a wide, open meadow sprinkled with late-blooming alpine wildflowers.

Nick shut down the chopper. He got out, encouraging Kari to do the same.

The falls, a rambunctious torrent of water cascading between jutting granite ridges, was no more than a dull roar from where they stood. A five-minute walk through massive stands of lodge-pole pines, past the distinctive orange trunks of Englemann spruce, would bring them face-to-face with the falls in no time.

She stared around her with a delighted smile. "It's beautiful."

"You haven't seen anything yet. Come on. I think we've got just enough time before sunset."

He headed off through the trees at a fast clip and Kari fell into step behind him. "Pop used to bring us up here on camping trips," he told her. "It's far enough off the beaten track that it doesn't get a lot of tourists."

The air grew damp and cooler as they wove through shadow and light and shadow again. Then the trees fell away and suddenly it was ahead of them, the base of the falls. Between the sheer rock walls, the rapids cascaded six hundred feet in a series of tiered drops, then plunged into a wide, deep pool. Late-afternoon light glistened on its surface, as though someone were skipping stars across the water.

"Oh, Nick," Kari said, sounding awed. "It's wonderful."

"This is my favorite place in the world. When I was in the service, stationed in the desert, you just couldn't seem to get enough water. I used to lie on my bunk and imagine myself here, stroking my hand back and forth across that pool. Kept me from going crazy sometimes."

"Do you come here often?"

"When I need down time. Or when things get too difficult at home."

He frowned, surprised by his own words. He wasn't in the habit of having these kinds of discussions, not even with the family. Maybe if he hadn't sensed her pain, he might have kept to the polite distance they'd agreed to, but it was too late now. And somehow, suddenly, it didn't seem so wrong.

She looked at him with troubled, searching eyes. "How are you and Tessa getting along?"

To deflect her scrutiny, he bent to pluck a stray wildflower. Pretty, but badly named. The elk loved lungwort blossoms, and this lonely flower was about the last one left where they stood. "Tessa and I are like two cats stuck in the same sack sometimes," he admitted. Then he laughed. "I suppose that comes as no surprise to you."

"Teenage moods are very mercurial. She'll come around."

"Soon, I hope. This business with her mother hasn't helped any, and I'm running out of inventive ways to ground her." He realized that he'd stripped the flower stalk of its blooms and tossed it away. 'Pop told me he caught her kissing Kyle Cambridge yesterday. I still haven't figured out how to handle that."

"Kyle Cambridge… The boy who got kicked out of school?"

"I see she's told you about him."

"A little. Mostly how unfair it all was."

He muttered a curse. He could just imagine what injustices Tessa had claimed. "She's too young to be involved with him, but I haven't been able to convince her of that. She's as thorny as a cactus when his name comes up. When we're in the middle of an argument, I don't even recognize her anymore."

She'd closed the distance between them without him really being aware of it. Her hand fell on his forearm, offering reassurance. "Fourteen is a very difficult time for teenage girls. Your body, your emotions, are out of control. You feel powerless. Try to be patient with her. I'm not really good with kids, but if there's anything I can do to help, I'd be happy to. Tessa's a lovely girl, Nick."

"She's very fond of you." He lifted one dark eyebrow. "I'll bet you're better with kids than you know."

She made a dismissing sound. "I'd make a horrible parent!"

There was a scattering of boulders just behind them, one of them a natural ledge, and Kari hopped up on it, letting her legs dangle over the side. She braced her arms behind her, closed her eyes, and inhaled deeply. He understood the impulse. The cool, pine-scented air, the earthy perfume of peace was irresistible.

"Why do you think you'd make such a bad parent?" he asked, coming up beside her and leaning against the rock.

Opening her eyes, she laughed. "If my mother was alive, she could give you a dozen reasons. I'm impatient. Stubborn. Disorganized. Impractical. I have no impulse control. Once my father promised to give me a pony for Christmas, and when I didn't get it, I went right into his study and tore up his latest chapter." She shook her head solemnly. "Luckily he had made a second copy, but I still ended up with no television for a month."

"Tough break."

She grinned. "Well, the punishment really only lasted a week. Dad convinced Mom I'd suffered sufficiently."

He caught himself smiling at her with a certain tender amusement. "I'll bet you were a Daddy's girl. Like Tessa used to be with me."

"And she will be again," she reassured him. "You'll see."

"You ever fight with your father?"

"Sometimes, but not often. He was always larger than life to me. As much as I hated that he could go off and leave us for weeks on end, I was proud of who he was. What he was."

"You and your mother never went with him?"

"Mom wanted to, but after I was born it wasn't very practical to drag me along. I know she resented my father for being gone so much of the time, and probably me, as well, for keeping her at home. As a result, the reception he got when he came back from a trip wasn't always very welcoming. Maybe that's why he found it so easy to leave the next time."

"Sounds as if she was the responsible one in the marriage. It's not very glamorous, but someone has to be."

He made the observation without thinking, and when he

saw Kari frown slightly, he realized she probably objected to it. Frankly, he thought that Madison Churchill, running off on grand adventures that could provide fodder for his next best-seller, coming back home to be greeted by his daughter like a king returned from exile, had probably gotten the better end of that marriage.

He wondered how much Kari recognized the resentment she'd had toward the man's career. She might have idolized him, but it had been his work she'd attacked in that fit of anger over the pony. She hadn't taken it out on his car or clothes.

It would be unwise to say anything like that, he decided.

"Oh, look," she said suddenly, pointing toward the falls. "Look."

He knew what to expect when he glanced back. It was one of the reasons he loved this place. Sunset had decided to put on a show of its own. The world went crimson and magenta, lavender and gold, painting the rocks with an artist's palette of color. Along the chute of the falls, the cascading water trailed mists like pastel veils.

They were silent for a while, soaking up the sight of it, the wonder that such a place could actually exist outside of picture books and Hollywood. He'd never brought any woman here. Not even his ex. He wasn't sure why he'd brought Kari. There were any number of places he could have taken her instead.

As though he'd called her name, she turned her head. She was so close he could see every tiny freckle the sun had laid across her nose, and her face was golden in the fading light. "Thank you for bringing me out here," she said. "My life feels as if it's had very little charm in it lately, and I needed something like this."

He watched her inhale a needed breath and let his gaze drift over her mouth, which was the richest soft red. Dancing at the edge of his consciousness, just out of reach, was the knowledge that he was enjoying this too much. He was too uncomfortably aware of her as a woman, but he'd missed the chance to keep himself aloof, and he knew it.

"I'm sorry you didn't find whatever it is you were looking for in Elk Creek," he said. "I sense it was important to you somehow."

She lowered her head a moment, then gave him an uncertain look. "If I told you why I initially wanted to go there, you'd think I was crazy."

He thought she was a lot of things, but crazy wasn't on the list. "Try me."

She remained silent for a long, long time. Then she said quickly, as though making the sudden decision to get the words out, "With every new book, my father kept a journal—ideas for scenes, plot points, but sometimes no more than his thoughts and observations about the research he did. The one for *Hours of Ice* was my last gift to him, but they never gave it to my mother as part of his personal…effects. Somehow, it got lost, and I really thought I might be able to find it. Of all the journals he kept, that one seems the most important now."

He shook his head. "There's no way it could have survived two years out in the elements. You realize—"

She held up her hand. "I know how foolish that hope was." She smiled. "Didn't I tell you I was impractical? Anyway, barring that possibility, I guess I wanted to visit Elk Creek Canyon because I thought I'd feel… I thought I'd be able to sense my father's presence there. That I'd make some sort of…connection. Not in a weird, ghostly sort of way, but just…closer somehow. I wanted to understand what had made him go there. But I didn't feel…anything." She bit her lip and put her hands on her thighs, as though bracing herself for some hurt. "Go ahead and say it. You think I'm crazy."

He wasn't good at this sort of thing. He didn't want to lie to her, but he knew he would handle it badly. He'd hurt her. And he didn't want to do that.

He exhaled a careful breath. "I don't think you're crazy," he said slowly. "I think you're a loving daughter who hasn't accepted her father's death yet. You didn't get to say good-bye. As much as I hate today's psychological buzzwords, it's only natural that you're looking for some kind of closure."

She stared at him. He watched her throat work. He thought she might cry then, and his gut clenched tight. But she kept her composure.

"I miss him," she said, and it was only because he was listening closely that he heard the catch in her voice. "In spite of all the ways he was careless with my mother's feelings, *and mine,* there isn't a day that goes by I don't wish I could see him just one more time."

He could see in the tightness of her mouth what that statement had cost her. She must have loved her father a great deal, and he was suddenly reminded of the way he'd felt when his commanding officer had called him into his office to say Sam had suffered a stroke. The plane ride home had felt as though it had taken forever, and all Nick had been able to think about was how many regrets there would be if his father died before he could see him one last time. The cramped terror in Nick's gut hadn't eased up until Sam had opened his eyes and tried to smile at him. But Kari hadn't been given that final gift, and he could imagine how much she had needed it.

He wanted the right response to come to him, but in the end, all he could think to say was, "I suppose we'd all make any bargain we could to get a second chance."

She shifted uncomfortably, as though trying to shake off her sadness, but unable to. "Isn't it awful sometimes…to realize that none of us get through life unscathed?"

Unwilling or unable to stop himself, Nick lifted his hand and brushed the back of his fingers along her cheek. He didn't know when it had happened, but somehow her pain and anguish had become his own. He sank down into the depths of that extraordinary moment, put his hand behind her neck, and pulled her close. Kissing her seemed the most natural thing in the world.

So much hurt, he thought. Just let me take it away. Just for a little while.

He kissed her gently, meeting her mouth in a long, sensuous caress. She made a little sound as her breath stopped in her throat, then she opened for him. He could feel her letting out her tension, letting her worries go as they tasted one another, in no great hurry, patient and slow and tender, content to explore.

It felt as if they were the only two people in a deserted universe. For a handful of heartbeats Nick was satisfied with the warm sense of serenity and purpose that flowed through him, but the mood suddenly became heated. His arousal was urgent and instant. He wanted all of her.

He lifted his mouth, searching her eyes. They had a cloudy, indistinct look that was new, and in them he read everything she needed and everything he wanted.

There was no need to say anything more.

He brought his hands up to the buttons of her blouse. His fingers felt thick, so clumsy that he cursed them, but in another moment he had pushed the material apart, exposing her lace-clad breasts. She shivered; whether it was from the cool, dusk air or her own desire, he didn't know.

"It's all right, Kari," he said softly. "I won't hurt you."

He touched his lips to her throat, feeling the wildness of her pulse beneath his tongue, sensing that the tide of her flaming blood was as strong and sure as his own. It had only been a matter of time, he thought. One way or another, sooner or later, this had been destined to happen.

But in the next moment she caught his hand as it settled over the clasp of her jeans. "Nick, don't," she said, her voice so low he almost didn't hear the words. "We can't."

He groaned, lifting his head. "I can't think of any reason why we shouldn't. You want this as badly as I do."

She brought her hands to either side of his face, searching his eyes. "I do. But I'm…not taking anything for protection. Do you have—"

"Damn it!" he swore, understanding with irritating swiftness. He took a step back from the boulder, dropped his head, and braced his arms on either side of her thighs. Anger—at himself—stretched its limbs inside his chest. "Just give me a minute," he said, breathing in a tight, controlled manner.

"I'm sorry."

He expelled one last, harsh breath, feeling his blood start to settle, but not soon enough to suit him. Not nearly soon enough. After a long moment or two, he shook his head at her, even managing a small smile of wry regret. "All these years of taking precautions, and for the first time in my life I'm completely unprepared."

He was gratified to see that she looked disappointed. "I'm sorry, Nick," she said again. "But I just can't."

He tossed her a black scowl. "I thought you were the woman with no impulse control."

"I grew out of it," she said, clearly trying for a lighter tone. As though realizing that didn't work, her features became serious once more. She touched his arm and he almost wished she hadn't. He had to strive very hard, *very* hard, to keep from pulling her up against him again.

"Please try to understand. No matter how much I would like—" She went scarlet, and began again. "I have certain goals for my life. I want adventure and travel and meeting new people. If I end up getting pregnant, being as tied down as my mother was, then I'll *end up* like my mother. Resentful and bitter. I don't want to feel that, in a year from now, all the really important events in my life have already happened."

He took a few more steps back, realizing suddenly that he wouldn't, *couldn't* run roughshod over that argument. Wasn't she doing him a favor, really? All those dreams of being like her father, footloose and free, no responsibilities to keep her anywhere she didn't really want to be. He knew better than to get involved with someone like her. Any relationship with this woman would turn sour in no time. She was beautiful and spirited and oh, so not for him.

Somehow he managed a rough smile and nodded. "Good enough," he said. In a gesture of pure impatience, he picked up her backpack. "We should get going. If we stay any longer, we'll both have to find out just what our convictions are made of."

CHAPTER THIRTEEN

THAT NIGHT Kari lay in bed, annoyed with herself for being unable to shake off the memory of what had transpired between her and Nick.

It wasn't that she wished it had never happened. Quite the contrary. It was that she wished they had been able to finish it. To finally get all that mysterious sexual tension between them out in the open. To explore the thrill and pleasure that two people attracted to one another could share.

But the fates hadn't been on their side and without protection, she wasn't helping. There was just no way Kari would willingly take chances like that. Not with her future on the line.

How horrible to have become so sensible! What good was that when it meant missing out on what could have been one of the truly great adventures of her life?

And why did Nick, who could be so contrary about everything else, have to be so darned understanding about her refusal? Any other guy, brought to the brink like that, would have sulked or gotten downright nasty. But he hadn't.

On the trip back, and tonight at dinner, he'd just acted as if nothing unusual had happened. In fact, in an attempt to keep the promise he'd made to her during their conversation at the National Park office, he gave her a slip of paper with a name and telephone number written on it. Walt was finally back in town. The old guy would be glad to talk to Kari, to see if he could shed any light on the circumstances of her father's trip.

Really, Nick had been quite annoyingly civil.

She fell asleep around midnight, then slipped into such a disturbingly erotic dream that it brought her awake with a jolt, sweating and out of breath. Frustrated and more annoyed than ever, Kari scooped her cell phone off the bedside table and punched in Eddie Camit's number. The photographer was a night owl who never minded a late-night call.

After the fifth ring Eddie picked up. "What?" he demanded. "I'm busy. Who the hell is this?"

Throbbing music and scattered background noise seeped around his words. He was likely at some nightclub—Eddie loved to dance. Clearly he hadn't been in bed, and the knowledge that he was having fun while she'd been fantasizing all sorts of foolish things in her sleep made her grumpy.

"Why haven't you called me?" she complained.

"Because I don't have anything to tell you."

"Is New Zealand on or off?"

"Still off."

"And Jamaica?"

"I told you I'd call as soon as I heard." He muttered something she didn't catch. "Damn, Churchill. Who peed in your cornflakes?"

She sighed, staring up at the ceiling. Even in the dark she caught a glimpse of that ridiculous red helicopter circling overhead like a giant mosquito. Sleeping in Nick's old bedroom wasn't helping a bit. Everywhere she turned, there he was. "I just need to get out of here. Save me, Eddie."

"Are you in jail?" he asked, his voice going low and serious.

"Of course I'm not in jail." She scowled into the phone.

"I'm just…eager. You call me the minute—the instant—you hear something. Okay?"

"Oh my God. You're not in jail. You're at a computer convention."

She had to laugh at that. She and Eddie had done a piece on computers once, and they'd both come away agreeing that there was no way to make the darned things look or sound exciting.

"Just call me," she said and snapped the phone closed.

After that, she felt a little better. Refocusing on her career was what she needed. What she'd said to Nick was absolutely true—she wanted the life her father had known, and anything else would be unendurable.

She put her hands behind her head, took a couple of deep breaths and tried to relax, an activity for which she had no talent. She wished she could move back into one of the upstairs guest rooms. Any place that didn't have so much of Nick's personal history stamped all over it. Every book he'd read, every medal he'd won. Those crazy model helicopters and planes. The photographs were the worst. She'd finally had to position them so that she didn't see them every time she entered the room.

Overhead, the helicopter glinted and started a slow spin. She narrowed her eyes at it.

Keep your distance, D'Angelo. I'm watching you.

But when she fell asleep a second time, she dreamed of rainbow-colored waterfalls and flying red dragons that chased her through dark forests that offered no escape.

KARI DIDN'T SEE NICK the next morning or that afternoon, which suited her just fine. After the weekend there had been a lot of check-outs, and while the dining room was unexpectedly slow, Sofia and her little band of housekeepers were as busy as ants at a picnic.

Kari had just put in the last load of towels when the older woman joined her. Moira, one of the maids, hovered at her elbow.

"Could you do me a kindness?" Sofia asked with a smile. "Will you take Moira home? Her father's been called back unexpectedly to his job and there's no one to watch her little brothers after school since her mother passed away. I'd ask Adriana to do it, but I don't think she can drive yet."

"Sure," she agreed. Renata was tough and had always treated her kindly, but Kari had to admit, she was partial to Sofia, who had a sunnier disposition and seldom had an unkind word for anyone.

The trip down the mountain was short and uninteresting. Moira made little conversation, and eventually Kari gave up her attempts to chat and concentrated on maneuvering some of the road's sharper turns. The girl's home was on a small tract of land on the outskirts of Broken Yoke, the town on the banks of the Lightning River. When Kari pulled the company van up in front of the plain, cramped-looking house and Moira got out, a trio of little boys exploded out the front door and came crashing against her legs.

Moira was clearly the mother figure in that household now, but she didn't seem to mind. She stood like a mountain peak among foothills of children, laughing at their antics and reaching out to touch them with loving hands. As quiet as she'd been in the van, it came as a surprise to see her so animated.

What must it be like, Kari wondered, to be part of such a large family or to be responsible for so many children? It made her realize how easy her life was. No one to pluck at you or to depend on you too much. No one to hold you accountable for anything. To just be able to pick up and leave anytime you wanted. She couldn't imagine how people like Nick and Moira did it.

With a final wave, Kari pulled out of the driveway. To get back to the mountain road, she had to drive through the center of town again. Broken Yoke had once been a wild frontier village, rich with silver, but it had clearly fallen on hard times in recent years.

Tourists in search of ski slopes and quaint shops didn't jump off the interstate to make a stop here. There were a few Victorian buildings on Main Street, a shady public park that ran right down to the edge of a sweetly gurgling creek, but little else of charm or interest.

She passed a small clapboard building that boasted the name Walt's Wilderness Tours spelled out in crudely cut pieces of wood. On the porch sat an elderly man in a rocking chair, reading a newspaper. This had to be the old guy Nick had told her about.

She parked, and even before she reached the front steps the man was getting out of his chair. He sported a beard that looked as if birds had once used it for a nest and had a plaid-shirted, homespun appearance that made Kari think of a retired lumberjack she'd once interviewed in Oregon.

"Are you Walt?" she called out.

"If I'm not, we're gonna have to change the sign. What can I do for you?"

"I'm Kari Churchill. I believe Nick D'Angelo spoke to you about me. I'm looking for information about a trip my father took out to Elk Creek."

"Yep. He said you'd probably be by to see me right quick. Which Elk Creek did your father hike into?" he asked.

"There's more than one?"

The old man grinned, revealing teeth that looked like piano keys. "Elk Creek Pass, Elk Creek Canyon, Elk Creek Falls, Elk Creek Meadow. They weren't too original in the early days around here. Which one you want?"

She couldn't help it. Her heart started to pound. "I thought I knew, but maybe I don't," she said. "Could we sort it out over a map?"

"Ain't too often I get a pretty young lady for company," he said, waving his hand toward the inside of the store. "Come on in."

FORTY-FIVE MINUTES LATER, Kari left Walt and got back in the car. She got no farther than the next block before she had to pull over in the parking lot of a drugstore. She felt breathless, almost dizzy.

The wrong place. Elk Creek Canyon had been the wrong place.

Or, at least, there was a good possibility. After she'd explained her interest to Walt, he'd told her in very colorful language that the damned young fools up at the Visitor Center had probably sent her to the wrong Elk Creek. Or maybe she'd misread the newspaper articles, or made the assumption that there was only one Elk Creek once she'd seen it on the map. Regardless, it was more likely she was really looking for the Pass—wild and beautiful and remote—not the Canyon.

Which could be why she'd sat out in that dreary, dull place yesterday and felt absolutely no sense of her father having been there.

And there was one more bit of potential good news, though she'd have to wait a day or two to get it. Walt knew all the guides in the area. He might actually be able to put her in touch with the one who'd led her father out to the forest. The thought made Kari's heart beat even faster.

That had always been one of the mysteries surrounding Madison Churchill's death. He had registered with the park service to camp at a popular tourist destination. But when he'd failed to check in after the unexpected snowstorm, the search team had not found him there. Valuable time had been lost and when they'd finally located him he'd been past saving. No one had ever been able to explain why he'd registered at one spot, only to turn up at another miles and miles away.

But Walt might be able to ferret out the answer to that one. Just give him a day or so, he'd told her.

Encouraged, Kari decided a celebration was in order. She spotted an ice-cream shop across the street. Nothing ushered in success like a heavy dose of hot fudge.

She was about to get out of the van when she spotted Tessa coming out of the drugstore. She entered the building next to it, a large plastic sack dangling in one hand. Maybe the girl would like to join her.

But then the sign over the building brought Kari up short.

Bus Station.

What business would the girl have there? This morning, none of the D'Angelos had mentioned a family member coming or leaving town.

A vague, uneasy feeling stole over Kari. She got out quickly and went through the glass door. It was a small, functional place, and in no time she saw Tessa standing near the bus bay. With a boy. Luggage lay around their feet.

They didn't see her approach. Both were absorbed in the contents of the bag Tessa held. They looked like kids exclaiming over Halloween treats. They *were* kids.

"…should be enough snacks to hold us until we get to Albuquerque," Tessa was saying as Kari reached them. "I got those chocolate-covered raisins you like."

"Tessa?"

The blond boy looked up and Tessa swung around. Her features went dead-white and her eyes moved like a trapped rabbit's. "Oh, K-Kari," she stammered. "Oh, hi."

"Hi." Kari kept her voice light and casual. "How come you're not in school?"

"My last class was at two-fifteen."

"Oh." She supposed that was possible. But all that luggage, some of it decidedly feminine. Without a doubt, she knew there was trouble here. "So…. You and your dad are in town?"

"No. Dad's in Denver. Picking up stuff for the lodge."

Kari jerked her head toward the front door. "I'm heading back there. Do you need a ride?"

"Uh, no. I'm just hanging out with Kyle." As though suddenly remembering her companion, the girl swung a look in his direction. "This is Kyle."

Kari held out her hand, which the boy shook limply. She noticed that his palm was sweaty. "Nice to meet you." She flashed a look around the bus station. "Not really much of a hangout."

"Well…actually…" Tessa began to explain.

"She's here to say goodbye." Kyle finally spoke up.

Kari's stomach flipped nervously. "Goodbye?"

"Yeah. I'm going to stay with my dad in Phoenix for a week. Tessa's just seeing me off."

Kari's eyes flickered down to the suitcases and backpacks. Clearly two sets. Wherever Kyle was off to, it wasn't alone. "Lots of luggage for one guy," she said. Then she smiled. "And they say *women* overpack."

The three of them laughed at that, though the two teenagers barely managed to make it sound normal. Tessa had gone from white to pink to beet-red. As for Kari, if she'd thought her heart was hammering before, she thought it might leap out of her chest now. She didn't have a clue how to deal with this situation. She just knew she couldn't walk away from it.

"I need to hit the rest room," Tessa said suddenly. "Excuse me."

She pushed past Kari, leaving her alone with Kyle, who looked distinctly uncomfortable. He spent the next few minutes trying to make small talk and failing miserably. He was good-looking in a rough sort of way, with small teeth and a spiky haircut that made him look as if he'd just gotten a shock. Which, with Kari's sudden appearance, probably wasn't far from the truth.

Divide and conquer seemed like the best approach. Whatever Tessa had planned, if she could be made to see reason at all, Kari would probably stand a better chance of convincing her with Kyle out of the picture.

She cut across the boy's meandering discussion of whether or not the area would have its first snowfall before Halloween. "I'll just make sure Tessa's all right."

"I'll go with you."

"Into the women's bathroom?" Kari asked.

"Oh. Okay. You go. But tell her to hurry up. Our—my bus is gonna be here pretty soon."

Kari pushed through the door of the rest room. When she didn't see Tessa right away, she nearly panicked, having visions of the teenager crawling through a window and running down an alleyway like some fugitive from a movie. Then she heard a distinct sniffle from one of the stalls. She went over to it and rapped lightly on the metal door.

"You all right in there?"

"Yeah."

"Want to come out and talk to me?"

"No. Jeez, doesn't anybody believe in privacy anymore?"

But in a few moments, the stall door opened and Tessa appeared. There was thunder in her eyes, along with a trace of tears. She'd tried to repair the damage to her mascara with tissue paper, but hadn't done a very good job of it. As unnerved as Kari was by this situation, her heart went out to the girl.

"You know, don't you?" Tessa said in an accusatory tone that trembled.

"What?" Kari replied, determined not to sound too much like a parent. "That you're planning to get on that bus with Kyle?" She nodded. "I suspected it when I saw the backpack with the little fairy keychain. Definitely not his type."

"Don't try to talk me out of it."

Kari crossed her arms and scowled. "Oh, sure. Like I can go back to the lodge and say to your father, 'Oh, by the way. I saw Tessa run off with Kyle this afternoon. That's not a problem, is it?' You think he was cranky toward me before?"

She'd hoped to get a smile from the girl, but evidently it wasn't going to be that easy. Tessa flung her tissue in the trash, then swung around on Kari so sharply that her long, dark hair slapped across her face.

"If you keep me from doing this, I'll just find some other way to meet up with him. You can't stop me. No one can."

She was probably expecting Kari to panic at that. She almost did. Somehow she said calmly, "If you're really that determined, then I suppose that's true. But why? What's Kyle got that the other boys you know don't have?"

"He likes me. A lot."

"Oh, come on. A pretty girl like you doesn't have any other boys after her? I doubt that. Is it just because he's forbidden fruit?"

"Huh?"

"The fruit that's just out of reach often seems the sweetest. Do you like him just because you can't have him? Because your father doesn't seem to like him?"

That got a reaction. Tessa tossed her purse down on the vanity. She gave Kari a hot look in the mirror. "I don't care what my father thinks."

"Why not?"

"Because he doesn't care anything about me! I've always suspected that Mom doesn't really want me messing up her life, but I never thought Dad—" She broke off, then started again. "He's just like her. He wouldn't be a bit sorry if I just disappeared off the face of the earth."

The words sent chilling fear and despair up Kari's spine. How could she ever hope to get through to the girl if her anger with Nick went this deep? She thought of the conversation she and Nick had shared yesterday, all his fears for his daughter so obvious to her. Oh, this foolish, foolish child! How could she believe her father didn't care?

Kari caught a breath and calmed her annoyance. She went to the sink and stood slightly behind Tessa, who was only making her waterlogged mascara worse with a handful of fresh tissues. She put her hands on each of the girl's shoulders. "You're so wrong, Tessa," she said. "How can I make you see that?"

"You can't. I know he doesn't care about me. He might want to *control* me, but he doesn't care about me."

"How do you know?"

There was a sharp knock on the door. Kyle's voice was nervous and impatient. "Tessa! Are you coming out?"

"In a minute," Tessa yelled.

"Tessa, I can't really speak for your mother's feelings, but how can you think your father doesn't care about you?" Kari repeated.

The teenager sniffed, opened her purse and withdrew a folded piece of paper. "Today is trash day. The night before,

Dad always bags up the trash in the kitchen and puts it in the bin outside. That's his routine. He never, never forgets."

"And?"

She held out the paper. "Last night I put this right on top of the trash. He couldn't miss it."

Kari took the paper, unfolded it and discovered that it was actually a brochure. A gynecological flyer about methods of birth control and how your body adjusts to them.

Uh-oh, Kari thought. How had Nick taken to such a clear indication that his little girl was growing up? Not well, she'd bet.

She handed the flyer back to Tessa. "Well, that's one way to break the news, I suppose."

"You don't understand," Tessa said with exaggerated patience. "That's not why I did it. I'm not having sex."

"So then why…?"

"I know Dad saw this because it had been moved to the kitchen counter. But do you know what he said about it?"

Kari could think of all kinds of things, but none of them fit for a teenager's ears. "What?"

"Nothing."

She had to admit, that surprised her a little. "And you think that somehow means your father doesn't care about you?"

"How could he? You know parents are always looking for signs that their kids are doing drugs or getting drunk or going off the deep end. But I guess Dad really doesn't care. He didn't say one word. I could be going to a hotel, having orgies, and he wouldn't care."

Kari snorted. "He knows you're not the kind of girl to do that. Even *I* know that." She turned Tessa around so that she could have the girl's full attention. "Oh, Tessa, you're so wrong," she said softly. "I don't know much when it comes to how parents and children are supposed to interact. But I do know your father is worried about you. Maybe he hasn't always done or said the right thing, but I've heard in his voice how much he loves you. I've seen it in his face—the way he lights up when he talks about you. I'm a journalist. I know how to read people. You're the most precious thing in the world to him."

Tessa shook her head wildly, fresh tears streaming down her face. "No, I'm not. Maybe once. He used to read me stories and teach me how to ride a bike and pretend to like playing Barbies. Now he hardly ever wants to be with me."

"Weren't you just complaining to me the other day because your father wouldn't give you more freedom? You can't have it both ways, Tessa."

She blew her nose loudly. "I'm not asking for that. There's a difference between wanting to run my life—that control-freak thing he's got going on—and wanting to spend time with me. I'm his daughter, but he doesn't seem to want me around—" Her voice broke in two, like a hard piece of sugar. "He didn't need Mom. And he doesn't need me. Kyle does."

As though he'd been summoned, Kyle poked his head around the bathroom door. He looked annoyed and worried. "Tessa, the bus is here! Come on."

"I'm coming!" she said with a sudden, harsh show of spirit.

Kyle disappeared without another word.

Tessa faced the mirror again and grimaced as she surveyed the damage to her makeup. "Kyle is going to think I'm such a freak. And a big baby."

Kari felt the first stirrings of absolute terror. If she couldn't talk the teenager into staying behind, what was she supposed to do? Call the police? Make a flying tackle as the girl walked toward the bus?

Splashing water on her face, Tessa wiped off the last of the mascara, then dried her hands. With a sigh, she swung around to face Kari.

Kari took her forearm, wishing she could shake some sense into her, but afraid to come on too strong. "Tessa," she said, reduced to begging. "Please. Talk to your father. Don't do this. You'll break his heart."

"That won't happen. He doesn't get hurt like you and me. He's tough. He just…keeps it all inside. Like when Mom left."

Kari shook her head. "Nobody pulls off that trick forever, sweetie. Sooner or later, pain always takes its toll. Can you really do that to your father?"

Fresh tears welled. One, dislodged from the rim of her eye, slid down Tessa's cheek. With the back of a hand, she wiped it away ruthlessly. "Why are you making this so hard? Why can't you just leave me alone?"

Was it possible that her voice didn't carry the same weight of confidence it had earlier? "Because I care about you, too. I know what it's like to have a father you don't always understand. But if you do this, you might not get a second chance to make it right again. Can you live with that?"

The girl stared at her for a long moment. Then she rolled her eyes and huffed out a disgusted breath. "We're not running away to get *married.* I just want to stay with Kyle at his dad's for a while. Just be together. But you're ruining everything!"

Suddenly she snatched her purse off the vanity and shoved past Kari, who followed her out of the bathroom at a quick pace.

"Damn it, Tessa," Kari said. "Tessa, stop—" She faltered as the teenager rushed to catch up with Kyle, who was gathering luggage. In the bay, Kari could see that the bus had come. "Oh, God," she muttered under her breath. "Oh, God." Now what? What should she do?

Kyle's eyes cut quickly to Kari and then back to Tessa. "You ready to go?"

Tessa picked up her backpack and slung it over one shoulder. "Actually, Kyle…no. I should have known I couldn't. You'd better go without me."

TESSA REMAINED QUIET and sullen all the way up the mountain. Kari noticed that her grip on the armrest was so tight that her knuckles were nothing more than white ridges.

Kari reached a hand across the distance that separated them and squeezed the girl's fingers. "It will be all right. You'll see. And I'll do whatever I can to help."

Tessa's mouth flattened into a grim line as if she didn't believe that, but she nodded as if she wanted to.

When they pulled up in front of Nick's cabin, the teenager swore under her breath. Nick's Jeep was in the drive. "Dad's home," she said, as if that fact spelled certain disaster.

In the next moment Nick came striding out the front door, car keys in hand and such a stormy look on his face that even Kari swallowed hard. When he saw the van, and Tessa in it, a moment of genuine relief crossed his features. Then he made a beeline toward them. As the girl slid from the vehicle he stopped and planted himself right in front of his daughter.

"What the hell's going on, Tessa?" he demanded. "Why were you at the bus station?"

Tessa gasped. "How did you know that?"

"Because Becky Tindall's mother just called. Becky did the smart thing and confessed that you were leaving town with Kyle Cambridge. You want to start explaining? It had better be good."

Kari had hurried around the front of the van, desperate to keep the situation from escalating out of control. "Nick, wait a minute—"

"Stay out of this, Kari," Nick said, stopping her with one outstretched hand. "I'm waiting, Tessa."

His daughter's mouth worked vigorously before she mastered enough control to get the words out. "I'm not explaining anything to you!"

She pulled open the back door of the van, yanked her luggage off the seat and stormed past her father. The front door slammed hard enough to make a statement. Nick was only steps behind her.

Kari caught up with him on the porch, pulling hard on his arm to bring him up short. "Nick, for God's sake, stop. Will you just listen?"

He swung around, jaw tight, nostrils flaring as though he couldn't take in enough air. "What's the story? Was she at the bus station?"

"Yes."

"With Kyle?"

"Yes. But obviously she didn't go with him."

"Because you talked her out of it?"

"She changed her mind. I think secretly she wanted to be persuaded."

He shook his head as if he were a dazed boxer trying to avoid a knockout punch. After a moment he said in a more controlled tone, "Thank you for that. I'm sorry to have involved you."

"What are you going to do now?"

He tossed a look back toward the cabin. "I'm not sure. But something unpleasant."

She grabbed his forearm, shaking it gently. "Don't go in there and read her the riot act."

"Why not, damn it? The little brat scared the crap out of me."

"Because it won't work."

He arched a dark brow. "I thought you were the one who would make a horrible parent. Suddenly you're an expert?"

She looked at him in exasperation. "If I didn't care so much about Tessa, I'd go back to the lodge and let you crash and burn. But I do so I'm going to overlook that remark. I talked to her, and I'll tell you what I think is the root of all this. Tessa believes you don't care about her."

"That's ridiculous," he snapped.

"Of course it is. But that doesn't mean she doesn't think it's true."

"Why would she?"

"She left a flyer in the trash. About methods of birth control."

"Hell, yes. It nearly stopped my heart when I saw it."

"She says she's not having sex. Probably not even thinking about it. Yet."

"Thank God for that at least."

"Why didn't you ask her about it?"

"And say what? I didn't know *how* to handle it."

"So you just ignored it and went off to Denver to pick up supplies?"

He made an irritated, impatient movement. "I didn't go to Denver. I've spent the afternoon with Leslie Meadows, an old family friend. She's a nurse, and I thought she could talk to Tessa. Explain…you know." He exhaled a harsh breath and rammed a hand through his hair. "Birth control. God in heaven, how am I supposed to deal with something like that?"

She felt a ridiculous sense of relief to know that he wasn't really as neglectful as Tessa had painted him. "That's a start," she said, almost to herself. "Maybe you're not completely hopeless."

"Do you have anything more you want to add?" Nick asked, scowling.

"Just this. Tessa mentioned several times that, unlike Kyle, you don't seem to need her anymore. You seldom spend time with her. Why is that? Are you too busy for your own daughter?"

"Of course, I'm busy, but—" He broke off, shifting slightly. He studied her with narrowed eyes, his expression stern. Finally he said, "The truth is, I don't know *how* to be around her anymore. When Denise left, Tessa was still just a kid. It was easy. But have you looked at her? She's almost a young woman. Everything she does and says and thinks is foreign. I don't know the language, and there's no woman around to teach it to me." He grimaced. "So I back off. Maybe more than I should, but…" He hesitated. Then he seemed to come to some decision. "I'm going to talk to her," he said, pivoting on his heel.

She made another grab for his shirtsleeve and refused to release it. He turned his head, frowning at her. "I've heard you, Kari, and I appreciate what you did. Now I have to get this straightened out."

"Nick, please," Kari said. "Don't talk. *Listen.* That's what she really needs and wants from you."

He gave her a short nod and pulled away. There wasn't anything else she could do.

She watched him go, praying for Tessa to be receptive and Nick to be wise.

CHAPTER FOURTEEN

SAM LAY IN BED and watched her undress.

He knew all of them by heart, these little rituals of Rosa's, developed over thirty-five years of sharing the same bedroom, the same life.

Fresh from the bathroom and the scented steam of her shower, she'd slip quietly around the room in her nightgown, gathering up clothes for the hamper. Then one hundred strokes of the brush against the black silk of her hair, until it crackled with life. Finally, lotion massaged into every finger and joint, across the backs of her hands. Rosie was vain as a peacock about them. They were beautiful.

He felt longing tug at him, the need so strong that he had to grit his teeth to keep from crying out. He wanted her, wanted an end to this terrible aching emptiness. Just the thought of never knowing his wife intimately again made something rip away inside him.

It was emasculating. How could Rosa torment him this way? Didn't she know he couldn't lie here night after night after night, doing nothing, *being* nothing? A piece of furniture had more presence in this room than he did.

With his good hand, he played with the automatic control that raised the head of his bed. First up, then down, then back up again when he couldn't get it just right. Frustration tore through him.

"Do you want me to do it?" his wife asked without ever turning around.

Enough!

"When I die," he told her in a tone determined to shock, "you'll be remarried before six months pass."

She looked over her shoulder at him, a questioning little frown marring her forehead. Recapping the hand lotion, she got up slowly and came to his bedside, perching on the edge of the mattress.

She took his hand and brought it to her lips. "When you die," she said softly, placing a kiss against each one of his fingertips, "I will mourn your loss forever."

"Ha! As if Burt Wickham will let *that* happen. He's had his eye on you for years. I'll bet he burns candles, praying I kick the bucket soon."

She smiled at him indulgently. "If he prays about you at all, it's that you'll quit harassing him about the need for a stoplight on Whisper Mountain Road."

"Don't be so quick to turn him down. You'll miss the chance to be a mayor's wife," he said, although he had to admit it was a poor argument. Wife to the mayor of Broken Yoke was hardly noteworthy.

"Ah, well," she said with a shrug. "I think I can live without such glamour and fame. Besides, I like the life I have here."

Well, I don't.

He pulled his hand from her grasp. "Fine. Do as you please. I'll be long gone anyway."

"Sam?" Rosa said, tilting her head to one side. "Is something bothering you tonight?"

"What could be bothering me? I'm all tucked in bed tighter than the skin on a grape. Pillows all fluffed. Medication close by. All I need now is one of those little mirrors you can put under my nose every so often to see if I'm still breathing." He realized he'd said more than he'd meant to. Worse, it had come out like a child's whine. Disgusted with himself, he straightened the blanket across his chest, then slapped his hands down and closed his eyes. "Good night!"

"Sam."

"What?"

"You might as well tell me. I won't be able to sleep until you do. Is it business?"

"No."

"Tessa?"

He opened his eyes again. "She'll be all right now that Nick's on to what's been bothering her lately." Tonight Nick had told them about the bus station incident and the heart-to-heart he'd had with the girl. Thank the heavens that Kari Churchill had been there to intervene.

"Nicholas, then?"

"No," he said sharply. "Although I never thought any son of mine would be such a lunk-headed fool that he can't see what's right in front of him." He scowled at Rosa, then stared up at the ceiling. "Are you going to keep talking all night? 'Cause I'm losing valuable sleep."

She shook his arm lightly. "Samuel Vincent D'Angelo, look at me and tell me what's wrong."

He brought his eyes back to hers. Might as well confess. There would be no sleep for either of them if he didn't.

"All right," he said in a no-nonsense tone. "You want to know, I'll tell you. You know how long it's been since we've had sex in this room? Or anywhere else, for that matter."

"Of course I do. But—"

"No 'buts' about it, Rosie. I'm tired of little pats on the

head, and little pecks on the cheek, and darned near nothing else. I may have had a stroke—"

"*Two* strokes," she cut in.

He waved away that comment. "Two, or a hundred and two, it makes no difference. It's not natural for a fifty-eight-year-old man to call it quits in bed. I gave up smoking and drinking and eating food that's bad for me. I don't see any reason why I should have to give up making love to my own wife."

"The doctor said no stress. Peace and quiet."

"There'll be enough peace and quiet when I get to the grave. As for stress, I'm suffering plenty having to lie here night after night with you so near and untouchable. This is *my* home. If it were a ship, I'd be the captain."

She laughed at him, the little witch. "Unfortunately, you married the admiral."

"Don't make light of this, Rosa." He drove one finger into the mattress, pointing to a spot beside him. "I demand you do your wifely duty."

She laughed again. "When you put it so charmingly, how can I refuse?" She bent low, brushing her lips against the side of his face, tugging his ear with her teeth. Finally she whispered, "My foolish, foolish Samuel. Don't you know I love you beyond life itself?"

She pulled back and his gaze moved across her face, feature by feature, fascinated. His heart bucked a little, but he didn't care.

He pulled back the covers, patting the bed. "Get in next to me."

"The bed's too narrow."

"You managed well enough in the back seat of my parents' car."

"I was thinner then." She smiled reminiscently. "So were you."

He reached out, running his fingers along the strong, fine line of her jaw. "You are still the most beautiful woman I ever saw," he said.

"Caro mio."

He reached up, pleased that his strength was there when he brought his fingers around the back of her neck. Sometimes his body was beyond coaxing or bullying.

"Kiss me, Rosie," he said, pulling her down.

"Are you sure, Samuel?" There was a little tremor of anxiety in her voice.

He nodded, catching her chin in his fingers so he could meet her eyes. "Don't torment me any longer. Can't you see that I would rather live one day as a lion with you than a hundred more as a sheep?"

KARI DIDN'T SEE NICK the next morning at breakfast. She was dying to ask if anyone knew anything about what had happened with Tessa yesterday, but the dining room was busy with guests and there was really no time for a quiet conversation. Besides, she wasn't sure just how much of his troubles with his daughter he would want to share with the family.

Around midmorning Sam rolled his wheelchair up to her in the kitchen and asked if she would mind driving one of their guests to Glenwood Springs since no one else was available. The chore was a no-brainer, a straight shot down I-70, but by the time Kari returned, it was two o'clock.

She felt at loose ends. Housekeeping duties were over for the day, and Aunt Renata had left tonight's menu taped to her bedroom door. Kari's Italian must be getting better because the names of the dishes didn't present a problem. She'd already checked her cell phone twice and discovered that there had been no call from Eddie Camit or Walt.

Truthfully, she was curious to know how Tessa was, whether she and her father had managed to work things out or if they were still at an impasse. She knew of only one sure way to find out.

She was on her way out the front door of the lodge when her cell phone rang. It was Walt from Wilderness Tours.

He didn't waste time with pleasantries. "Miss Churchill, can you come down to my place? I got some information for you."

"I'm sort of in the middle of something right now. When?"

"How about tomorrow?"

They set a time to meet. "Did you find out anything?" Kari couldn't resist asking.

"Yes, ma'am, but I'll warrant this is something you're gonna want to hear in person. Won't take too long."

"All right," she agreed. "I'll see you tomorrow then."

She disconnected, wondering about Walt's need for mystery. But surprisingly, she realized she could wait to find out. Right now, her main concern was finding out how Tessa had managed.

She made her way down the drive that led to Nick's cabin. The afternoon was gorgeous. Between the trees she caught glimpses of Lightning Lake, glinting in diamond-cut sunlight. She saw that a couple of guests had taken out the lodge's canoe and were lazily stroking their way to the opposite shore.

That picture-book scene made Kari realize that, in some ways, she was going to miss this place after she left. The beauty that took your breath away. The peace. The purity of air so clean that it almost stung your nose to breathe it.

And the people, too. Rose and Sam. Addy with her high spirits and eternal optimism. Tessa, who could always remind you of the best things about being young, even when she was driving you crazy. Even the Zias, who were so different in temperament, but like two halves of the same person.

And Nick—his touch so electric that it could make her flinch. Something in his voice that nearly always caused her heart to quicken. No point in denying that she'd miss him. Miss the possibilities.

She knew that later, when she was in New Zealand or Jamaica or wherever the job took her, the memories she'd gathered here would play in her mind like a slide show she couldn't control.

His Jeep was in the drive. She jogged up the wide planks that formed the front steps and knocked. She heard movement inside, then the door swung wide so fast that she took a step back. Nick stood there in jeans and a navy polo shirt as dark as his eyes, his hair mussed as though he'd plowed a hand through it a dozen times. He was barefoot.

Darn her heart. It just wouldn't behave sometimes.

"Hi," she said, wondering why she suddenly felt a little nervous.

He didn't look surprised or disappointed to see her. "Well, hello there. Don't tell me you escaped the Victorian sweatshop?"

"I just thought I'd come down to see how things went yesterday. With you and Tessa, I mean."

He shrugged. "She talked, I listened. Just like you ordered. All this time trying to figure out what the hell is wrong between us, and you show up and figure her out in a week." He brought one hand up to give her a mock salute. "Nice work, Dr. Churchill."

There was something wrong. His flip, overly casual attitude didn't ring true. Was he irritated with her?

"It wasn't like that," she said. "I think she just needed someone different to talk to. Someone outside the family." She made a show of looking beyond him to the interior of the cabin. "Is she around? I thought I'd just say hello."

"Nope. I let her call off school today so Addy and Aunt Sof could take her shopping in Denver. Tessa specifically asked that I not go with them." He lifted his hands. "So here I am."

Was Nick feeling vulnerable because Tessa hadn't wanted him to go? Was that the reason he was like this? "Well…" she said, clearing her throat. "That's probably a good thing. It shows that you trust her and are willing to relinquish a little control. That's very important to a teenager."

"Then fine. I relinquish everything. I'm no damned good at it, anyway."

She looked at him sharply. "Are you all right?"

"Right as rain." Then he turned away, leaving her standing there.

She hesitated a moment, then walked inside, closing the door behind her. He wandered through the foyer and Kari followed, feeling unnerved and confused. What was wrong with him?

The foyer opened up into a living room that was chic and yet cozy. Hand-hewn logs for walls, of course, with high, cross-beamed ceilings. There was a huge flagstone fireplace in one corner, and lots of windows that brought in the outdoors. Kari had only a moment or two to absorb these things before her eyes fell on the large coffee table in front of the leather couch.

"Oh." The sound escaped her before she could call it back.

Two bottles of wine sat there, one of them drained completely, its mate nearly empty, as well. A half-filled goblet sat so close to the edge of the table it was a miracle it hadn't toppled off.

As though surprised to see that she'd followed him into the room, Nick turned toward her and did a little double take. He picked up the glass. "Wanna drink? Italians always have excellent wine handy for any occasion." Something he saw in her face—probably surprise—made him frown at her. "What's the matter? Now what have I done?"

"Nothing. It's just that I've never seen you drink much before."

He drained his glass in two swallows, then made a satisfied sound. "Stick around. I plan to be stinking drunk before the night is over."

"Do you think that's wise?" she asked. She hated that she sounded so prim, but it had honestly never occurred to her that someone as controlled as Nick D'Angelo would ever drink too much. This thing with Tessa must have rattled him more than she'd thought.

"Wise?" he asked, as if he'd never heard that particular word before. "No, but I'm sick of trying to be wise. Too much work."

"Nick, every parent must occasionally run into stumbling blocks with their kids. You and Tessa—"

"It's not just Tessa," he said with a grimace. "It's everyone. Every *thing*. Since I came back here, I've built my whole life around trying to hold this family together. Trying to make the future safe for them. Trying to keep the business afloat in spite of Dad's mountain of medical bills and leaky plumbing and ski seasons without enough snow to bring in the tourists."

"And it's what you do best. Everyone says so."

He sank down onto the couch. It made a whooshing sound as air escaped. Resting his elbows on his knees, he ground the palms of his hands against his eyes, then let his fingers dangle between his legs. "Then they don't know what the hell they're talking about," he muttered. "I'm just a mediocre juggler who can't keep all the balls in the air."

She came to stand in front of him, feeling the coffee table

hard against the back of her legs. She touched his shoulder. "Well, you don't drop very many."

He looked up at her. "I've dropped a bunch of them lately."

"You mean Tessa?"

"For one."

"That happens. No parent—"

"Brandon O'Dell killed himself," he interrupted in a quiet voice.

Her stomach floated, though she had no knowledge of that name. Maybe it was the look in Nick's eyes. Dark and haunted and devoid of any vitality. "What?" she asked on a small breath of sound. "Who?"

He settled back, letting his head fall against the cushion. He closed his eyes, and she watched his throat work. "God, wine used to make me feel good. Now it just makes me sour and maudlin. Go back to the lodge, Kari. I'm not fit company right now."

"I'm not going anywhere," she said. She took the seat beside him, their knees almost touching. "Tell me what you mean. Who killed themselves?"

He opened his eyes and lifted his head to look at her. "Brandon O'Dell, an old army buddy of mine. His girlfriend called this morning. Told me they'd found his clothes on some beach in California. They're still looking for the body, but the chances are slim because of the currents…"

"Was there a note?"

"No."

"Then it could have been an accident."

"Not likely. I spoke to Bran not long ago. He was drunk, talking crazy. He wanted me to come out to see him. I told him no. Later, I said. I was so damned caught up in my own life—"

She wrapped her fingers around his forearm, squeezing a

little because he seemed to be drifting out of her orbit, lost in his own misery. "It's not your fault, Nick. You couldn't have known what was going on in your friend's head."

"I wish that was true," he replied. Then he shook his head wildly. "God, I wish it was true. But we went through a lot together. Some of the same demons Bran has struggled with for years have been—"

He broke off and looked away from her, clearly uncomfortable with the conversation and unwilling to elaborate. She remembered what Addy had said about Nick's reluctance to share his innermost thoughts and knew it was true.

"Have been what?" she pushed.

"I've played our conversation over and over again in my head, and I realize now that I should have seen the signs. Hell, even his girlfriend thought this was a possibility. But I told her no. I blew it off. I blew *him* off. Because I didn't want to have to deal with one more problem. I think that may have been one of the most selfish moments of my life."

"Nick, don't. Don't take on this burden of guilt."

"Why not?" he asked with a harsh laugh. "I'm a guy who prides himself on being responsible, aren't I? Have to take the bad with the good. Swallow it all down." He frowned. "Now where's that medicine?"

He tipped forward, groping for the wine bottle.

She placed her hand over his, just enough to still his movements. "Don't."

"Why?"

"Because it won't help."

"It will. For a little while."

"You don't want to be like this when Tessa comes home."

"They're spending the night in Denver. For one of the few times in my life, I can do anything I damned well please." He shook off her hand and lifted the bottle. "And this," he said, pouring another glass, "is it."

She watched him gulp it down, not knowing any way to stop him.

He turned his head to look at her. He gave her a fierce scowl. "Either drink with me or go home. I don't need an audience."

She took the glass out of his hand and set it back on the coffee table, far out of reach. "It would serve you right if I *did* go back to the lodge, but I'm not going."

"Why?" he asked, giving her a loose, devilish smile. "Because you like being with me?"

"Because if I leave you here in this condition, you'll probably fall down and crack your head open, and all your brains will fall out—assuming you have any left. One way or the other, I'm sure I'll get the blame for it."

He ignored that statement. He was busy staring at one bare foot that he'd brought up against the edge of the coffee table. He wiggled his toes, frowning, as though he'd never seen them before. "I have big feet."

"Enormous."

His glance slipped to her, and he lifted one brow rakishly. "You know what they say about a man and the size of his feet, don't you? Big feet mean..."

"You'll never be 'Lord of the Dance'?"

Squinting at her dangerously, he shook his finger in her direction. "You are a very cruel woman. I've always said that about you."

"I'm sure you have. And probably a lot more. Now come on, Sasquatch. Can you get up?"

"I could, but why should I?"

"Because you can't go on like this."

She'd run out of patience. How was she supposed to function in a world where a tough, sensible operator like Nick D'Angelo could fall apart like a cheap sweater? It was unnerving.

She reached out, pulling him toward her. He didn't resist, but when she put both hands under his arms to lift him up, it was like trying to move a wall of solid rock.

"Come on, Nick," she said, groaning. "Stand up."

He complied, though his grip on her nearly pulled them both over as he swayed. "Where are we going?" he asked.

"To the bedroom."

"Why, Miss Churchill, are you making an offer I won't refuse?" He snorted. "God, do you have any idea how many times I've dreamed of this?"

She glanced sideways and shook her head at him. "You are really going to hate yourself in the morning."

"Probably," he agreed. Then his hands tightened around her. "But right now I want you to kiss me." His head was tucked into the curve of her neck. He blew a soft breath against her throat, and she was aware of the pungent odor of good wine and the earthy, male scent she'd come to think of as pure Nick. "You know you want to," he said in a throaty, low tone.

The terrible thing was, whether he was drunk or not, she *did* want to kiss him. She answered him thickly, her head swimming a bit, as if she'd been the one to drink too much wine. "Later."

"I'm holding you to that."

"I think it was safer when we were enemies."

"But not as much fun," he said, nuzzling her ear.

She pulled away, desperate now to steer him in the direction of the bedroom. If she could just get him to lie down, sleep this off… She realized suddenly that she didn't have a clue where his bedroom was. When she asked him, he pointed toward the ceiling. Second floor.

She swore softly. They'd never make it up the stairs. Already her arms were quivering with the effort it took to keep him from sliding down to the floor.

"Do you have a bathroom with a shower down here?" she asked, searching for an alternative.

"Uh-huh," he said, flinging an arm in the general direction of the kitchen. "So I don't drag mud or snow through the place."

"Perfect. I've got you. Now walk."

Nick started off steadily enough, then cursed as he tottered and threatened to fall over. Together they lurched past the kitchen, down a long hallway, colliding noisily every so often with walls and doors until they reached a bathroom off the mudroom. There was a small shower stall in the corner. With one hand supporting Nick, Kari used her other to slide the plastic curtain back. Little by little she managed to get him propped against the back wall of the shower. As soon as she turned loose of him, he slid into a sitting position.

His head fell back, hitting the wall with an audible thunk. He lifted it, blinked slowly, looking around. "This isn't my bedroom."

Breathing heavily, Kari crouched on her heels in front of him. "No, it's not. But I just want you to remember, I'm doing this for your own good."

"Doing what?"

Instead of answering, she gave him a quick, hard kiss on the lips. Then she stepped out of the shower, pulled the curtain closed and stuck her hand back in to fumble for the faucet. The one marked "cold."

Nick yelped as the icy water hit him, then blistered the air with a string of curses that bounced off the walls so loudly Kari wanted to cover her ears against the sound. She sat on the toilet, listening to him groan and sputter and curse some more. The water ran and ran, and long minutes passed.

Eventually Nick grew quiet. Just when she thought she should probably check to make sure he was all right, the water stopped running. Metal rings screeched across their rod as he yanked the curtain back. He was still sitting on the tile. Soaked, of course. Water streamed from his hair, running down the long length of his neck. His clothes were matted against his body as though they'd become a second skin.

He didn't look happy. Not angry, really. But definitely not happy.

"Are you all right?" she asked.

"Do I look all right?"

"Are you sober?"

"Close enough."

He blew water away from his lips and pulled his legs against his chest. His feet made little splashes of sound as they settled into the puddles on the shower floor.

"Good. Then you can manage from here, right?"

She made a move to leave the room, but he reached out and grabbed her arm. "Wait a minute. Not so fast."

"Hey!"

The room tilted and she somehow ended up seated beside him on the tile, their legs entwined. Water soaked through the material of her jeans in no time. She struggled to put a little distance between them, but it was hopeless.

"This is no way to thank someone," she said.

He took one of her hands, touching his lips to the back of her balled fist. His eyes lifted to hers. "Thank you," he said softly.

She flushed. She was very much aware of his physicality, the glimpse of dark hair where the wet fabric of his shirt had parted, the way water lay in the hollow of his throat like a tiny pool, the strength of his hands, feeling like a burn in spite of the cold water.

"You're welcome," she said in a tight voice.

"Was I a complete ass?"

"The worst."

"I'm sorry. I haven't been drunk since…well, I can't remember the last time. You haven't been seeing a very good side of me lately, have you? First with Tessa. Now this."

"At least you have one," she remarked, hoping for a lighter tone. "I used to think you didn't."

He looked at her sharply. His mouth stretched into a small smile. "Life is full of surprises, isn't it?"

"Uh-huh. Sometimes some pretty big ones."

He brought one hand to her face, letting his fingers drift over her cheekbones, then her lips, while the last of the water plinked from the shower head. She couldn't take her eyes off him. There was no logic in allowing him to touch her here, now, but she felt bound by some impossible magic, some strange inertia.

"Have you ever made love in the shower?" he asked.

"No. I'm strictly a bathtub kind of girl."

He grinned. "That can be arranged."

"Nick…"

"You owe me a kiss."

"How do you figure that?"

"I didn't forget *everything*," he told her, lifting a wry eyebrow. Then his face became very serious. "I'm going to kiss you now. If you're going to say no, it may be too late."

"I'm not going to say no."

"Good."

He kept his promise, pulling her closer, holding her face

in his palms as he kissed her so thoroughly that it gave her an insane rush of pleasure. She heard her breath come in little gusts. She felt unnerved and powerless, while her blood moved thin and hot in her veins.

He smiled at her as he pulled away at last. "That was nice. But I can do better." His fingers plucked against her blouse. "Shall we get these clothes off?"

"Nick…"

He pulled her against him again, his hand moving to gently cup the underside of her breast. Her legs drew up, coming against the wetness of his jeans, sliding along the length of them and finding the sensation oddly sensual. She moaned.

"Shh…" he whispered as he laid a trio of kisses against the side of her face. "I'm going to take good care of you, Kari. Protect you. Upstairs. An entire drawer full of protection." His light laugh reverberated in her ear, making her stomach quiver. "We just have to get there."

As though in a dream, she tilted her head away, allowing him access to her throat. He nipped and kissed and showed her his intentions, the palm continuing to travel in a slow, tender circle against one nipple even as his mouth found the turn of her neck. His touch—oh, she could not get enough of it.

Her senses slowed. She opened her eyes, looking down. "You're right. You do have big feet."

"What?" he asked, barely lifting his head.

"Nothing."

She gave up trying to make sense of any of it. Desire such as this had been a long time coming. She had fought and struggled and yearned to find magic in her life, and finally here it was. She wasn't going to deny it any longer. There was something, something she had to find out—she couldn't name it, but could identify the longing.

Somehow it was all connected to Nick. This charming, dangerous man who had come roaring into her life. She turned her head quickly and kissed him back. Hard, wanting him to know how much she needed this.

She felt the twitch of his mouth as it curved into a smile.

She'd been wrong earlier. They *could* make it up the stairs and to his bedroom.

Eventually.

CHAPTER FIFTEEN

A LONG WHILE LATER, in the dusky lavender of twilight, Kari
sighed. Even to her own ears, it greatly resembled a con-
tented purr.

"My sentiments exactly," Nick whispered, touching his
lips to her cheek.

They lay naked in his bed, bodies tucked close, satiated and
warm beneath the covers. Their clothes, both wet and dry, had
been discarded with little fuss. They had made love, slept a
while, and now there was just this soft silence between them.
A sweet silence. The kind neither one of them felt compelled
to break.

For one insane moment she wished they could remain
like this always. This pleasure upon pleasure, the feeling of
weightlessness and freedom—the sensations Nick had
coaxed from her body were exquisite. And so, so much
more powerful than she had ever dreamed possible. It felt
strange and raw, to be filled with such a terrible need for
his touch.

And when she went away, when she left Lightning River
Lodge and Nick D'Angelo far behind her…what then?

Emotions she couldn't begin to sort out pounded through
her head. The one thing she was certain of was that, in his
arms, her body surged ahead of her brain and she felt lost. A

though a tornado had picked her up and then deposited her in some strange land.

The telephone rang and Nick stretched to answer it. She hoped it wasn't Renata, looking for her. Kari had already called from her cell phone, asking for the night off. How easily a lie had come to her lips with Nick's mouth teasing her throat. Of course, the older woman had said yes. They could manage. Kari was free to do as she pleased.

And oh, she had. With Nick, she definitely had.

She waited, her head pressed against his chest, her fingers absently stroking across the silky dark hair that whorled around one nipple. She could tell whoever was on the line wasn't family. His words were sharp and short, and beneath her ear, his heart went into trip-hammer rhythm.

"Thanks for calling me," he said. "I'll be in touch soon." Then he replaced the receiver.

He remained quiet, but she felt his arms tighten around her, as though he could take strength from that embrace.

"Everything all right?" she asked.

A long moment. Then he said, "They found Bran."

The silence, so wondrous only minutes ago, seemed suddenly oppressive. She waited for Nick to continue, but he didn't. She lay still in his arms, watching the moon through the window moving up in the night sky like a huge white coin. For a moment she teetered between regret that this beautiful interlude had come to an end and a feeling of bottomless sympathy for what Nick must be going through right now.

"He's not dead," he added in a bemused tone, sounding as though he couldn't really absorb that news.

She lifted up on one elbow. In the coming darkness, his features were nearly indistinguishable. "That was Roxanne," he said. "Bran's girlfriend. He's in a rehab center in San Diego. Checked himself in to get help for his drinking."

"What about his clothes on the beach?" she asked in surprise.

"He told her he'd intended to kill himself, but after he got into the water and sobered up, he'd realized he couldn't do it. The current took him out. Some fishermen picked him up, stark naked. They loaned him a pair of shorts and dropped him at the nearest dock. Bran walked down to a pay phone and called the local center for alcoholic rehabilitation." He blew a gusty, relieved breath against her hair. "Damn his sorry hide. I could kill that bastard with my bare hands."

Elated for his sake, Kari slid closer, planting soft kisses against his chest, across the line of his collarbone. "Oh, Nick. That's wonderful. Wonderful."

"Yeah," he said. "Yeah, it is."

He seemed in shock, as though he'd never considered the possibility of a happy ending for Bran. Kari settled against him again, and they remained like that for a long time, just holding one another. He let his fingers play through her hair, rubbed his hand gently along her arm again and again, and when those movements finally ceased, she thought he might have fallen asleep.

But then, suddenly, in the softest of voices, he said, "Bran and I flew Black Hawks together. In the war."

"Desert Storm?"

She felt his nod against her hair. "In Bosnia, too."

"Were you close?"

"Closer than brothers. You get that way in places like that."

She was relieved to hear him talk of the relationship at last. She sensed that whatever burden he carried from the past, it needed to be taken out of isolation and set free. "Was it horrible?"

Nick paused, then said, "You have no idea what men will do to one another for a cause they believe in. We were young, scared most of the time and trying not to show it." He snorted. "I think the guys we were picking up were more scared than we were. When we came over a sand dune to scoop them up, you could see they wanted to weep, they were that glad to see us. Bran and I thought what we were doing there was important. Not because of any political statement being made. Just in support of the guys who needed us."

"There can't be any better reason than that."

"There was this time, just once, when I doubted…"

He stopped, and she felt his chest rise quickly as his lungs hitched for air. She angled her head up at him, trying to find his eyes. "Nick, please talk to me. I want to help if I can."

"I've never believed in rehashing the past. Especially when there's nothing you can do to change things. But Bran…maybe if he'd talked to someone, maybe if we'd both talked about it…"

She reached up, cupping the side of his face with her hand. "Talk to *me* about it. Let it out. I would never judge you."

He was silent so long she thought he meant to refuse. She forced herself to keep quiet and wait. Just wait.

"We were in Iraq," he said at last. "Orders came through to do a hot extraction of some coalition forces trapped in the Euphrates River valley."

"Hot extraction? You mean, get them out?"

"Yeah. They were in the middle of a firefight, getting the crap knocked out of them by the Republican Guard. As soon as we got there, we could see that our guys were pinned down in a drainage ditch in a field. There were dead goats and camels everywhere—some of the Bedouin shepherds were firing on our men, too, because they thought they'd get cash rewards from the Iraqi army. It was chaos."

His lips came against her temple, as if needing contact. She wondered if he was even aware that he'd touched her there. "An F-16 came up to give air support. Dropped a cluster bomb right on top of the enemy to shake things up. It only got worse after that. Everyone running for cover, flares going off to mark positions."

"I can't imagine what that must have been like."

"It was like hell. Smoke and confusion and men screaming. Bran and I just wanted to pick up as many as we could and get out of there, but I couldn't *see* the ground, much less land the bird. I knew Bran was having the same trouble. He was yelling for his door gunners to get ready for the hit. He slammed down, then I landed almost on top of him. So close, I swear I could see the freckles on his copilot's nose. I told my gunners to lay ground cover. Then our boys started scrambling into the bay. Some of them were getting picked off even as they climbed aboard."

"I don't know how anyone goes through something like that," Kari whispered. Her heart was hammering in her chest.

"The thing is, it's all happening so fast. Your body just reacts, even if your mind can't accept it." He sucked in a deep breath, as though trying to gather courage for the rest. "So there we were, bullets ripping into the birds, men yelling and trying to find some corner to get into. The smoke and dust started to clear a little. Then over the radio I hear Bran yelling, 'Watch it, Delta Two! Watch it!'"

"You were Delta Two?"

"Yeah. Only I couldn't see a damned thing and neither could my gunners. Bran shouted to his miniguns, 'Left flank! Left flank! Take 'em out. Get 'em the hell off of us!' So they did. They just started firing."

He stopped. Took another deep breath. The images were

in Kari's head now, too, unbearable, and she could barely breathe herself.

"It was just a couple of frightened shepherd's kids, running through the smoke, probably trying to find their folks. A boy and a little girl, probably no more than six." When Kari gasped, he moved against her, as though trying to both give comfort and find it. "We lifted off right after that." A pause. "I always thought that from the air they looked like rag dolls, just lying there as if someone had thrown them out in the trash."

Horrified, Kari shut her eyes momentarily, trying to dislodge the picture from her mind and finding herself unable to do so. "Oh, Nick—"

"You don't have to say it. I've replayed it in my mind dozens of times, what we could have done differently, how we could have known. But I know it wasn't anyone's fault, really."

"No, it wasn't," Kari said firmly. "It was just the…the horrible tragedy that war brings sometimes."

"Bran blames himself, of course. Says he can still see those kids coming out of the smoke at the last moment before the minis went off. That he should have waited one more split second before giving the order to fire. That he shouldn't have panicked."

"How could he have made any other choice, given those circumstances? He was trying to save lives. Yours included."

"I've said the same thing to him, but I don't think he believes me. His drinking has gotten worse since he got out of the service. He can't hold a job. Looking back now, I realize I should have tried harder to get him real help."

She hugged him closer. "Bran is alive. It's not too late to help him. And you will. You know that you will."

"Roxanne says he can't have visitors for at least a month

with the program they've got him on. But yes, after that, I plan to go out there. See what I can do to help."

A month. In a month she'd be long gone from here. Most likely, she would never see Nick again. She could not contain it, the pure pain of loss that cut deep into her heart.

What was she feeling for this man she'd known less than two weeks? A man whose past was still so much of a mystery and whose future was one she couldn't imagine sharing? It didn't seem possible. This was lust, not love. And yet, she was suddenly filled with amazement that, against all odds and common sense, she might very well be in love with Nick D'Angelo.

He sighed heavily and made a fretful movement. "I don't want to talk about this anymore. Not now."

She recognized that she couldn't press him any further. Deliberately she gave him a more playful glance. "All right. What *would* you like to talk about?"

"Who said anything about talking?" he asked, a smile buried low in his voice.

He pulled her suddenly on top of him. In the calculated way he moved against her, Kari realized that he was determined to put all talk of the past behind them. No more tales of death or pain. His touch was almost a desperate reach for life.

His hand traveled over her ribs, down the yearning swell of one hip in a slow, delicious invitation. Through the eroticized patchwork he made of her nerves, she somehow managed to catch his fingers and bring them to her lips. "No…" she said on a whisper of sound. "Let me…"

She nuzzled her face against the warmth of his chest, then stretched to trail the tip of her tongue over his lips, feather-light and teasing. Slowly her mouth worked its way from the corner of his smile, then to his ear, along the firm, raspy line of his jaw, then back to his mouth again. She kissed him deeply, as though he were the source of life, and as she did so she slipped one hand beneath the covers and laid her fingers lightly upon him.

There was a quiver of response beneath her touch. An indrawn breath, quickly taken. "Kari," he said in a husky, tight voice. "What are you doing to me?"

She let her fingers play, unleashing a tender, sexual prowling meant to arouse. "Oh, dear," she replied, pretending to be worried. "I thought you'd know."

He captured her face between his palms. His dark eyes were gentle with passion. "I'm not sure I'm up to this just yet."

"Oh, you're up to it," she said as she tightened her hold. Involuntarily he moved against her and already she could feel his hard welcome. "Don't you agree?"

A hoarse explosion of sound escaped between his lips. "Yes…" he said on a growl. "Oh, yes."

Then he covered her mouth with his and slid easily, effortlessly into her again.

THE NIGHT PASSED like a heavenly dream.

There were parts of it that remained quite clear to her— the laughter and quiet, nonsensical conversations. The hour spent in the kitchen when hunger struck, sharp and sudden in spite of their best attempts to ignore it. Those moments, when they got past everything and found the child in themselves again. Those would remain with Kari forever, she thought.

They touched and tempted one another. She enjoyed watching Nick sleep, finding it painfully sweet, like trying to drink thick honey. Sometimes they grew quiet and simply lay side by side. She had no idea where his thoughts took him, and she was determined not to ask because she could not bear to ruin this idyll.

When Kari woke near dawn, feeling embarrassingly lazy and self-indulgent, she found Nick was gone. She ran her hand across his pillow, feeling no warmth there. A dull ache began to beat against her rib cage. She missed him already.

Where had he gone? He hadn't mentioned any early morning task, but anything was possible with the weight of responsibility he shouldered.

The dream began to slip a little. Suppose morning had brought regret? Nick was so practical. Did he view the night they'd just passed as nothing more than fun, terrific sex? The result of catching him at an emotional low point—when he'd been drunk and feeling sorry for himself? She didn't want to believe that.

The sound of her cell phone ringing made her jump. She wound the bed sheet around her and scrambled to find it in her pile of clothing that still lay on the floor. She sat back on the bed, hoping it wasn't Renata looking for her. The bedside clock said it was almost five-thirty.

"Hello?" she said tentatively.

"How soon can you be on a plane?" a male voice asked, the connection less than perfect.

"Eddie?" she said, speaking up.

"Who else?"

"New Zealand came through?"

He made a dismissive sound. "Who needs New Zealand, mon, when we can have fun in the sun in Jamaica?"

"So it's Metcalf's treasure ship."

"As promised. You can thank me later."

"That's great," she said, a little surprised by the lackluster response. What was wrong with her? She should be delighted.

Evidently, Eddie thought so, too. "You don't sound as happy as I thought you would."

"Sorry. It's still early here. I'm happy. Tell me more."

"Metcalf wants to meet with us as soon as possible. He's very nervous about the whole thing—I think it's starting to sink in just how much a find like this can affect his future. Next thing you know, he'll be walking around as cocky as Indiana Jones. Without the Harrison Ford looks, of course. Wait until you meet him, Kari. He's only forty, and I swear, his face is so leathery I expected to find the name of an Italian shoemaker burned into his forehead."

In spite of the way her pulse raced at the idea of leaving here so suddenly, she couldn't help laughing. Eddie was so…Eddie. "So when do I need to be there?"

"Take all the time you need," he said generously. "Just be here by tonight."

"What?" She wiped hair out of her eyes, sitting up straight. She hadn't been expecting that kind of deadline.

"Do you want this or not?" he asked in an aggrieved tone. "And, anyway, aren't you the one who was begging me just the other day to save your sorry butt?"

"I was. Because I knew if anyone could get me out of this place it would be you. And of course I want this. I'm thrilled. You always come through for me."

"I do, don't I?" He sighed, sounding pleased with himself. "I'm a saint, really."

"You're my hero, Eddie."

"That's better. So do I need to make arrangements to get you here tonight or can you manage that on your own?"

"I'll call the airline as soon as we hang up."

"Good. I'm at the Clayborne Inn in Port Antonio. In spite of that dreadfully dull name, it's got a decent restaurant, a great view and a spa. The masseuse has hands that can play your body like Mozart."

"Sounds like heaven," she said, knowing Eddie would want that kind of reaction or he'd pout. "I'll see you later tonight."

"This is going to be a big one, Kari. Don't plan on going to bed as soon as you get in. We're celebrating. What's your pleasure? Hard liquor or champagne?"

"Champagne, of course. What's a celebration without that?"

She closed the phone and just sat there on the bed.

Tonight. She had no idea how she could manage that. Even if the D'Angelo family could see their way clear to turning her loose. The airport in Denver was always a mess. She still needed to meet with Walt down at Wilderness Tours. She wasn't prepared, really, to interview Antone Metcalf tomorrow morning.

She called a halt to that kind of thinking because, truthfully, the only thing she wasn't prepared for was leaving here. Leaving Nick.

But suppose she told him about the assignment and he asked her to stay?

No. Not likely. It was pointless to nourish such a hopeless thought.

Disgusted, she tossed the phone onto the bed, then stifled a gasp of surprise. Nick stood leaning in the doorway, watching her. He was fully dressed, looking as handsome as ever. She had no idea how long he'd been there or what he might have heard of her conversation with Eddie. As usual, his eyes held that maddeningly unreadable quality they often had when he looked at her.

"Good morning," she said, schooling her own expression.

"Sorry," he replied. "Didn't mean to eavesdrop."

"That was Eddie, the photographer I usually work with."

"Sounded like he had good news."

"He did. We've got an assignment in Jamaica. Some salvager bringing up a Spanish galleon. Supposedly it's loaded."

He looked at her steadily. "Hard to beat that kind of excitement."

"I need to be there tonight."

"So I heard."

"I don't want to leave the family in a lurch. I made a commitment to your father and—"

He made a dismissive gesture with his hand. "Don't worry about it. We'll manage."

"So the family—Addy—will be able to handle the rest of the preparations for the wedding and everything?"

He nodded. "Your parole has come through."

She flushed, stung by his slightly bitter, flat tone. "I wasn't thinking of it like that, exactly."

"The family will be sorry to see you leave."

So tell me not to go, she sent the silent message. *Give me a reason not to get on that plane. Just one.*

He didn't. He just stood there staring at her, waiting, while she looked back at him, wondering how much of her heart was showing in her face.

"I'll miss them, too," she said at last.

The telephone on Nick's bedside table rang. As though hating the interruption, he frowned and strode over to the bed to answer it. He listened for less than a minute. Then he said, "Okay. I'll be right there. Just leave it alone for now."

He hung up. From the top of his bureau, he scooped up his cell phone, a few items for his pocket, not saying a word. She waited for a long, breathless moment, wondering if they were really going to part like this.

"Nick—"

He swung around. "I have to go. Aunt Renata can't get the griddle to heat. God knows what we'll do if the guests can't have pancakes."

"It's the plug. It's shot, I think. I meant to say something yesterday, but I completely forgot."

"Too busy dreaming about the next great adventure, I imagine."

She frowned. "Do we need to talk? About this…" She inclined her chin toward the bed. "What we—"

"I don't think there's anything to say, really. You want a life full of adventure and excitement. I've had my fill of that."

She wanted to be tough and brave, but it hurt all the same, to see how easily he could put what they'd shared behind him. In spite of her best intentions, she couldn't help asking, "So that's it? We're just…what? The old cliché of two ships passing in the night?"

"It was good. But having great sex can't change who we are inside and what we want out of life. Nor should it."

"That doesn't mean—"

"You deserve to be happy, Kari. I hope you find what you're looking for, but this…" He looked away a moment, then back at her. "We always knew this was just temporary."

CHAPTER SIXTEEN

KARI HURRIED BACK to the lodge, arriving in the kitchen just as the dining room opened for breakfast. The room was busy enough that Renata didn't have time for questions. No one seemed to notice that Kari was slightly out of breath, her appearance less than stellar or that she was so distracted that she had to be reminded by one of the guests to fill water glasses.

To the outside world, she probably just looked a little frazzled. But inside, her spirits had plunged to the lowest desolation.

When the dining room emptied, she went into the kitchen and grabbed a plate of scrambled eggs from the warmer Rose kept filled for employee meals. Kari supposed she should tell the family she was leaving, but it didn't seem the right time just yet. With Addy, Sofia and Tessa still in Denver, the atmosphere was subdued, even though Rose and Sam seemed to be in particularly high spirits. Nick had fixed the griddle and quickly disappeared. He hadn't returned, but that hardly seemed an issue. They'd already said their goodbyes in the bedroom, hadn't they?

"Kari, are you all right?" Renata asked from the sink, where she was just drying her hands.

"Sure," Kari said, trying to keep her smile breezy. "Why do you ask?"

"You've been very quiet this morning."

Nothing left to say. Except goodbye.

"Just a lot on my mind lately," she said, hoping that vague answer would suffice. Renata had a nose for trouble like a bloodhound.

Sam, seated across from her and eating a bowl of cereal, used his spoon to point in her direction. "Renata's right," he said with a piercing glance. "You're much too quiet. Has that foolish son of mind done something to upset you? Something new, I guess I should say?"

Oh, if you only knew.

"Kari?"

She looked at Sam, hoping the color she felt blooming in her cheeks would be mistaken for the heat in the kitchen. "No, he's done nothing," she said quickly. "Not a darned thing."

Inwardly she cringed, because those last few words had sounded very sarcastic. So much for pretending.

With fresh resolution, she straightened her spine, disgusted with herself. Really, she'd been through difficult times before. So Nick didn't want to give them a shot. Tough, but that was life. How much worse could it get? And when she arrived in Jamaica, fully immersing herself in Metcalf's fantastic adventure, she'd soon forget about the silly wanderings of her heart.

Before she came under anyone else's radar, she scraped back her chair and excused herself.

When she got back to her room, there was a message waiting on her cell phone. Although she hoped it was Eddie, giving her a little more time, it wasn't. It was Walt, reminding her of their appointment today.

All the way down the mountain Kari wondered what had made Walt sound so mysterious yesterday. But if he'd really located the guide who had hiked her father into the park, or just where he'd really camped, it was ironic that the information wouldn't do her much good now. If she intended to check out the area, she'd have to come back.

It hit her quite suddenly that she'd never want to do that. Not as long as there was a chance of running into Nick. It would be unbearably hard to see him.

She went into Wilderness Tours, not knowing what to expect. She liked this place, the cozy feel of it, the smell of good wood and old fires. The plank flooring creaked as she trod across it to greet Walt.

"I'm glad you came, Miss Churchill." He inclined his head toward the chairs huddled around a fireplace. "This is my grandson, Kenny."

She hadn't noticed the second occupant. A tall, thin man— no, a boy really—unwound from one of the high-backed chairs and came forward to shake her hand. Closer, she saw that he was probably past the age of consent, but the way he smiled hesitantly and rolled his eyes made him look no older than Tessa.

"I go by Kenneth," he said. "I stopped being Kenny when I got out of high school."

Kari returned his smile. "Very nice to meet you, Kenneth." She cut a glance to the older man. "What's this about, Walt?"

Nobody said anything for a long moment. Walt looked at his grandson expectantly. "Get it out, boy. Clear your conscience, and you'll sleep like a baby tonight."

"Miss Churchill, I've been trying for two years to get up the nerve to contact you," the young man said. His tone was respectful, but nervous. Every bit of his body language indicated that this conversation was difficult for him. "When Grandpa told me you'd come around asking questions, I knew I couldn't keep it to myself any longer."

Kari was curious now. "Keep what to yourself?"

"I'm the guide who took your father to Elk Creek. The Pass, not the Canyon. You did have that wrong."

"My father hired you?" She realized how skeptical she sounded. He hardly seemed old enough. "I'm sorry. I didn't mean it to come out that way. It's just that you're…rather young."

"I know. That's why it's a little more complicated than it should be. I've been waiting to get registered with the National Park as a guide for a couple of years now. But you need a lot of experience."

His grandfather, watching the conversation closely, gave a sharp nod. "All in good time, Kenny. All in good time."

The boy bit his lip, then said softly, "On the day your father came into the park office, I was there. I overheard him sign in for the trip to one of the canyons. I caught up with him in the parking lot, told him I knew a better place than that if he wanted to see some spectacular scenery and stuff."

"So he hired you to take him."

"Misrepresented himself, is what he did," Walt said, though his tone carried no censure.

Kenneth looked very uncomfortable now. "I told him I was one of Grandpa's guides. I mean, I've been hiking this area since I was old enough to walk. Elk Creek Pass is remote, but it's not dangerous. It's the snowstorm that made it that way." His words came faster, as though speed would make the explanation more palatable. "Your father was crazy about the place. Said it was just what he was looking for. I never thought it would end up the way it did."

Walt reached out a hand and placed it on his grandson's forearm. "Slow down, Kenny-boy. No sense rushin' the tellin' now."

Kenneth nodded, then looked at Kari again. "Anyway, I hiked him in. And then I came home."

"So my father never went to the original place, or told the park service he planned to camp someplace else?"

"No, ma'am. As far as I know, he didn't. I asked him not to 'cause the park service doesn't like freelance guides hanging around trying to pick up business."

"I see." She remained silent a moment, digesting this information. She could imagine her father making a deal like that. If possible, he wouldn't want to see the usual, touristy places in the park. The book he'd planned to write would require research of a more rugged kind. Something with an edge to it.

But almost immediately after she had that thought, she felt her stomach take a swooping dive. She fixed a razor-sharp look on Kenneth and from his face, she could tell he knew the next question.

"Are you telling me that when he turned up missing after the snowstorm, and the search-and-rescue team tried to find him and couldn't, you didn't inform them that they were looking in the wrong place? You just kept quiet about him changing his itinerary? Let him stay out there—trapped—until it was too late?"

"No, ma'am!" the young man said excitedly. His face went paper-white. "I swear I didn't. I would have said something if I'd known."

"You didn't know he was missing?"

"No, ma'am. I was down in Mexico with some of my friends. That's why I needed the money your dad paid me. To be able to go off with them and have fun."

Her pulse settled a little. From years of interviewing, she thought she could read people well enough to know he wasn't lying. "When did you find out what had happened?"

"When I got home my mom told me everyone was looking for him. I didn't know he was a celebrity." He reddened, looking embarrassed. "I don't read all that much."

"Go on."

"Anyway, I *did* call the park service, but I don't know if they believed me. I didn't tell them I was the one to take him out to Elk Creek Pass. Maybe if I had, they would have looked sooner, I know. But I was scared to."

Walt made a disgusted sound. "They wouldn't a' listened. Those guys are all a bunch of block-headed bureaucrats who you can't tell nothing to."

"Well…" Kenneth continued, "then, it didn't seem to matter anyway, because the word came over the news that they'd found him—still alive and all."

She nodded, trying to picture it. "So that's what you've had on your conscience all this time? That you took him out there and it ended badly?"

"No, ma'am," the boy said, his voice low and soft. He looked down at his feet a moment, then back up at her. "I wish that was all it was. What's really been eating at me—" he reached into the inside pocket of his denim jacket "—is this."

He offered the book to her. She took it, watching her hand stretch out slowly, almost disembodied, as if all this were happening in a dream. She knew what it was, of course. She'd seen it, or one just like it, so often on her father's desk, tucked in his suitcase, peeking out from the top of his camping gear.

She blinked, staring down at the red cover with its rounded corners and cracked leather. She wanted to cry.

She looked back up at Kenneth. "This is my father's journal."

His Adam's apple bobbed a couple of times, and he nodded. "I figured it was something important. I didn't read it. Well, not much of it, anyway."

"How did you get it?"

He didn't answer. Between them she could sense Walt willing the boy to come out with it, to just tell the truth, although she suspected she knew it already.

"How did you get it?" she repeated, feeling a little breathless.

"I stole it."

"How?"

"I knew a couple of the guys with search-and-rescue," he told her at last. His tongue slid across his lips nervously. "When they brought your dad in, I was down there waiting to see if he'd say anything about who took him into Elk Creek Pass. I didn't know he wasn't gonna make—" He took a deep breath. "So the stretcher came off the helicopter first, then your dad's personal stuff, just a few things I guess they'd scooped up. I saw the book…so I just took it."

"Because you thought he might have written something about you that would get you in trouble."

"Yes, ma'am. I didn't know what they'd do if they found out I was the one who took him there. I mean, your dad was famous."

She lifted the journal slightly. "And is your name in here?"

"No," he said with a shake of his head. Then more quickly he added, "I just skimmed it is all. I didn't see my name anywhere, but I could tell it was personal, so I just left it alone."

"Why didn't you give it to my mother? She was at the hospital for a week before my father died."

"I should have. I *know* I should have. But the longer I kept it, the more scared I got. Then your dad—I know it was wrong. Honest. I just couldn't do it. So I've been holding on to it, thinking enough time would go by that I could send it someplace, or call someone. Then Grandpa told me you were in town."

Walt nodded, looking at her. "I've known something's been

eating at the boy for a long time. Just didn't know it had anything to do with this."

"I'm really sorry, Miss Churchill. Really sorry. For everything."

Kenneth looked undone, so miserable that Kari wondered
if the boy would *ever* be able to forgive himself.

"It's all right, Kenneth," Kari said, and made the startling
discovery that she meant it. Her father was gone, and there
was nothing to be gained by weighing this young man down
with more guilt. "I can imagine how it happened. And if Elk
Creek Pass is as beautiful as you say, I'm sure it pleased my
father very much."

"You thinking of going out there yourself?" Walt asked.

"No," Kari told him. "I don't think that will be possible
right now." Her fingers tightened on the journal. "And perhaps, not even necessary."

SHE GOT ALMOST HALFWAY UP the mountain before she had to
pull over into one of the scenic overlooks. She could feel her
pulse increasing with every breath she took. She stopped the car,
then picked up the journal where it lay on the passenger seat.

She didn't want to look at it. Not right now. This last communication from her father was too important for a quick
read. It deserved time and calm, clear thought. But she
couldn't resist just touching it.

The pages were well-thumbed, slightly soiled. When she
let her fingers drift through them, she swore she could smell
her father's familiar, manly scent.

The bold strokes of his penmanship brought a smile to her
lips. The sharp S's that looked like lightning bolts. The cap-
ital letter T no more than lazy hammocks. The looping way
he wrote an O, as though it wore a little cap of importance.

All her life she'd seen his hand at work—in postcards and autographs and hurriedly dashed off notes to the editor as he wedged the latest manuscript into a delivery box.

A few pages from the back of the book, she came to the end. The writing ceased abruptly. She knew what that meant. The words swam out of focus as her vision blurred. Oh, God. To think that this was the last…

She couldn't help it. There was no well of bravery she could draw from in that moment. She bent forward and laid her head against the steering wheel. The tears came, harsh and without grace, but she didn't try to stop them.

WHEN SHE GOT BACK to the lodge, Kari knew she'd have to hurry if she wanted to make her flight. She packed, gently sliding the journal into a side pocket of the backpack that would go with her on the plane. It was too precious to trust to the baggage handlers, more valuable than any treasure Antone Metcalf could scoop up from the bottom of the ocean floor.

Finally, there was nothing left but to say goodbye to the D'Angelo family. She hoped her sudden departure wouldn't leave them short-handed, and that Nick had already told them she had to leave. He'd probably already made arrangements for additional help.

Hearing a vague commotion coming from the kitchen, Kari went to check it out. She was glad to see that Addy, Sofia and Tessa had returned from their overnight stay in Denver. She wouldn't have wanted to leave without saying goodbye to the three of them. Nick was nowhere around, but that hardly seemed to matter now.

She watched and listened as the three travelers laughed and shared their stories about the trip. It was clear they had no idea she was on her way to Jamaica. They spoke over one another, rapidly, with lots of hand gestures, and Kari kept quiet for the moment, not wanting to drop her news in the middle of such joy and steal their thunder.

She'd never seen Tessa so animated and happy. A few comments she made regarding Nick made Kari believe there might be real hope for them. No matter how she felt about him right now, she didn't doubt for a minute that he would make every effort to help his daughter find her way.

Eventually, the stories wound down. Everyone seemed content to linger in the kitchen and sample Rose's latest batch of *choux* pastries that she intended to offer that night at dinner.

Kari cleared her throat. "I guess this is as good a time as any to say this. I'll be leaving in a few minutes. My next assignment. I have to be in Jamaica tonight."

Absolute silence as several pairs of eyes stared at her. The only sounds were the beverage cooler fans humming and some custard concoction of Rose's bubbling on the stove.

She filled the awkwardness of that moment with a larger explanation of the salvage of Metcalf's ship. No one looked the least bit impressed.

Finally, Tessa spoke up. "Well, I'm just going to say it. This sucks!"

"Tessa," Rose said, throwing a warning to the girl. She crossed the room to Kari. "This is wonderful news. We're very happy for you, but sorry to see you go."

"She means that," Renata said. "We all do. You've been a breath of fresh air around this place. Livened it up."

Kari felt color creep up her neck. She hadn't expected such a compliment from Renata, who didn't indulge in sentimental foolishness.

"I don't know what to say," Kari stammered out. "I expected—I didn't think you'd be— I've felt so responsible for what happened to Addy."

"Nonsense," Rose said. With a glance toward her daughter, she added, "Whatever guilt you felt, it has been more than atoned for with your help here. And it certainly wasn't yours to bear alone, as Addy well knows. Put it from your mind now, and let us send you off with a proper goodbye."

As though given a cue, the Zias gathered around Kari, as well. She found herself in an Italian embrace worthy of a papal appearance. They exclaimed over her lucky opportunity to see an actual treasure ship and offered advice on the best ways to survive foreign food and drink. She sensed they were happy for her, but she didn't think she was kidding herself—they were genuinely sorry to see her go, too.

Tessa continued to sulk in the background. Addy looked stunned. Sam looked furious.

When Kari's gaze collided with his, he said loudly, "I agree with Tessa."

"Sam," Rose said.

"Me, too," Addy added.

"I thought you liked it here," Tessa said.

"I do. But I have to make a living."

At that moment Nick walked into the kitchen. Seeing everyone, he came to a halt. She noticed he didn't bother to look in her direction.

"Did you know anything about this?" Sam asked. "Kari's leaving."

"We spoke this morning," Nick said calmly.

"And…?" his father prompted.

Sam's face was thunderous. Nick looked suddenly annoyed.

The last thing Kari wanted was a fight between family members. She moved quickly to Sam's chair. "*And*…believe it or not, after our shaky start, Nick's just as sorry to see me go as you are, Sam. But there's no help for it. Now, even though I can't turn in a two-week notice, will you still give me a good reference?"

She smiled, silently begging him not to make this any more difficult. Evidently he got the message. After a single muttered oath, he took one of her hands in his. "You will always be welcome in this house," he told her, his voice solemn and firm.

The look in his eyes made a lump form in her throat. This was something else she would miss about this place. The feeling that, given half the chance, she could have belonged here. But that kind of option wasn't being offered.

Everything went quickly after that. Before she knew it, Kari was in her rental car, saying one last goodbye as everyone waved from the driveway. Even Nick was there, though she suspected he didn't want to be. Perhaps it would have looked churlish if he had refused to see her off.

Rosa rushed up to the driver's window and pressed a folded piece of paper into her hand. "My cannoli recipe," she told her. "I know you liked them." Then she winked. "*Cannoli.* Not calamari."

At the last moment Addy was there, too, holding on to her sling to keep it from banging against the car door. "You'll come visit us?"

"I will."

Something in Kari's face must have tipped Addy off to the fact that a return trip seemed very, very unlikely. She frowned. "You won't come back. Damn that brother of mine. Somehow this is his fault, isn't it?"

Kari shook her head at the young woman. "No. It's no one's fault. Some things just aren't meant to be, Addy."

Before Addy could say anything more, Kari put the car in

gear and pulled away with a last wave to the family. Glancing in her rearview mirror, she saw them still standing in the driveway, watching her go. It was sweet and touching and difficult. The D'Angelos were like no family she'd ever known before. She had come to care about them deeply.

Just before her car bumped onto the main road, she looked back for the last time. While everyone else gave her a final wave, Nick had already begun to walk away, separate and contained, no doubt already turning his attention to some long list of responsibilities.

And evidently finding it so easy to turn her loose.

CHAPTER SEVENTEEN

THE *MAGDALENA* was a brilliant find.

Below its sand-and-algae-covered decks it carried enough treasure to make Metcalf and his backers filthy rich, enough items of historic importance to please the academic world, and enough mystery in its tragic past to thrill the public.

Four days after Kari arrived in Port Antonio, she stood on the dock with Eddie Camit and watched the salvagers from the ship pack the latest haul into water-filled containers. From there, the goods would be transported to a warehouse where Antone Metcalf's team of scientific experts would catalog and inspect every item.

A TV crew jockeyed for a better position on the rickety dock, eager to catch sight of the most recent load, some of which had been pretty spectacular. Silver stirrups, incense burners, a bronze cannon, solid bars of both gold and silver that could fund a small country, gem-encrusted pendants, rings and even a pair of rosary beads studded with emeralds. Metcalf had hired a security detail to keep the salvagers from being mobbed, but Kari suspected they were going to be woefully inadequate. Everyone wanted to know more about the *Magdalena* and the treasure it held.

"And we're the ones with the inside track," she heard Eddie say gleefully beside her.

A self-satisfied smile stretched his lips as he sipped a local beer. He'd been insufferable since she'd arrived. He'd worked hard to get this job, and it would be quite a feather in his cap. Hers, too. As he frequently reminded her.

"Should have taken your advice," he said with a grimacing hiss as he gently touched his sunburned nose. "When you go home tomorrow, leave me your sunscreen."

Home. That meant Florida and her condo. Probably a pile of bills on the kitchen table, sour milk in the fridge and a couple of dead plants if Mrs. Marston across the hall had forgotten to water them. The idea of returning didn't hold much appeal.

"Maybe I'll just stay here," she told him. "The article's wrapped up, but since you're going to stay and take more pictures, I could tag along and keep you company."

He tilted his head at her, eyes narrowed to slits. "You've got something going with Metcalf, don't you?"

She didn't have a clue what he was talking about. "What?"

"I've seen the way Antone's been watching you the last couple of days. The man's crazy about you."

"If he's watching me, it's to make sure I don't steal any of his blasted treasure. The guy's more paranoid than Fox Mulder."

"Can't say that I blame him. But that doesn't mean you couldn't have him—" he snapped his fingers "—like that. *If* you'd put forth a little effort and stop looking so serious all the time."

"I'm not interested in putting forth a little effort."

"Why not?"

"Because I…" *Because I want Nick,* she thought. *Nobody else. Just Nick.* She gave herself a mental kick. For Pete's sake, she sounded like a child whining over the loss of her favorite toy. When was she going to get past this ridiculous yearning for something she couldn't have? "Just because," she finally said.

"Oh," he replied with a short laugh. "As long as there's a good reason."

"Stop badgering me, Eddie."

They watched as the salvagers tried to maneuver dozens of cannonballs into the crates. Beyond the dock, boats bobbed like floating seagulls in the turquoise bay.

"For a woman who's just witnessed a fortune in treasure get dragged up in buckets from the bottom of the sea, you've been very solemn this trip," Eddie said.

"It's not like it was *my* fortune in treasure."

"Could be," he said with a teasing gleam in his eyes. "If you'd give Metcalf half a chance. I admit the guy looks like an old shaman from an Indian tribe, but you could work on his skin problem. A little moisturizer…"

"I am *not* interested in Antone Metcalf. Or anyone else."

She looked away for a moment, feeling slightly uncomfortable. It was one thing to tell lies to yourself, but she and Eddie had gotten close over the last couple of years. She never lied to him.

"Oh my God!" Eddie gasped so suddenly that Kari looked back at him and one of the salvagers lifted his head. Eddie pulled her aside and gave her a piercing glance. "You're in love."

"No, I'm not."

"Yes, you are. I can see it in your face. Who's the lucky guy?"

She crossed her arms. "There *is* no lucky guy."

When Eddie remained silent, watching her, she uncrossed her arms and started to walk up the dock. A light breeze stirred her hair, bringing with it the warm scents of the ocean. She wished she could inhale the air so deeply that it would sear away every thought she'd ever had of Colorado and a dark-eyed man who could make her howl with frustration and hurt.

She became aware that Eddie had come up beside her as she headed back toward their hotel.

"How long have we known each other, Churchill?"

"Six years, give or take."

"Long enough not to kid one another in matters of the heart, wouldn't you say?"

She stopped and stared at him. No point in hiding anything from Eddie. "If I thought I was in love, I don't anymore," she admitted in a quiet voice. "It didn't work out. It didn't even get a chance to because he wasn't interested."

"The myopic bastard. You're a damned fine catch."

"Thank you. I could kiss you for saying that."

"Don't get any ideas," he said, the old Eddie again. "I'm completely loyal to Buzz."

They sat near the ocean, watching a couple of teenagers work their way out of the water with swim fins and snorkels and a netted bag of sea treasures. The beach here was rocky, not like home at all, but it was still quite beautiful. In another hour sunset would be sliding down the thatched roofs of the hotel, painting everything with a rosy glow.

"How do you feel about Las Vegas?" Eddie asked as he polished off the last of his beer.

"Hot. Touristy. Why?"

"I have a friend who knows Wes Sanderlin."

"The actor?"

He frowned at her, looking disappointed. "Of course, the actor. How many Wes Sanderlins are there with two Academy Awards, six ex-wives, a boatload of money and every studio producer in Hollywood in his back pocket?"

"What about him?"

"They're shooting his new movie in Las Vegas. All the trades are saying it's going to be a contender next year. The studio is looking for some early coverage, and a buddy of mine brought our names up as possibilities. I thought we might be interested."

"I don't know, Eddie… Can I think about it? I haven't been home in a while…"

She stopped because he looked surprised by her hesitation. It wasn't like her.

"Sure. We can talk about it later." He tossed his beer bottle into a nearby trash can. They walked up the two flights of stairs that led to their rooms. In the corridor, Eddie said, "I'm going to take a shower and change for dinner. Thirty minutes. Okay?"

She nodded and went to her own bedroom. The shower felt wonderful, and she let the water run longer than she needed to. Even if you weren't on a boat, when you were this close to the ocean it always seemed as if the breezes left a fine film of salt on your skin.

She dressed and did something simple with her makeup and hair. Eddie would knock on her door when he was ready to go down to the restaurant.

With a little time to kill, she sat on the bed and pulled her father's journal out of her backpack.

Since leaving Colorado, she'd spent long hours in the night dissecting every passage. It had only been in her possession four days and already she knew whole parts of it by heart.

This journal was the only one she'd ever have. She didn't know what had happened to all the others. None of them had turned up in her mother's things after her death. Kari suspected that Laura Churchill, filled with bitterness and anger toward her late husband, had destroyed them.

So this was the last. The one Kari had given him the Christmas before his death. And now it was hers again, forever.

She leafed through the pages, going past the beginning of the book quickly since more than half of it dealt with the creation of *Hours of Glass*. Then the tone of the writing changed. Every day of the trip into Elk Creek had been detailed down to the tiniest leaf and rock, even after the snowstorm hit. But then finally, a week before her father had been found and airlifted to the hospital, the tone changed again, to a diary.

Reading it had been difficult. It was clear to Kari that Madison Churchill had known his chances for survival were slim at best, especially after he had fallen on an ice-covered patch of ground and broken his leg. From there his writings had gradually spiraled down to grim acceptance of his fate. Her father might have been a dreamer, but he was realistic enough to know that what he wrote on those final pages of his journal might be his last communication.

Most of it was addressed to her mother. Passages from the last few pages stood out to her, making her stomach kick and tighten as she read them:

I know now that I have frittered away my time on earth, searching for a life that was fuller and richer than any I ever deserved, thinking that everything unknown must surely be new and glorious to me. That I have hurt you in unspeakable ways until there is nothing left in common between us now but our incompatibility.

I have felt homeless in my own home, but this has been a result of choices I made—none of them were yours. I have never stretched out a hand to you again for fear of being bitten, and in doing so I will never feel your hand stretched out to me again in love…

Most of what matters has taken place in my absence.

Our sweet Kari has paid the price. I know that you loved me, Laura, but I was not worthy of it and no love can survive neglect...

And finally, with her heart beating hard and rapid in spite of the numerous times she'd read it:

I will tell you now that you and Kari will be in my life forever and hereafter, that personal relationships are the important thing, the only thing, really, not this life of distance and regrets that I have so foolishly chased after. I hope with all my heart that you can find it in yours to forgive me...

Tears filled Kari's eyes. No matter how many times she read them, these words filled her with sorrow. All those wasted years. When her mother's love for her husband had turned to bitter stone. When her father, so careless and wrong-headed, had squandered their love. How could two people have allowed it to happen? Why hadn't they tried to find a middle ground? Surely that had not been impossible?

And now, it was too late.

"Are you coming?" Eddie's plaintive voice came through the bedroom door, followed by a sharp rap. "There's a piña colada waiting with my name on it."

Quickly, Kari wiped away a tear and closed the journal with a soft snap. "Right behind you," she called.

THE RESTAURANT WAS crowded and stuffy, but the food was delicious and a steel drum band played enthusiastically in one corner.

Afterward, feeling too full to sit any longer, Kari allowed Eddie to lead her for a stroll around the pool. The moon was out, but the ocean was no more than a soft, rushing sound as small waves gathered and spilled on the shore.

The light on the pool water made it sparkle and dance. Pretty, but it didn't move her somehow. She couldn't help thinking about King's Creek Falls, where Nick had shown her what real magic could be like.

A waitress in an outfit that looked more Hawaiian than Caribbean found Eddie. He'd ordered the house specialty before they'd left the restaurant.

He frowned down at the trio of flowers and fruit that covered the top of the glass. "Good Lord, I don't know whether to drink it or plant it," he said. He plucked the decoration out of the glass and tossed it away. "You want one?"

She shook her head, having barely made a dent in her own small goblet of white wine. "Too sweet. I'll stick with this." She lifted her glass, enjoying the way moonlight caught the liquid and turned it golden. "'Wine makes a symphony of a good meal,'" she quoted.

Eddie gave her an odd look. "Where did you hear that?"

She hid a smile, thinking of the day Rose had tried to teach her about all the different wines offered on the lodge's menu. Her brain had spun for three hours afterward. "Just a friend," Kari said.

After the waitress departed, Eddie lifted his face skyward, inhaling deeply. "Look at that moon. You can't tell me you get views like this in Florida. Not since the developers moved in and started running things, anyway."

"Not many," she agreed.

She realized suddenly that she couldn't remember the last time she'd gone down to the beach in front of her condo. Or even stood on the balcony and watched the sunrise. When had she forgotten to appreciate the beauty around her own home? And why had it never been enough?

Eddie must have sensed her mood. "Come on, Churchill. Liven up. If I wanted to be around someone this gloomy I'd have brought my accountant."

She turned toward him. "Do you ever think about what we do, Eddie? This career—always living out of a suitcase, jet-lagged all the time, never putting down roots. Never spending the holidays with family."

He made a scoffing sound. "Come and spend Thanksgiving with my parents. That will cure you of that wish once and for all."

"I'm serious."

"Of course I think about it. And you know what? I think I'm the luckiest guy in the world." He took a sip of his drink. "Okay, so there are a few drawbacks, but think about it. We get to travel, meet new people all the time—*interesting* people, famous people. The money's not bad." He gave her a sharpened look. "You'd be miserable with some white-bread, middle-class life built around a passel of kids and the neighborhood block party."

"With the right person—"

Eddie shook his head quickly, as though he'd finally lost patience with her. "There *is* no right person for people like us. Sure, I'm crazy about Buzz, but he knows the job comes first because that's the way I want it. As for you, you need to remember that this is the life you chose for yourself. And it's a good one. You're building a fine reputation as a journalist." He winked at her. "You have a great partner, so what's the problem?"

"I don't know—" She broke off, aware of Eddie's eyes on her

She felt cross suddenly, and a little lost, because she had always counted on him to give her good advice. But nothing Eddie had said to her felt right anymore.

"What don't you know?" he asked with a long-suffering sigh. "You wanted what your father had, and now you've almost got it—well, except for the bestselling novels part, because you stink at writing fiction—but you've found your niche. Freedom and adventure and excitement—you're Mad Churchill's daughter, all right."

Instantly she could see those last pages of her father's journal as though she held it open in her hand. "In the end, it didn't bring Dad happiness."

After giving her a sour look, Eddie took a couple of swallows from his snifter glass. "You know what I think?" he asked, his voice rife with suspicion.

"No, but I'm sure you're going to tell me."

"I think this is Mr. Wonderful screwing with your psyche."

"Mr. Wonderful?"

"The guy in Colorado with bad judgment. You're still moping over what might have been, when what you need to do is thank the fates for looking after you. You would have hated all the responsibility of a home and family. You should be glad he rejected you."

"He didn't reject me exactly. Not in those words, I mean."

He did a funny little double take. "Well, in what words, then? Did you talk about marriage?"

"No."

"Did you say anything about being in love?"

"No."

"What *did* you say?"

"Nothing, really. We slept together. You called to tell me to come down here. He knew I was leaving. I asked if we needed to talk, but he said he always knew that our time together was temporary. End of discussion."

Eddie blew a gusty breath. "So you never told him how you felt?"

"No."

"Then can you please tell me how you know he didn't want a relationship?"

"It was just something…I knew."

"When did you get psychic?"

"Don't tease me," she said, looking away in discomfort and then back again. "I feel bad enough as it is. You weren't there. You don't know how humiliating it is to realize you love someone and they don't love you back."

One eyebrow rose. "So you love him?"

"Yes, damn it! I do." Her voice shook far more than she liked. This discussion invited pain, but it felt almost a relief to say those words. To have them out in the open at last, where she could mourn them and then pack them away like treasured pictures in a dusty scrapbook.

More calmly she said, "But I couldn't say anything. I didn't want to get hurt any more than I already was. I couldn't see the sense in laying my heart out on the ground for him to do a tap dance on it. So in the end, I didn't say anything, and he didn't say anything. I didn't look at him, and he didn't look at me, and that was that."

Eddie scratched one cheek thoughtfully. "Well, that's one way of handling it, I suppose," he said in a careful tone. "Although next time you decide to fight fire with fire, you might want to remember that the fire department usually uses water."

"Your point?" she asked, her tone pure acid now.

He sat his glass on a nearby patio table. Gently he took her arms in his hands. In all the years she'd known him, Kar didn't think she'd ever seen Eddie look so sweetly concerned. "My point being, you might have considered swallowing your pride and telling him how you felt. Just laid it on the line to see what he had to say." He shook his head, giving her a sad little smile. "You couldn't have ended up any more miserable than you are right now, could you?"

THE PROBLEM WITH WEDDINGS and receptions, Nick decided, was that they lasted too long.

Bad enough that it took months of preparation to put on a decent one, with a flurry of tears and panic and confusion from everyone involved as the days wound down to the big date. So when that day finally came, when you'd listened to the pledges of undying love and trembling "I Do's" exchanged, the darned thing ought to end right there and then.

But no. Then everyone had to stand in line to congratulate the happy couple, listen to a bunch of silly toasts, eat until they popped, dance until they dropped, and finally, see the bride and groom off in a snowstorm of confetti.

Such determined, choreographed gaiety was ridiculous as far as Nick was concerned.

Sour, man. You're way too young to be this sour.

With arms folded across his chest, he leaned against one of the stone columns near the portico and watched the festivities.

Chuck Graybeal, the bride's father and the D'Angelo family dentist, had booked the entire lodge and was spending thousands of dollars to make this wedding memorable. The gazebo—decked out in blue netting and bows—had made a pretty backdrop for the ceremony. The dining room had been too small to hold this many people, so the reception was being held outside, too, on probably one of the last pretty days of autumn they were likely to get at this elevation. Maybe next year, Nick thought, if things went well, they could add a small banquet room to handle this kind of function.

A dance floor had been set up near the grassy clearing that overlooked the trails to Lightning Lake. The band, with shimmering gold aspens making a curtain behind them, had gone into a set of old standards. What they had lacked in talent, they'd made up for in noise level, so it was nice to finally hear something that didn't make his ears bleed.

He became aware of movement behind him and turned his head. It was Pop, wheeling down the front ramp Nick had added last year.

Crap. In the bad mood Nick was in, he didn't want to talk. Of course, considering his mood lately, if he waited for a better time, it might never come.

The old man spent a few moments watching the crowd on the dance floor. "They look beautiful, don't they?" he said, indicating the happy couple, who also happened to be friends of the family.

"Uh-huh." Frankly, Nick thought the bride looked wilted, and the groom seemed downright shocky. Maybe reality had finally kicked in.

"Weddings are such a renewal of hope for the future."

Nick didn't say anything to that. The relationship between the two of them had been edgy of late, and he didn't want to make it worse. But he had a feeling he knew where this conversation was leading.

To distract him Nick asked, "How's Mom making out in the kitchen?"

His mother and the Zias had put on one heck of a feast. Everything from antipasto to *Mussels Tarantino* to *Pollo Marcato* to *Wandas*—little Italian pastries in the shape of bow ties.

"It's winding down now that the cake's been cut," San

said. "Even Addy had to pitch in for a while. She's getting very good at managing that sling, but we could have used an extra hand."

Again Nick didn't respond. His father was as subtle as an anvil falling on your foot. Nick knew perfectly well whose "extra hand" he was referring to.

"When do you fly them to Steamboat Springs?" Sam asked. The newlyweds had planned an elaborate honeymoon.

"Tomorrow at nine. They're spending tonight in Number Twelve. Should be memorable. Aunt Sof's got champagne and chocolate waiting. The sheets are covered with rose petals flown in from California."

"Chuck has spared no expense, it seems."

Nick made a face, his gaze falling momentarily on the groom, Danny Myers. The silly ass was trying to dip the bride, but he kept tripping over her train. She didn't look a bit happy about that. "Hope the marriage lasts longer than the credit card bills Chuck's going to be faced with."

He heard his father sigh heavily. "You know, son, if losing Kari makes you this bitter, then I really think you ought to do something about it. Before it poisons you for good."

Nick glanced down at his father, frowning. "I didn't *lose* anything. She has a career, remember? And she couldn't wait to get back to it."

"You don't know that."

But he did. He had only to recall the sound of her voice on the telephone when she'd spoken to her photographer buddy. Thrilled. Eager. And if Nick thought he'd misread that attitude, all he had to do was remember the actual conversation. Her side of it, anyway.

Hearing those words had brought a halt to any foolish ideas he'd been entertaining. Who could compete with a life like that?

"Did you even *ask* her what she wanted?" Sam's features conveyed disdain, as though Nick had behaved very badly.

"Didn't have to. It was pretty clear. And I didn't see any reason to try to convince her otherwise. No sense in embarrassing us both."

"*Idiot!* Why not? Do you think your mother said yes to me in the beginning? Some women need convincing. The good Lord provides a worm for every bird, Nick, but He doesn't throw it in the nest."

Nick held up a hand. "Pop, don't. There's nothing to be done about it now. Even if I wanted to. And I don't."

Sam brought his balled fists down on the arms of his chair. "Well, of course something can be done about it. It's never too late. You could call her. Tell her how you feel. I'll tell you the truth, son. When you face death as I have, you finally know what life is all about. Sleeping alone may be quieter, but it's not warmer."

As much as he wanted to refute that fact, Nick suspected his father was right. Nick had slept alone for years, and he hadn't thought for one minute that he could actually miss having a woman in his bed. But when that woman had been Kari...

Annoyed that his father simply refused to leave the subject alone, Nick decided it was time to get tough. He turned toward Sam.

"What was I supposed to do, Pop? Tie her up and keep her here against her will? Beg her to stay? What kind of happiness would that have brought either of us? I learned my lesson when I was married to Denise. You keep someone in a relationship they don't really want, and no one wins."

"You don't know she couldn't have been happy here," Sam said stubbornly.

"I know she wants adventure and thrills in her life. In case you haven't noticed, around here we're a little short in that department."

"You're a stubborn fool, son," his father said. "Kari is a rare gem, and you're going to make one of the biggest mistakes of your life just because you won't take a chance. A ship is safest in the harbor, Nick, but it's not meant for that."

He subsided into sulky, indignant silence.

Nick took a ragged breath, unwilling to discuss it any further. He needed something else to occupy his mind, something to blot everything out. Memories of that one night in his bedroom were always lurking just beneath the surface, sharp as a knife.

Kari had been a demanding, tempestuous lover, tantalizing him slowly, encouraging him wildly. Her movements had taken the last of his control away, until he'd stretched out on her, his body flat and pressing hard, until he imagined he could feel every feminine muscle, every tiny bone. He went deeper and deeper, plunging inside her so suddenly, so completely, that a long, uncontrollable shiver of passion had passed through them both.

He had known it could only be temporary that night. He had wanted to make the experience something she would never forget. To brand his imprint on her thoroughly, so that she would always remember him and those hours.

Instead, the truth, unadorned and ugly, was that *he* was the one who couldn't seem to cure himself of remembering every tiny detail. He lived for only one thing now. A day when he could cut Kari Churchill as cleanly from his heart as she had swept him from hers.

"So what do you think?" a voice said beside him, and Nick came out of his reverie to discover that Addy had joined them.

His gut twitched in fresh irritation. His sister was even

worse than Pop. Over the past few days she'd taken him to task half a dozen times for allowing Kari to leave. As if all he'd had to do was tell her not to go.

"What do I think about what?" Nick asked cautiously.

"You don't listen to a thing I say," she complained.

"That's because you're like a broken record lately."

"Tell him again, Adriana," Sam interrupted, obviously Addy's willing accomplice. "Maybe he'll actually hear you this time."

Addy sighed. "*I said,* the TV's been running a lot of coverage about that treasure ship. It's the perfect excuse to call Kari. You could find out how she is. See if she's happy. See if she misses us at all. It would open the lines of communication between the two of you again. What do you think?"

He wanted to strangle her. And Pop, too. Why couldn't everyone in this family leave well enough alone?

Nick gave her a hard look. "I think you ought to mind your own business."

"I'm just trying to help."

"Well, don't. The last time you interfered in my decisions I ended up short one helicopter." He touched her sling. "And you ended up in that." He looked around for an excuse to leave them and found it when the band's microphone made a screeching whine right in the middle of "Smoke Gets In Your Eyes."

"I need to check the sound system," he said, and headed off across the lawn before either of them could stop him.

He could avoid them for the rest of the day, but if he knew those two schemers, they'd soon call for reinforcements—maybe Mom and the Zias. He'd go down to the heliport in a few minutes. Work out his frustration by replacing Raven Two's fuel line.

He'd almost made it to the speaker setup when a hand

came down on his arm. He swung around, not in the mood for any more advice. *"What?"*

"Hi, Dad," Tessa said. Then, taking one look at him, she asked quickly, "What's wrong?"

His face relaxed into a smile. Who would have guessed that his daughter, once such a worrisome problem, would be the only one in this family who *wasn't* driving him crazy right now?

"Nothing, sweetheart," he réplied in a calmer voice. Then he lifted a questioning brow. "Unless you're going to try to talk me into calling Kari."

Her nose scrunched, making her look very young. "Do you want me to?"

"No," he said firmly.

She held out her hand, giving him the sweetest smile. "Then would you like to dance? I need practice for the homecoming dance."

"I'd be delighted," Nick said, seizing on that idea with desperate gusto.

He pulled Tessa into his arms. They'd been making headway in their relationship lately, and if nothing else in his life seemed sane and normal, at least there was hope for the two of them.

She looked pretty today, animated and fresh-faced. He supposed it had something to do with the fact that he'd finalized arrangements with Denise that would allow Tessa to visit her mother in Boston. "Are you happy about spending some of Christmas break with your mom?"

Unexpectedly, his daughter shrugged, a lackluster response. "I guess."

"Your mother's eager to see you—"

"Dad, it's okay," she said quickly, halting his automatic defense of Denise. "I know Mom goofs sometimes. And I know you try to make it right so I don't get hurt."

He felt a tightness inside his throat and his belly and chest. No matter how he had failed with Denise, they had produced this beautiful child. "I love you, Tess."

She grinned. "I love you, too, Dad." They moved around the dance floor a little while, then Tessa tilted a glance at him. "Can I tell you something?"

"Of course."

"I was hoping you'd ask Kari to stay. I wanted you to."

He jerked back a little. "You did?"

"Uh-huh. I think she would have been good for you. And I liked her a lot. But I'm not really surprised you didn't."

"Why not?"

Her dark eyes, so like his own, glittered. "Because just like Nonno Sam says, sometimes D'Angelos have more pride than sense."

CHAPTER EIGHTEEN

RIGHT UP UNTIL the moment Kari stepped out of the rental car in the Lightning River Lodge parking lot, she had been sure she was doing the right thing.

She knew how she felt about Nick. With absolute certainty, she knew.

But now, walking up the sun-dappled driveway, she was suddenly struck by how many ways it could all go wrong. The pretty, optimistic pictures she'd painted in her mind on the plane back from Jamaica began to run into a jumble of water-colored fantasies that could not be trusted.

Suppose she'd misread every look and touch? Suppose by leaving here she'd ruined any chance for a future? What if he simply didn't want her in his life? A shiver whistled through her. There was no way to think about any of it without touching upon something frightening.

She ordered a halt to such negative thoughts, resolving to lay off this bad habit of doubting herself. She had come all this way. There was only one thing to do. If she let fear and pride stop her now, it would be her own fault. No doubt about it.

The crowded party on the front lawn of the lodge caught her attention—it must be the Graybeal wedding. It looked to be a success, with people laughing and eating and dancing, and the newlyweds hanging on to one another as if they'd been welded together.

And then she saw Nick.

He was dancing with Tessa, near the edge of the portable dance floor in front of the band. A sweet flicker of pleasure went through her at the sight of him. When he bent his head to catch something his daughter said, then laughed, that flicker turned into a fire, licking at her insides. Just seeing him again—all that pure, masculine grace and power—made her take a mental step backward.

She lost sight of him. As she craned her neck to spot him again, someone touched her arm and she turned.

"Oh my God, it *is* you!" Addy said beside her.

Sam was just behind Addy. Whatever Kari feared Nick's reaction might be, there was no doubt in her mind about how these two felt about Kari's return. Their eyes were sparkling, their smiles wide enough to shame a shark.

The two women hugged one another. "After making all those darned candy baskets, I had to see how the wedding turned out," Kari said. She slid a glance back to the dance floor, hoping to spot Nick again.

"When did you arrive?" Addy asked excitedly. "How long can you stay? Does Nick know you're here?"

Before Kari could answer any of those questions, Sam tugged on his daughter's sleeve. "Adriana, hush up. Can't you see she's not here for us?" He made a shooing motion toward the dance floor with his good hand. "Go on, girl. They've been dancing a long time. Tessa could probably use a break. And if that son of mine says anything at all objectionable, you come get the two of us. We'll settle his hash once and for all."

Giving them both a smile of thanks, Kari headed for the dance floor. She was so focused on Nick that she barely registered anything else. She was hardly aware of the tinkle of laughter around her, disinterested in the swell of achy music as the band began a new tune, oblivious to the sharp scents of autumn that promised frost before the week was through.

She wove through the crowd, coming up beside Nick and Tessa. Before he was aware of her presence, she tapped the girl lightly on the arm. "Mind if I cut in?"

Her eyes never strayed from Nick, but she heard Tessa's gasp of surprise. "Kari!" the girl exclaimed. "You're back!"

"I couldn't stay away," she said. "May I borrow your father for this dance?"

"Sure. Cool." The teenager gave Kari a hopeful smile and then quickly disappeared into the crowd.

During that short exchange Kari was aware that Nick had not moved. Not a centimeter. He stood staring at her with startling intensity, as though he were assessing her from the inside out. Her heart began to beat so high in her chest that she would have to clear her throat to talk.

She put her hand up in an invitation. When he didn't take it right away, she said, "I think I should warn you. If you make a scene, or refuse to be nice, D'Angelo reinforcements will be all over you like the Indians at Little Big Horn."

She'd hoped for at least a smile, but Nick didn't even blink. His eyes held hers captive, but the awful stillness of his features tore at her heart.

She ruffled her fingers. "Come on, Nick. It's just a dance, not the end of the world."

He took her fingers in his, then she slipped into his arms. He kept her at a polite distance, she noticed. As if they were strangers.

"Tessa looks well," she said.

"She's fine."

"How are you two getting along?"

"Better."

So they were back to minimalistic conversations, too. Not good. But she wasn't going to allow him to lapse back into that kind of non-communication. She'd come too far to be turned aside so easily. Even anger was better.

Deliberately, she moved her hand from his shoulder to the back of his neck, and pressed closer to him, whether he wanted her to or not.

Laying her cheek against his chest, she sighed. "This is nice," she said softly. "When I was in Jamaica, I fantasized about doing this." She touched her lips against his throat in a gentle kiss and felt his heartbeat, strong and fast. "Tell me you missed me."

He made a little sound and pulled away. He didn't turn loose of her hand, however. Instead he said, "Come with me. We can't do this here."

Do what? she wanted to ask. Fight? Kiss?

He wove between other couples on the dance floor and she followed in his wake. He led her along the trail that edged the lake, finally stopping at the same spot where they had once worked together to repair the fence. Leaning against the log railing, he waited while a few stragglers from the reception strolled by. Music and laughter drifted to them on a light breeze, but the air still seemed to throb with tension. It felt as though an ocean of space lay between the two of them.

When the guests were out of earshot, Nick crossed his arms and tilted his head at her. "Why did you come back here, Kari?" he asked in a gruff tone. "What do you want?"

His eyes seemed like such a shut door, so much so that for a brief moment she considered telling him something other than the truth. But she couldn't allow herself the luxury of indecision. Too much was at stake here. She swallowed hard and came toward him, stopping when no more than a couple of feet separated them.

"I suppose," she said slowly, "I could lie or pretend. Make up something that might sound plausible—though what that would be I can't imagine. But I promised myself that I wouldn't do that." She bit her bottom lip. "I came back here for you, Nick."

His reaction threw her completely. His features remained blank, a mask she couldn't penetrate. She felt a drowning sensation creep into her soul, a powerless sinking beneath forces she might be unable to fight.

In spite of shivering inside, she said, "I was hoping for a little more enthusiasm than this."

He scowled. "You came back...for me." It was a statement, not a question. He spoke briskly, stripping the words of any emotional content.

She took a deep breath, determined now. "I guess I mean, for us. That night in your bedroom—I realized that I didn't want it to ever end. It meant something to me, and I want to believe that it meant something to you, too. I can't explain it, or understand it. I know it wasn't just sex. When I was with you, I felt like I'd finally found something worth fighting for, something I've been looking for all my life." She lifted her chin. "So that's why I've come back."

"You shouldn't have," was all he said.

The shivering threatened to become an icy paralysis. "Why?"

"You can't be happy here."

"I think I should be the one to make that decision."

He shifted, as though annoyed. "What about your career? All those thrills you want?"

"I've thought about that. A lot. These past few days I've

watched a fortune in jewels and gold being brought up from the bottom of the sea. But that's *all* I did, Nick. I just stood by and watched. They weren't *my* adventures. They weren't *my* thrills. They belonged to someone else."

"You're still a part of it."

"I get to be an observer for a little while. Then it's over. So how have I enriched my life? What have I gained? Nothing."

"So this assignment wasn't the perfect one," he said with a shrug. "A new thrill, a new adventure, will come along sooner or later. You need that in your life, Kari."

"I thought I did," she conceded. "I used to dream of going with my father, and I was so angry with him for refusing to take me with him. But I've finally figured it out, Nick. I wasn't angry with him for going to those places. I was angry with him for refusing to stay home. With us. Refusing to be a real family." She studied him, hoping that she was getting through to him somehow. "Don't you see? There's no adventure waiting for me out there that can compare to being here. With you. If you'll just let me."

"There's no adventure *here*," he said with a shake of his head. "There's only work and commitment and so many mundane tasks that even *I* want to chuck it all sometimes. But this is the life I've made for myself and my daughter. This is who I am."

"And that's the man I fell in love with," she said a little desperately. "I'm not saying it would be easy. I'm not saying we'd get it right all the time. But I want to try." She looked at him closely. "Just tell me this. Do you love me at all?"

He made a frustrated sound and looked away for a moment. "God, Kari...the things you say."

"I know this may be sudden," she added quickly and moved closer. "I can hardly believe I'm asking. But I don't believe it's wrong to say these things. I can't lose by loving. I can only lose by holding back." She touched his sleeve. "Couldn't we try to work something out?"

"No."

She stood frozen, in quiet shock. When she finally found her voice, the words came out so softly, they were almost a whisper. "You're saying no, then."

She stood taut and trembling, her knees gone weak. She had to get away from here before she disgraced herself completely. She started to turn, but Nick's fingers closed around her arm.

"I'm saying no. I don't want to *try.* I don't want to experiment with a relationship. I want to marry you."

With a gasp, she lifted her head. "Marry me?"

"Don't tell me that for once I've finally left you speechless," he said with a half smile.

"I'm sorry. It's just—I wasn't expecting that."

"Kari—" His voice was soft and textured, his features serious once more. "Everything you've said about that night in my bedroom holds true for me. I knew it then. I know it now. I love you. I've loved you for so much longer than I could ever admit to anyone. Including myself."

"Then why did you let me go?"

"I thought you wanted your father's life. How could I hold you back?"

She went into his waiting arms. "Oh, Nick, I've learned so much lately. About what's really important. I can't bear to think of making the same mistakes my father and mother did. They loved one another, but they wouldn't work together to save their marriage."

He coasted his hand along her cheek. "I want you to be happy here, Kari. I want us *both* to be happy, with no regrets, ever. You need to be sure about this."

She laid her head against his chest, hearing his heartbeat thunder in her ears. "Do you remember that day in the kitchen, when your father told me how he had saved your mother from the river?"

"I'll never forget it. I remember glancing down from the ladder and seeing your face as you listened to him. You were so still—enthralled, really—and I thought I'd never seen anyone so beautiful. Why?"

"Do you remember what your mother said? About how she was so frightened. But then your father told her to trust him, and she looked into his eyes, and she jumped across the distance to catch his hand. A leap of faith, she called it."

"I remember."

"That's what it will be like, Nick. A leap of faith for both of us." She pressed her hand against his heart. "But I believe that, as long as we're together, we can handle anything life throws our way."

He hugged her close. "I'll do whatever I can to give us that chance, Kari. I can't change who I am—"

"I don't want you to!"

"—but I can change some of the ways I handle things. I can ease up on trying to control every aspect of my life. It hasn't been working all that well lately, anyway." He brought his hand to her chin, lifting her eyes to his. "I can't ask you to give up what you love just to stay with me. Sooner or later you'll want to take some assignment that will take you away from here. I can accept that." His fingers coasted along her cheek, the most delicate of touches. "Who knows? Maybe I'll even tag along, if you don't mind the company."

"You don't understand. I would love for us to be able to travel together sometimes," she responded readily. "But that's not really what I want anymore. In fact, I was thinking that I want to try to write my father's story. Not just a bare-bones biography. Something more personal. His editor has expressed an interest, and who would have a better chance of knowing the real Madison Churchill than me? I think I can do it, Nick."

"Of course you can. I've seen you. You can do anything you set your mind to. And I'll do whatever it takes to help make it happen. I'll add on to the cabin, give you a real office to work in. What would you prefer? A view of the forest or the lake?"

"It doesn't matter. As long as it's here and you come with it." She turned her face until her lips found the warm center of his palm. "Because this is where my heart is."

"I know we can make it work," he said huskily. She felt his lips on her hair. "Can I assume your answer is yes?"

She smiled up at him and nodded. He kissed her then, and for a little while the world dropped away. She felt tears of joy star her vision. She wiped them away and pulled back to look at him again.

"I'll be such a good wife. You can teach me Italian, and I'll help Sam with his physical therapy. Your mother can show me how to cook. *Really* cook. Maybe I could even learn to like calamari."

He laughed. "Let's not get carried away."

"Will you make love to me at King's Creek Falls? At sunset?"

He touched his lips to her temple. "And sunrise." Then her cheek. "And noon." Finally at the corner of her mouth. "And in the middle of the night."

When she could think again, she gave him a earnest look. "I'll try so hard to be a good mother to Tessa, Nick."

"I don't doubt it for a minute. And maybe to a few of our own?"

"I hope so. I know I'm not Italian, but I'll make your family glad you married me."

"They already think of you as family," he said, giving her one of his heart-stopping smiles. "You can't imagine the hell I've been going through since you've been gone. I'd hate to see which way they'd vote if it ever came down to a choice between the two of us."

She shook her head. "It never will," she said solemnly.

"No, it won't," he said. His voice was thick and love-filled. "Oh, God, Kari…all the years ahead of us…all the moments in the rest of my life, I give them to you. I don't know why you want the kind of love I have to offer. I don't know what the future holds, but if there are adventures out there waiting, we'll find them…"

"Together," she told him, and he nodded.

The breeze rose gently, like the sweetest, purest song. It stirred through the aspens behind them, set them shimmering in a golden splendor that awed Kari every time she witnessed such magic. Farther out, Lightning Lake lay in iridescent blues and greens, as though it somehow, impossibly, contained within its chilly depths the essence of light.

Soon she would come to know it even better. She'd found her place here in these mountains. And among all this beauty she would create a world of her own adventures. With Nick.

He let go of her long enough to reestablish her at his side, one arm tucked around her waist. "Let's go home," he said.

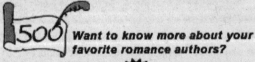

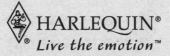

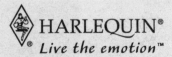

Men of the True North—
Wilde and Free

The Wilde Men

Homecoming Wife
(Superromance #1212)
On-sale July 2004

Ten years ago Nate Wilde's wife, Angela, left and never came back. Nate is now quite happy to spend his days on the rugged trails of Whistler, British Columbia. When Angela returns to the resort town, the same old attraction flares to life between them. Will Nate be able to convince his wife to stay for good this time?

Family Matters
(Superromance #1224)
On-sale September 2004

Marc was the most reckless Wilde of the bunch. But when an accident forces him to reevaluate his life, he has trouble accepting his fate and even more trouble accepting help from Fiona Gordon. Marc is accustomed to knowing what he wants and going after it. But getting Fiona may be his most difficult challenge yet.

A Mom for Christmas
(Superromance #1236)
On-sale November 2004

Aidan Wilde is a member of the Whistler Mountain ski patrol, but he has never forgiven himself for being unable to save his wife's life. Six years after her death, Aidan and his young daughter still live under the shadow of suspicion. Travel photographer Nicola Bond comes to Whistler on an assignment and falls for Aidan. But she can never live up to his wife's memory...

Available wherever Harlequin books are sold.

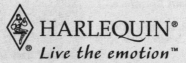

HARLEQUIN®
Live the emotion™

THE WEDDING PLANNERS

Where weddings are all in a day's work!

Have you ever wondered about the women behind the scenes, the ones who make those special days happen, the ones who help to create a memory built on love that lasts forever—who, no matter how expert they are at helping others, can't quite sort out their love lives for themselves?

Meet Tara, Skye and Riana—three sisters whose jobs consist of arranging the most perfect and romantic weddings imaginable—and read how they find themselves walking down the aisle with their very own Mr. Right...!

Don't miss the THE WEDDING PLANNERS trilogy by Australian author Darcy Maguire:

A Professional Engagement HR#3801

On sale June 2004 in Harlequin Romance®!

Plus:

The Best Man's Baby, HR#3805, on sale July 2004
A Convenient Groom, HR#3809, on sale August 2004

Available at your favorite retail outlet.

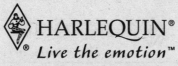

HARLEQUIN®
Live the emotion™

Visit us at www.eHarlequin.com

HRTWP

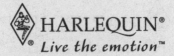